MW00794931

JEALOUS IN PARADISE

PARADISE SERIES

BOOK 18

DEBORAH BROWN

This book is a work of fiction. Names, characters, places and incidents are either the product of the author's imagination or used fictitiously. Any resemblance to actual persons, living or dead, or to actual events or locales is entirely coincidental. The author has represented and warranted full ownership and/or legal right to publish all materials in this book.

JEALOUS IN PARADISE

ISBN-13: 978-0-9984404-9-1

Cover: Natasha Brown

PRINTED IN THE UNITED STATES OF AMERICA

JEALOUS IN PARADISE

Chapter One

A scream ripped through the night air.

Creole, who was sitting next to me, stood and pulled me to my feet in one swift movement.

"Was it too much to expect that we'd get through the grand opening drama free?" I asked my husband. Now there was a word I never tired of thinking or saying—husband.

Before he could answer, another scream followed. He grabbed my hand, and we turned and ran toward the sound. This time, I recognized it as coming from my mother, who stood in the doorway of the room she'd been assigned. From the horror etched on her face, it wasn't an oversized cockroach that had her making the bloodcurdling sound.

Creole maneuvered us around the guests, who'd been partying around the pool in the middle of the u-shaped property and now turned to stare, all probably thinking the same thing as me: "What's going on?"

Mother's husband, Jimmy Spoon, flew to her side, getting there steps ahead of me. He wrapped his arms around her, and she buried her face in his chest and mumbled incoherently.

He peered into the room over the top of her head and pulled her away.

"She's dead," Mother whispered faintly, cocking her head towards the open door.

I poked my head inside and saw a blonde-haired woman face down on the floor in the entrance to the bathroom. She was naked, and other than the bed strewn with her clothes, nothing else in the room had been disturbed.

"I'm certain she's just passed out drunk," I said. "I'll take care of it."

After months of "hurry up and wait," Creole and I and our best friends, Fabiana Merceau and her husband Didier, had been the winning bid on the old run-down motel in the heart of Tarpon Cove in the Florida Keys. We had renovated it in record time and named it Beachside for its location across the street from water access. We'd agreed on most things, except when a vote was taken about who would handle guest relations and any irksome problems that were bound to happen. It was decided three to one that everything could be pushed off on me.

Creole, who'd stopped to check on Mother, appeared by my side and also glanced inside. "We need to figure out if the woman is a registered guest who wandered into the wrong room, and if not, figure out what we're going to do with her. All the rooms are booked, and it's not a good idea to set a precedent for guests sleeping their drunk off by the pool."

"I'll roust her and, if necessary, call her a cab." I entered the room and was overwhelmed by the sick smell. Groaning inwardly at the cleanup that would be needed, I grabbed her dress off the bed and crossed the space. Suddenly, a pair of hands grabbed my upper arms and jerked me back, turning me away, but not before I saw the revolver lying next to her hand and the pool of blood around her head.

"Babe, I'll take it from here." Creole led me back to the door. "We need to keep everyone out." He waved his arm, motioning to Didier, who stood a foot away, Fab by his side.

Already, several people had gathered at the window and were peering inside, a couple of them holding up their phones to take pictures—of what, they didn't know, but that wasn't a factor.

"Keep these people back," Creole told Didier, lowering his voice to add, "We've got a body." He took out his phone and called 911, going into cop mode, which was familiar to him from his days as an undercover officer before injuries sidelined him and he decided that he'd had enough.

"You okay, Madison?" Fab asked, and put her arm around me. I nodded. "I'll be right back." She went into the room and closed the drapes, much to the annoyance of the lookie-loos. Then she came back out and stood by my side. "Do you know what happened?"

"It looks like suicide. We need to make sure that none of the guests skip out, in case the cops want to talk to anyone." I looked over her shoulder and took a head count. "Maybe they won't be questioned, since it's self-inflicted and not murder, but I'd hate to guess wrong and be in trouble."

"Once news of this gets out, our bookings will skyrocket. Not that they're not good already," Fab added at my horrified look.

Didier appeared next to Fab and hooked his arm around her, kissing the top of her head and brushing her long brown hair over her shoulder. "I'll see to the guests and make sure everyone gets a drink refill."

"Will you check on Mother?" I asked Fab, knowing that she could get information out of her faster than anyone.

"Too late. She and the husband lit out of here," said Fab, who never missed a thing. "I got as close as I could to eavesdrop and still remain unobtrusive." She smirked. "Spoon tried to get her to stay, telling her the cops would have a few questions, but she wasn't having any of it and about tripped out of her sandals getting off the property."

I'd never hear the end of it now. Mother had dragged her feet RSVPing for the opening gala, and as a result, she'd gotten the last room, which was rumored to be haunted. It was also the nicest room, in my opinion. When she figured out which room she'd been assigned, she flipped. Even though she thought the whole ghost story was nonsense, that didn't mean she wanted to sleep in the room.

The property had an interesting history. Two men with a long business history had partnered and built the motel in the early 1950s and turned it into a profitable venture. Several years later, one of the partners suffered a heart attack and died. The other, seeing an opportunity to make a higher profit, turned it into an adult motel, planning to triple the revenue with a pay-by-the-hour plan, not factoring in either the seedy element it would attract or losing out on the traffic of those wanting to avoid late-night antics, who moved on down the road.

Isabella Sloan, the widow of the dead man, had been swindled out of her half of the property by the so-called family friend and partner. Even worse, he'd left her penniless, and she was eventually forced to sign the family home over to the bank. One night, with nowhere to go, she'd checked into the end room with her three small children and refused to leave. Days later, after a screaming match between her and the partner, her body had washed up on the beach. It was ruled a homicide, but no one had ever been charged.

The motel's colorful history had it that Isabella had never checked out of the room, and she could still be seen at times, gazing out the window. Some claimed they'd seen her around other parts of the property. It was also rumored that she wasn't always a gracious hostess and often didn't allow guests a good night's sleep, instead choosing to throw objects around the room.

The only odd occurrence that had happened since we acquired the property had taken place during the re-painting of the room, which was to be restored to its original appearance at my insistence and painted white, rather than one of the colors that had been chosen for the other rooms. The painter had mistakenly hauled in a container of blue, and before he could dip his roller, it had overturned. He swore he'd been a foot away when it happened. Thankfully, the flooring was getting replaced anyway.

Police cars screamed closer and double-parked out front. Sheriff's Deputy Kevin Cory got out of the first car, his partner behind him, and was the first to come through the gate. We'd torn down the rickety fencing and put in a low brick wall that didn't obstruct the view and doubled as seating for the truly bored, who could count cars as they crawled by, depending on traffic flow.

I waved Kevin over. We tolerated one another and made feeble attempts not to bother each other, but sometimes, irritating each other was too good to pass up. "If you had accepted our invitation and taken the night off, you'd already be here," I said when he got closer.

"Opening night and already a triple murder." Kevin laughed at his hilarious self. Oftentimes, he was the only one to find his jokes funny. Did it bother him? Oh, heck no.

"When word of that exaggeration rolls around town, I'll know who to blame." I waved him over to Creole.

"Anyone cut out the back?" Kevin asked.

I flinched, knowing he was referring to the times law enforcement arrived at my bar, Jake's, and those with warrants beat it out through the kitchen exit. "Just my mother, who was the one to discover the body. You know where to find her."

Kevin nodded and caught up with Creole.

I hung back, not sure what to do next. I'd been through enough police investigations to know they preferred that people stay out of the way and not tamper with evidence.

"What do I do if someone wants a refund on their room?" our portly, grey-haired resident manager asked, having barked at a few people to move out of the way, to which they grudgingly responded by moving an inch or two, refusing to do more than that lest they miss out on something good. Cootie stared down at me, a concerned look on his face, and fidgeted from one foot to the other.

We'd advertised for a couple to manage the property, and only eccentrics had shown up, and that was putting it nicely. It was also my suspicion that that was why I got voted problem-solver. Ready to give up and not willing to run the place myself, I'd decided to hire the next person in the door. Enter an acquaintance, Cootie Shine, who'd helped Fab and me out of a bad situation in Card Sound. He was perfect for the job—outgoing personality, oddball rapport, didn't take sass, and packed a Glock that he knew how to use.

Glancing around at the lookie-loos, I didn't think that would be a problem. I'd hate to ask those who continued to stare eagle-eyed at the room door what their preference was. Multiple bodies? A smoking gun or two? "Since this was an invitation-only event and I know everyone here, you send anyone asking for a refund to me." I shook my head. "They're lucky we don't charge extra."

"Did you know the deceased?" Cootie asked.

"No, and I'd like to know how the woman got access to the room and why she showed up on this night, of all nights, to off herself."

"I did my best to keep an eye on things, but she must have got past my radar somehow."

Rude Banner had rushed up in time to hear my question. Rude, short for Gertrude, was Cootie's almost-wife by her own definition, insisting that they'd marry one of these days. The short, grey-haired woman never failed to speak her mind and was a handful, according to Cootie, which he said with a twinkle in his eye. The pair had met while hibernating in the mangroves and been on and off for a number of years. Both were vague as to how many.

More patrol cars and a forensics van pulled up, along with an ambulance.

"Keep everyone busy with food and drink," I said to Rude. "I'll ask Creole—he'll know what's going to happen next. We should be prepared to have the cops tell everyone to leave."

"Don't you go worrying none," Rude said. "This night is going to be the talk of the town, more so since it went down in the haunted room."

Chapter Two

A number of the party-goers gathered around the pool the next morning after only a couple of hours' sleep. It had taken law enforcement most of the night to finish their investigation. Once the detectives and forensic technicians arrived, they'd photographed, mapped, videotaped, and collected evidence before removing the body. All the guests were cooperative when questioned and gave their names, addresses, and contact numbers so they could be interviewed later if necessary.

Conspicuously absent was Mother, who'd called earlier and suggested that the meeting be moved to her house. I'd known when she called at an indecent hour that she was requesting a change of plans, so I didn't answer, knowing she'd burn up Creole's phone and relieved to let him be the mean one. When his phone rang, he'd glanced at the screen where her picture had popped up and growled at me. I skirted around him and out the door to wait in the SUV.

Mother wouldn't ask. She would, however, hunt me down later and insist for the umpteenth time that the property be sold.

"You so owe me." Creole had slammed the door. "In case anyone asks, you left ahead of me."

Anyone. I'd bit back a laugh. Mother wouldn't ask.

During the remodeling process, we'd decided to enlarge the lobby area to accommodate tables and comfortable seating for an early continental breakfast. The dead space on the other side of the front desk had been turned into a one-bedroom apartment, another reason Cootie had been a good choice, as he'd just been rousted out of the mangroves for squatting and had no issue with relocation, only negotiating a parking space for his Airstream.

After we arrived, Creole corralled Didier for an update while I sniffed the air for a coffee scent. Fab shook her head, unamused. The sliding pocket doors to the office were pushed back, and Fab and I made ourselves coffee from one of the individual machines, grabbed muffins, and went to sit by the pool.

My brother, Brad, and his unofficially adopted son, Liam, who looked alike—fresh off the beach, tanned, with sandy brown hair—though they weren't actually related, had grabbed enough chairs for everyone and sat arguing over some sports score. A student at the University of Miami, Liam lived on campus, but often made the drive south to the Keys for social occasions and family events.

Creole and Didier stood less than a foot away where everyone could hear, and grilled Cootie for anything they might have missed in the few hours we'd left to get some sleep. They were just about done when Rude flew in out of nowhere and flitted around in a tutu, celebrating some obscure holiday or other. She'd come with a warning that she celebrated as many of the official days as she could.

"Where's my favorite niece?" I asked Brad. He'd gotten custody of his daughter after it was proven that he didn't kill her mother.

"Mila's at preschool," he said, a *you didn't expect me to bring her here* look on his face. "Anyone got an official update on last night?" Brad appeared quite pleased with himself, which probably meant he was in possession of news ahead of everyone else. I sat back in my chair and squinted a glare designed to make him squirm. He laughed, used to my antics.

Everyone claimed a seat.

"Creole and I have decided that making friends with the local sheriff's deputy should be assigned to our problem-solver," Didier said, humor dancing in his blue eyes.

"Oh, great." I rolled my eyes at the two of them. "Kevin's been my tenant for how long? And we've never passed the stand-off stage. Here's the woman for that job." I pointed as Mac ran in from the rear of the property, tutu over her workout leggings. Great, she'd gotten the memo about the prestigious day. I foresaw her and Rude one-upping each other. No tennis shoes for this woman. She had on fish-shaped somethings that could be construed as shoes and were slowing her down as they slapped the concrete.

Mac Lane managed The Cottages, a ten-unit beach property that I owned and rented to unusual characters—guests and regulars alike. If she ever tried to leave her job, I'd be forced to hunt her down and restrain her in some way that left her still able to maintain a semblance of order there.

The woman skidded to a stop and flounced into a chair, pulling a banana and a bottle of water from under her shirt. "You gotta start over if I missed anything."

"It's been decided that I'm to get all friendly with our favorite law enforcement officer," I said.

Mac wrinkled her nose. "Your personalities don't bump and grind. Leave that to your bro and Liam—saw the trio shooting hoops this morning."

"I thought someone rolled off with the thousand-pound hoop?" Fab said.

"Brad replaced it." Mac beamed.

I rubbed the middle of my forehead.

Fab groaned. "Madison does that when she's getting a premonition, in case you didn't know."

Most gave a courtesy laugh, and all eyes turned to me.

"I'm guessing that Brad's got the latest update

about what happened last night." I flourished my hand. "Take it away."

"Rebecca Herd is the deceased woman's name, and no, she wasn't a registered guest or on the party list. It appears she snuck in and met her untimely demise. At first glance, one would think she offed herself, but not so fast. Kevin didn't divulge why the investigators thought otherwise, only that the coroner would make the final determination."

"If she didn't off herself, then that leaves murder," Fab said, her interest piqued.

"Typically, the officers and detectives on the scene would be able to quickly determine if a person has been murdered or committed suicide," Creole said. "When a murder is staged to look like a suicide, things are arranged in ways that promote the murderer's deception. But most murderers don't have the experience of seeing dozens of real death scenes and real suicides, like detectives do. What the murderer thinks a suicide should look like may not be the way it looks when a person really kills himself or herself, patterns officers have seen many times before. The murderer is likely to get the details wrong in a way that is obvious to the police."

"A staged suicide, and whoever it was chose our motel," I said. "I wonder what made Beachside the ideal location?"

"I'll ask the psychic down the street if murder is a good omen for opening night." Rude chewed her bottom lip.

"The one that's always got the closed sign lighting up the window?" Liam laughed. "That's some prime real estate going to waste with that crumbling building sitting there waiting for a good storm to blow it apart."

"You sound like you're gearing up to join the family business." Creole, who was sitting on the other side of Liam, clapped him on the shoulder.

Brad, Creole, and Didier ran our family real estate business, which specialized in developing property in Tarpon Cove. Mother, Spoon, Caspian, Fab's father, and Fab and I were silent investors.

"Kevin and I checked the security feeds last night and didn't come up with anything," Fab said. She had designed the system and overseen the installation. "I've decided that we need a few more cameras around the place, as not all locations were visible. There were a couple of hidden corners."

"When you were shooting hoops, did your friend happen to mention when the cops would be releasing the room?" I asked Brad.

"As soon as they were done early this morning, you were free to go in and clean it up."

"I've got a crime scene cleaner on speed dial for that gruesome task." I wrinkled my nose. "I used to be a regular client; wonder if he's missed me."

Fab and I gave a grim laugh at the not-so-pleasant memories.

"It's too bad the door wasn't crisscrossed with crime scene tape," Rude lamented. "Word would have gotten out and we could have sold tickets to the lookie-loos who came by with an excuse to peek in the window."

"What a great idea," Didier said, his tone saying clearly not.

"If you're going to turn the room into a roadside attraction, I suggest you get the drapes rigged to open and close by remote." Brad laughed, pleased with his idea.

"Sorry to squash all these good ideas, but the room will be ready for occupancy in a day," I said.

"Maybe we shouldn't rent it out until it's no longer a story," Fab mused.

"Bad idea," Mac said and smiled at Fab's glare. "You got to jump on that baby, jack up the room price, and milk it while it's hot news."

"I'm speaking for the partners—this isn't the kind of start we wanted, and we're not capitalizing on it, since we don't want to be known as the murder motel," Creole said. "I'm going to get with Kevin and keep updated on the case, especially if it's ruled a homicide."

"I'll have a background report run on Rebecca, so we'll know everything about her, and turn it over to Fab if there are any further questions," I said, as Fab had been a licensed private investigator for years.

"If it turns out to be murder, I'll be delegating. I'm trying to make good on my promise to Didier—" Fab smiled at him. "—to pause before leaping into dangerous situations."

"I had a little more in mind, such as calling me first, so I have the opportunity to talk you out of anything risky," Didier said.

Good luck to that.

"Cootie, are we set for real guests in two days?" I asked. I'd learned his real name was Milton but had been sworn to secrecy.

"No cancellations, if that's what you're asking. Don't worry, I've got this handled."

"I suppose now is a good time to bring this up." Mac rubbed her fish shoes back and forth on the concrete. "Rude and I got to talking..."

I bet.

"Anyway..."

"You might want to speed this up. We've got a meeting at the office. New client," Fab announced.

Oh goodie, a new one!

Didier pinched her arm and got a frown in return.

"You know how I'm always arranging tours for The Cottages' guests? I say we buy a short bus and do our own."

Liam raised his hand. "I'll drive it on weekends."

"What about the other days?" I asked.

"I'll be able to find someone," Mac said, as though it would be a no-brainer job to fill.

"That better not be code for a drunk who needs a day job." I locked eyes with Creole, who shook his head and grinned, letting me know I was on my own. "Run the numbers and give them to me," I told her.

"Any more issues to bring up?" Creole asked.

"It was nice having a meeting out here," I said. "Since we won't be able to do it again once we have guests, I suggest that in the future, we use Fab and Didier's house. They can send out for food."

Didier laughed. "Good idea. We've got plenty of room."

Chapter Three

Everyone split up and went their separate ways. Fab and I headed to the office for the next meeting of the day, with Fab taking a new shortcut down a side street and an alley. The woman must cruise the streets at night, ferreting out these alternate routes. She wasn't one to take a direct way if another one would shave off a whole minute.

Fab had bought two warehouse buildings down in the seedy area adjacent to the docks on the other side of the Cove. She and Didier had converted one of the buildings into office space. I'd also recently carved out an alcove to conduct business. The other building had thus far been ignored.

A half-block from the property, Fab hit a button on the visor that opened the security gate. She drove through and parked in the garage next to a black Escalade with limo-tinted windows.

I turned in my seat. "Nice SUV. Who does it belong to?"

"*Our* new client," she said with a secretive smile. "He also requested you."

"That's swell." I wasn't about to ask who,

choosing to be surprised. Fingers crossed it wasn't a criminal or a whack-job. I got out and followed her up the steep steps to the offices on the second floor.

Before we got to the top, the door opened and Xander stood on the threshold, beckoning us inside. The enormous open space had been divided, albeit subtly, into Fab's private investigation firm, FM Associates, on one side, and Didier's real estate offices on the other. Color was what differentiated the two. Fab's side was white and chrome. Didier's was also chrome, with black and splashes of blue and grey.

Xander ran the office and had given himself the title of VP. I'd hired him after his failed attempt to snatch Fab's purse, thinking if he was half as smart as he said, he'd take the opportunity and fit right in. With his impeccable computer skills, he got an interesting assortment of jobs thrown at him besides the background checks. I'd warned him before he accepted employment with Fab and me that the exact description of the job was "a little of this and that." So far, it had lived up to the description.

"I've got a job for you," I said as I passed him, going inside and doing a double-take at seeing Gunz sitting behind Fab's enormous glass-top desk.

Theodore Gunzelman—though no one would dare call him that to his face—was a long-time sketchy friend of Fab's. He swore he'd gone legit, but being a money lender at exorbitant interest rates would raise eyebrows as to how legit. He patted his shiny bald head and pasted on a sneaky smile that would have most taking a step back. When I first met the man, he'd been into hair paint, which was messy and didn't look the least bit real.

Gunz hoisted his considerable bulk out of the chair. "Ladies."

"You let him in?" I said to Xander. "That was brave of you."

"Only because Ms. Merceau called ahead of time." Xander let out a nervous laugh.

"You call me by my first name, why not her?" I nodded in Fab's direction as I curved around the corner into the cubbyhole at the far end that was my office and threw my briefcase on my ten-foot-long desk, which Fab had had custom made from recycled shiplap. I could sit in my cushy office chair and enjoy the view of the water—the main selling point, in my opinion. I'd also decorated the space with a few beach accents, which I had to get permission for from Ms. Picky, who hadn't ixnayed any of my choices.

"You're nice to me," Xander whispered.

"I heard that," eagle ears shouted. "I'm as nice to you as I am to anyone else."

Xander flinched.

"'Hey you' also works." I laughed at his pink-tinged cheeks, then stopped teasing him and asked, "You ready to take notes?"

He pulled out his phone, and I told him about the suicide/murder from the previous evening and that I needed him to find out everything he could about Rebecca Herd. Also, anything he could find out from police reports, as long as he didn't run the risk of being charged with a felony. I didn't want the recently turned twenty-one-year-old getting arrested.

"It's rude to keep our client waiting," Fab called from behind her desk. Gunz had moved to the opposite side and sat facing her.

I grabbed a water out of the kitchen refrigerator before sitting at the far corner of Fab's desk. "So, you're the new client?"

"I asked for a meeting." Gunz drank from an aluminum water bottle. "Besides, it was a good excuse to come for a look around, since I hadn't been invited."

I glanced at Fab, who shrugged at his high-handedness. We waited for him to continue.

"As you two know, I have a rather large family, cousins and such, who run amok, as we like to say." He laughed and slurped more of the contents from the bottle.

I'd met the sisters, and they were C-crazy, and of course, they hated Fab. When I tried to get more information about them before accepting the job, the details had been sketchy. At the time, I was happy to get away from the pair in one piece.

"Rarely a day goes by that my phone's not

ringing with some crisis that needs my attention. That's where the two of you come in. I'd like to hire you as 'fixers' for my family issues. I'll field the calls; you clean up the mess. The last couple of jobs that I sent you out on went well from my perspective, in that they didn't require anything hands-on from me, and I'd like to keep it that way."

"I'm not available for exclusive service. I have other clients that I'm not willing to end my association with at this time," Fab said.

Who? But I didn't voice the question. Hopefully, she didn't mean the troublesome millionaire acquaintances from her previous life that called with illegal requests.

"Lucky you." Gunz flashed a sly look. "Because my phone doesn't ring off the hook every single day with problems."

"We'll talk about it and get back to you," Fab hedged.

"Did I mention that I pay better than anyone in town and always in cash?" Gunz grinned.

Cash was the way we both liked to do business.

"I'm surprised that this offer includes me," I said, breaking up the staredown between the two. "I didn't think I was one of your favorites. Or even on the list."

"You've grown on me, and you have odd-people skills that will be useful in handling my family." Gunz's smarmy smile returned, and he focused it on me. "You've proven to be a decent mediator, and you have the ability to keep Fab from shooting one of my more annoying relations. Not that they wouldn't deserve it. I can't thin out the herd by killing them off, though; I'd lose my favorite status."

Herd? I bet they'd love that description.

Fab shrugged, letting me know she didn't have any more questions.

Not even one?

I straightened in my chair. "Cash is nice, but we'd need assurance that we'd also have access to the perks that come from an association with you. I was pleased that you got the Hummer repaired and back to me looking like new. I hope you conveyed my thanks to whoever."

"That goes without saying. Fabbie knows she can call anytime." Gunz beamed at her.

"We'd also need an understanding that you agree to divulge all aspects of the case, good and bad, in advance. If a case goes sideways and we end up dodging bullets, running for our lives, or other pesky issues like that and we find out that you knew in advance, that would terminate the relationship and you might find yourself staring into the eyes of an alligator." Why was it being left to me to negotiate these details?

"You're threatening to have those prissy husbands of yours feed me to some reptile?" Gunz boomed out a laugh.

"You might outweigh our husbands—" *By*

more than a hundred pounds I left unsaid. "—but don't think they would hesitate to shoot you. In the future, any mention of either of them is off limits."

"Calm your skirt. You got my word I won't be sending you into any dangerous situations, period. I get any hint of that, and I'll take care of it myself."

"I'm going to need you to keep your word on that," Fab said adamantly. "If I have to choose between this company and my husband, I'll close up shop."

I smiled at my friend's decision, knowing that she'd given it a lot of thought and it wasn't an easy one to make.

"While you two are discussing how great it would be to be my personal fixer, I've got a job." Gunz eyed the two of us and continued. "My aunt lives in a rundown house outside of Marathon and is hearing noises in the attic. When her daughter tried to question her, she clammed up and said it was probably the kids next door throwing rocks at the back of the house. She's old, and it's probably the television." His phone pinged, momentarily drawing his attention away. He glanced at it, then shoved it in his shirt pocket. "What I'd like the two of you to do is talk her into letting a contractor come out and do an inspection. I'm hoping she can be talked into getting a few repairs done. So far, she's shrugged off every suggestion I've made. I'd also like you to pay the neighbor a visit and stop the rock business if that story turns out to be true."

"Welfare check again?" I asked. "The last job we had like that, the person was dead. Murdered. We don't have such a great track record on these kinds of jobs. Wasn't the killer a mental patient?"

Fab shrugged, making it clear she didn't want to rehash old cases. "Stop, you're making my head ache." She made a face. "Let's hope it's not rats."

Gunz shuddered. "You've got carte blanche to get whatever the problem is fixed."

"This afternoon?" Fab asked me.

I nodded.

"Give this arrangement a chance, and I'll be your star client," Gunz boasted. He picked his phone out of his shirt pocket. "I'll send you the information you'll need, and I'll be calling my aunt, Fern Wallace, to let her know you're on your way. When she pitches a fit, I'll tell her that I can't stop you because you've already hit the road." He stood. "You got a card?" he asked Xander. "If you're as good as you say, I can maybe throw work your way."

"Nothing illegal," I said inflexibly. I leaned forward, grabbed one of Fab's cards, and pushed it across the desk. "Write your number on the back. And just so you know, Xander is family."

"Got it." He hugged Fab, then pulled an

envelope out of his shirt and tossed it on the desk.

I stayed seated and waved.

"Call with an update when you're leaving Fern's house. I'm hoping you can talk sense into her." Gunz crossed to the door and clumped down the stairs in his motorcycle boots.

"You need a business card," I said to Xander. "Design something cool and use our printing company. Charge it to the office."

"I think I'll copy yours and just change the number. Maybe add a name—VP. Let people think it's my initials or whatever they want to think."

Chapter Four

According to the GPS, Gunz's aunt lived this side of Marathon, which suited me. It wasn't often that Fab got a client that didn't require a drive to Miami. We hadn't gotten far when my phone rang. I retrieved it out of the cup holder and was a little surprised to see Billy's face on the screen. "Billy," I told Fab. He worked for my step-daddy. It'd shocked everyone in the family when I first used that term... except for the man himself, who laughed and shook his head. Billy was one of the few people that we could call and ask, and he would do, no questions asked. He was also roommates with Xander.

"You never call; must be important," I said after answering.

"No one's dead or anything." Billy growled a chuckle. "Can you stop by later so I can cash in one of my favors?"

When I first moved to the Keys, I'd found that my favorite aunt had bequeathed me a fistful of IOUs in addition to a new life. Better than money, they'd come with the promise of favor-doing. I'd since amassed a pile of my own and had spread my personal chits about town.

"Fab and I are headed to a job that shouldn't take long." Fingers crossed. "I'll call when we're headed back. Do I get a clue?"

"There's no fun in that. See you later." Billy hung up.

"Thanks for putting it on speaker," Fab huffed. It was standard MO for us to put calls on speaker, except when it was either Creole or Didier.

"He's cashing in an IOU and wants a face-to-face later. Happy now?"

"Good thing I have free time or you'd have to reschedule."

"Yeah, okay."

On the outskirts of Marathon, we turned off the highway and onto a gravel road. One-story houses dotted one side of the street, a continuous row of trees on the other side. The address turned out to be a lime-green one-story house with pink trim that had taken years of weather abuse with no attention to repairs. The small yard sported dead grass and a few struggling cactuses. Fab pulled into the gravel-filled driveway behind an older model sedan. Peering out the windshield, I saw that the upstairs attic sported a shuttered window on one side.

"I'll follow your lead," I said. "Since I don't know what the heck we're supposed to be doing. Pretend exterminators." I scrunched up my nose.

"Just be prepared with one of those folksy inanities of yours." Fab shut the car door before I could respond.

I got out and followed her through the weeds and up the unstable concrete path. Fab knocked politely on the door.

I snickered. "I'll teach you a real knock later."

"She's old; I don't want her dying, thinking a SWAT team is on the doorstep."

A grey-haired oldster stuck her head out the door, toothy grin on her face. "Whatever you're selling, not interested. Got more crap in my house than I know what to do with."

"We're— " Fab started.

"I don't need saving, either." She shut the door.

I stepped in front of Fab and cop-knocked.

The door flew open. "That was unfriendly."

"Fern Wallace?" I asked, just in case we had the wrong house. She nodded. "Gunz sent us. You want me to call him and report that you were unfriendly?"

"Why the hell didn't you say so?" Fern opened the door wide. "Watch where you step. It might look like junk, but you never know."

"I'm Madison and that's Fab." I tipped my head toward her.

The large, dark living room didn't scream welcome—more like creepy, and I was only a few steps inside. It could be best described as cluttered and dust-filled. Several inches, in fact.

Opening the drapes and windows to let the fresh air blow through would have been a good start and possibly help to dissipate the scent of animal pee.

"I missed the family meeting where we voted and made him king," Fern huffed. She sat in her recliner, barely missing a little mutt dog, who barked a reminder: *Look where you're sitting*. He looked at us with disinterest and went back to sleep. "You got three minutes, and then you're out the door like the last one. Except that one never got in. Course, he didn't threaten me, either."

The woman didn't offer, but not about to stand, I perched on the end of the couch, trying to avoid animal hair, which was impossible. In her usual style, Fab crept slowly around the perimeter, checking everything out.

"This is our first job for Gunz." It wasn't, but I was going for the sympathy factor. Maybe she'd cut us a break and cooperate. "It could be a lucrative account if we do a good job." I rubbed my fingers together. "We're two hard-working women with children to feed." Well, me anyway. She didn't need to know they were four-footed. "She's going to do a quick property inspection." I pointed to Fab. "We'll report back, and Gunz can send someone to fix any issues we find." I nodded to Fab to pick up the pace.

"She won't steal anything, will she?"

"We can have her empty her pockets before

she leaves, if that would make you feel better," I offered.

Fab turned her head and growled. She started her room-to-room search, which took less than a minute, then went out the back door.

"Lived here long?" I asked. Small talk was better than staring at one another.

"My husband and I bought this house and the one next door fifty years ago."

I glanced around the room and took note of the original finishes. Nothing had been replaced or updated. From my vantage point and bending a bit, I could see into the kitchen, where the countertop dipped to one side. It was a wonder that the appliances—rusted-out relics—were still functioning.

"Gunz would like to send out a contractor to make repairs for safety and structural issues. Are you amenable? I wouldn't want to send someone out and have you scare them off like you did us."

"That worked out well," Fern said grumpily.

"The benefits of accepting Gunz's largess are that he'll send someone who knows what they're doing and he'll pick up the tab. Two reasons to cooperate." I pasted on a smile that I hoped conveyed friendliness.

"It's not that I can't pay for it. I'm saving for my old age. When I'm dead, it's in my will that I want to be buried with it." Fern cackled.

"That gets around, and people will be digging you up."

"Greedy bastards."

Fab was back. "Which side do the rock-throwers live on?"

The woman looked confused, then unleashed an embarrassed laugh. "I made that up to stop the interrogation by my daughter. Wanting to know this and that. I'm a grown woman, for pity's sake."

Fab rolled her eyes. "It's good to have a daughter that cares enough to worry."

"I suppose. But when I ask nosey questions about her personal life, where does that get me? She changes the subject. So, I figure she's owed payback and a lie or two."

Fab and I heard the noises coming from the attic at the same time and stared up at the popcorn ceiling, which was lumpy in places.

"Rats," the woman said.

Fab and I exchanged a look. The noises were too loud to be rats.

"You know, they can eat your house down." I stood and removed my Glock from the waist holster. "The attic?" I said to Fab. She nodded to the hallway and drew her Walther. I leaned toward Fern. "You go out the front and stay out of the way," I whispered.

"You can't shoot 'em," Fern screeched.

Footsteps, followed by a loud crash, and a gun went off. The ceiling opened up, and a man fell to the floor. Dazed, he groaned and tried to sit up, but instead, settled for rubbing his head.

The woman squealed. "You fat ass, look what you've done. You're going to fix it, too." She waved her arms and started to rush him.

I grabbed the back of her housedress and stopped her from advancing on the man.

Fab kicked the gun out of the man's reach and put her foot in the middle of his chest, her Walther staring him down. "Call Gunz and find out what he wants done," she said to me. "You got a name?" she asked the man, who groaned. She kicked him, and he groaned again.

I took my phone out of my pocket and called Gunz.

He answered on the second ring. "Yeah."

I hit the highlights of what had just gone down, pausing to ask the woman, "You know him?" She shook her head. "Truth?" I demanded.

"I don't know him, dammit. I don't even have a ladder tall enough to get up there."

"Good thing." I shook my finger at her. "You're never to go up there."

"I'm sending the cops," Gunz barked. "Call me back when they've left." He hung up.

Cops. He's calling, I mouthed to Fab. "I'll get the handcuffs." I ran out the door to the SUV, pulled the cuffs out of Fab's work bag, and rushed back inside, handing them to her.

Fab cuffed one of the man's arms to a kitchen chair she'd dragged over.

He hadn't moved, and he also didn't take his eyes off the Walther.

"How did you get in?" Fab demanded. When he didn't answer, she aimed her gun at the wet spot on his pants.

He flinched, waving one arm. "Don't shoot me. I climbed up the ladder outside. I wasn't hurting anything. I just needed a place to sleep."

"How long have you been in residence?" I asked.

"About a month. I didn't move around much during the daytime, waited until night when the old girl went to bed to come down and use the kitchen and bathroom."

"You've been without any amenities for that long?" I said in shock.

"I got food and water at the convenience store. It's open all night. Peed out the window. There's a hole I could see the television through, and she had it up loud enough since she can't hear anything."

I turned at the sound of cars pulling up.

"Let's go outside," Fab told the woman. "You got anywhere we can take you until this mess gets cleaned up? You pack a bag, and we'll drive you."

I nudged Fab. "You deal with the cops." Two of them had gotten out of their cars and walked across the grass. I put my arm around the woman. "Plan on being gone for a few weeks. Even if Gunz has someone out here tomorrow, and he will, it takes time, and I'm going to suggest having the house tented in case you do have rats. You want me to call your daughter?"

"I'm not going up there. She lives in Orlando and has enough to worry about. My sons live out of state, so forget that. I'm staying here. I'll live in the bedroom."

"Forget that notion. It's not safe until the living room is cleaned up. Besides, you and I both know you wouldn't stay out of the way."

"You don't know me."

"I know your ilk. That's good enough."

"Ilk, huh?" Fern got a big smile on her face. "I like that."

"I'm going to come up with Plan B. You're going to cooperate, and if you don't, I'll kick your butt." Her eyebrow went up. "I'll have someone else do it."

Fern hooted. "I like you."

"I'm going to remind you that you said that."

One officer had gotten the man to his feet and led him to the patrol car, where he put him in the back. He came over and drew Fern off to one side. The other one motioned to me.

"What's your version of events?" he asked.

Before I answered, I said, "I have a gun in my waistband and a permit to carry in the car."

"Doesn't surprise me, working for Gunz." He laughed at my surprise. "Don't make any sudden moves." He laughed again.

I answered all his questions in succinct fashion and had a few of my own. "How do you know Gunz?" came to mind, but I refrained.

When he was done, I asked, "Is it okay if Mrs. Wallace sits in our SUV, out of the heat? When we're done here, we're relocating her until repairs can be made."

"No problem. We won't be much longer."

Fab sidled over and stood next to me. "Turns out there's an outstanding warrant on our freeloader. Can you believe breaking and entering and burglary?" She nodded toward Fern, who, rather than joining us, was leaning against the bumper of her car and glaring at the house. "What are you doing with her?"

"She's not cooperative and will go right back inside if we take our eyes off her. Where does Gunz live?"

Fab roared with laughter.

I took my phone back out while Fab recovered. "This is Madison," I said when Cootie answered.

"I figured that out when your name came up on my screen."

"Do we have a room available for a few weeks?" I asked.

"Yep. Had a couple of murder cancellations. Got squeamish when they heard the news. Didn't think it was funny when I told them the blood had been cleaned up. Course it hasn't, but what do they know? Scaredies."

Laughing only encourages such behavior, but I couldn't hold it back. "So…" I told him what happened and my bright idea to put Fern up.

"Maybe assign Rude to her to make sure she doesn't go off the rails. She's the aunt of an important client of Fab's, so we can't have her wandering in traffic."

"Between the two of us, we should be able to keep her from being mowed down by a bus."

I knew Cootie was perfect for the job. "And extra pay."

"We'll keep the light on."

I turned to Fab. "You deal with Gunz and the added expense. You need to tell him to get on the repairs pronto. No foot-dragging."

"One thing about Gunz—he wants the job done, so you won't hear any complaints about additional fees as long as he doesn't have to deal with anything." Fab got on her phone and updated Gunz, then shot me a thumbs up.

I walked over to Fern, who wasn't happy to see me coming and didn't bother to hide it. "I got you a motel room up the highway in Tarpon Cove. You can stay there until your house is inhabitable."

"Nothing wrong with it." She kicked gravel around, acting like a petulant child. "Who's going to pay that bill?"

"The king. You can either pack a suitcase and come with us or I'll send Gunz."

"That would be plain-ass mean."

I'd had enough and a headache was creeping in. "Be careful where you step when you go inside, and when you come out, be sure to avoid falling plaster. You know, just in case."

I got two steps away when she said, "Hold on. I'm going, but I'll drive. I'll need to check on things here, make sure everything is going smoothly. You sure Gunz is paying?"

"I'm sure. Does that run?" I pointed to the rusted Ford Falcon that appeared to be on its last tire despite still having four.

"Kind of."

What the heck? "You'll ride with us, and I'll arrange transportation for whenever you need to get around." And an escort, which I left unsaid.

The cop who'd questioned me came over. "I wouldn't go inside; more of the ceiling could come down. Any questions, give me a call." He handed each of us a card.

"I'll secure the house. You..." Fab pointed at Fern.

I ushered the woman inside and helped her pack a bag, which consisted of her tossing items of clothing at me, which I stuffed in a couple of tote bags. I led her back outside and helped her into the back seat.

"Otis," she yelped. At my confusion, she said, "My poodle."

I went back inside. The dog hadn't moved off the chair and was still asleep. It appeared to be as old as its owner and desperately in need of a bath. I went into the bedroom and jerked the comforter and a pillow off the bed, carried them back into the living room, and wrapped up the dog, who took manhandling by a stranger in stride. I carried him out to the car, settling him next to his owner.

"You're good at this," Fab said as I walked around her to get in the car.

"Now I know why Gunz included me in this job. He knows I have more patience for this kind of drama. You would have shot her and been home already."

Chapter Five

Fab flew down the Overseas Highway back to the Cove. To our collective relief, Fern fell asleep, and Fab turned up the music to drown out her snoring. I checked her into a room at Beachside, introduced her to Cootie and Rude, and reinforced that she could call anytime. I instructed Rude to take her anywhere she wanted to go, except back to the house until Gunz gave the okay.

"The guys aren't going to be happy that we didn't call," Fab said once we got back in the SUV. "Where to now?"

"I'm going to find out right now." I texted Billy: *Where do you want to meet?*

Shooting pool at Jake's was the response, which I showed Fab.

I called Creole. "Are you with Mr. Merceau?" I laughed. "Speakerphone." That was a heads up to let him know that Fab would be listening.

"We were just talking about you two and about to wager how much the bail would be."

Fab snorted.

"This wasn't meant to be a busy day, but it got

that way fast." Creole groaned, which I ignored. "We're both bullet-hole free. The other guy will live but with a sore butt. He discharged his weapon, making a hole in the ceiling, and fell through."

"If this was anyone but you two, I'd think you were joking," Didier said.

I told the guys about the newest client, debating whether to mention Gunz's name and deciding to toss it in in a way I hoped came across casually.

Total silence.

Fab raised her brow and smirked.

"Well then," I said. "We're meeting my next appointment at Jake's, and then we'll be home. Do you want me to bring dinner?"

"*You* have a client?" Creole asked.

Didier laughed in the background.

"You don't have to say it like that." I sniffed theatrically, happy he couldn't see the amusement on my face.

He must have covered the phone to say something to Didier because his next words were muffled.

"That is so rude," I huffed. "You suck at letting us listen in, and now the pet peeve of all is coming—you'll have to repeat every word you just said."

"No need to order dinner. Didier and I have something else in mind."

"What would that be?"

"You'll see." Creole blew a kiss through the phone and hung up.

"Wonder what they're up to?" I glared at my phone before shoving it in my pocket.

"You're so suspicious."

I restrained my eyeroll. "A dollar says I'm right."

"A dollar!" Fab laughed. "Do people just assume that Westin is Creole's last name? Didier gets called Mr. Merceau all the time."

"The first time, he laughed. Now, he answers to it."

Creole, aka Luc Baptiste, had retained his undercover moniker when he left the force. And Didier, who'd used only his first name as a fashion model, had also decided not to take up his last name again when he left that industry.

Fab turned into the driveway of Jake's, slowing and perusing the property I owned. The short block consisted of several businesses. The bar sat at the back of the lot. On the right side, an old gas station had been turned into a garden antiques store called Junker's. In the other corner was Fab's lighthouse, which had appeared one night in lieu of payment on a job, with no other details forthcoming. Thus, I also claimed ownership. So far, it hadn't garnered any interest from the cops, and that made me happy. Currently, Gunz rented it as office space for whenever he needed a desk to meet a client. Passersby often stopped there for photo-ops. At the front curb was a pink roach coach, Twinkie Princesses, which sported a sign saying, "We fry anything." That might be true if they ever opened.

Every parking space close to the building was full, so Fab pulled around the back and parked next to the kitchen door. We entered Cook's domain. Cook—Henry to two people that I knew of, one being my four-year-old niece; the one and only time I called him by his first name, he growled at me—ran the kitchen efficiently, and I never interfered. His office door was open, and he sat behind his desk on the phone. When I waved, he nodded at me.

Fab and I went down the hall and stopped at the bar, where Kelpie, the pink-haired bartender, was holding court, leaning over to offer a generous view of her assets as she shoved a tip in her bra top. The stools were filled with regulars, and the few tables dotted around the room were also filled.

"Hey, Bossaroo." Kelpie waved.

I stabbed a cherry and held it up, code for soda. I glanced out the open doors to the deck, happy to see that my reserved table was empty and the other outside tables were also empty.

I'd long ago had a sign made, but more often than not, people ignored the tented placard with a gracious "Don't sit here" on one side, "Reserved" on the other.

Fab jerked my arm and nodded to where Billy

was shooting pool. I walked over, made eye contact, and pointed to the deck, then walked outside, overturned the sign, and took a seat, Fab across from me.

Billy came through the door, tipped his beer bottle to me, and grabbed a seat. "Thanks for meeting me." He was a man who blended in with the masses... until you screwed him and he handed you your head. "Here's the deal. This is about Xander, and who better to help him, since you know all the players involved?"

"He's not in trouble, is he?" I asked.

"What did we miss?" Creole and Didier came through the doorway, beer in hand, and sat down.

"Are you checking up on us?" I asked indignantly.

He leaned over and laid a loud kiss on my cheek. "I wouldn't put it that way. Sounds unfriendly." He nodded to Billy, who smirked at the unfolding drama.

Didier hooked his arm around Fab, who flashed him a moony smile.

"Billy has a right to client confidentiality," I huffed.

"Don't care about that, as long as we're agreed that no one embarrasses Xander if my idea doesn't work out," Billy said. Everyone agreed. "Crum used his connections to get the kid into some highbrow university out in California to finish his degree on a scholarship. Snarked that

Xander was wasting his talents working with stupenagels."

"What's the problem?" Creole asked.

"Hon-nee, he's *my* client," I reminded him with a raised eyebrow.

"Oh yeah. Carry on."

The guys laughed.

"The kid likes hanging with the stupenagels and considers us family. He knows the California deal is an opportunity he can't turn down but doesn't want to be away from his cobbled-together family. He's had enough loss for someone so young."

Xander Huntington's father had died without leaving a will. He was in college at the time, and his step-mother didn't pay the tuition and didn't tell him until he got his notice to move out of the dorm. That's also when he found out that he was penniless and on his own. He'd realized in short order that life as a criminal wasn't his calling.

"What do you want these two to do about it?" Didier asked.

"I want Madison to go and light a fire under the professor's ass—get him to get the same offer closer to home. And no derogatory terms hurled at the kid, like he's wont to do. He tosses 'sissy' around quite a bit. If he can't do it, fine, a polite 'no, I'm not as smart as I claim' and move on. I'd do it, but I'm itching to kick his ass, and it wouldn't bother me that he's an old man."

"It would make it so much easier for me if you

could restrain yourself," I said. "To assure myself of a positive response, I'll offer up an IOU to the professor."

"Client." Creole snorted. "This is favor-doing. I hate this IOU system of yours, except for the ones that I've currently amassed."

I frowned up at him.

"Am I interrupting? Sorry." Clearly, he wasn't. "Continue."

"Why didn't Xander come to one of us?" Fab asked.

Conversation came to a halt as Kelpie crossed the threshold, tray in hand, and set down fresh drinks, taking away the old ones. She winked at Billy and left quickly.

"Xander would never ask," Billy said. "Besides, he doesn't know I concocted this idea. If he did, he wouldn't want me to approach you. He holds you in high regard." He nodded at me.

"What about me?" Fab demanded.

"You scare the hell out of him." Billy made a disbelieving face, as though it should be a no-brainer. "You only have yourself to blame. Didn't you threaten to shoot him one day when Madison wasn't around?"

"You didn't." I glared at Fab.

"Shoot, not kill."

"I'll take care of the curmudgeonly professor. I'll enjoy twisting his arm," I said. "I'll have Crum present the option to Xander to finish his degree in South Florida. He can claim credit for the idea, which will appeal to him. If he hedges in the least, I'll have my sidekick with me." I shot Fab a sneaky smile. "By the time she's done scaring the snot out of him, he'll be on board."

Fab made a trigger finger and blew on it. She winked at Billy.

"No one says a word about any outside manipulation." I shot a stern eye around the table. The guys smirked. "Just so you know, I'm going to be calling Xander later, pitching a side job," I said to Billy. "It will take me a day or two to get with the professor."

"He enjoyed the last job." Billy laughed. "Besides, he wouldn't turn you down anyway. More pet-sitting?" he asked, referring to a job from one of Fab's clients who had more money than sense, needed a pet-sitter, and thought of her first. Well, not exactly. They couldn't find anyone else. It might not have been a problem if they'd chosen a domesticated animal as a pet instead of an oversized rodent. I shook my head. "That's too bad. I got invited to the mansion and indulged in living like the rich for a day." He stood. "I appreciate this."

"Happy you called on me." I smiled at Billy. "Order dinner and eat here or take it out—on the house."

"Sounds good." Billy went back inside the bar.

"Do you plan on feeding us?" Fab asked the guys. "We missed lunch."

"Favorites?" Creole stood. At our nods, he said, "I'll put in the order."

Chapter Six

I'd warned Fab the night before that I wasn't available for early morning anything. To my surprise, she held off until almost lunchtime, when my phone beeped with a text from her: "Five minutes."

I slid on a pair of sandals, grabbed my bag, and went outside, surprised that Fab wasn't already waiting out front. She'd obviously been by earlier, as she'd left her Porsche, which I hated to drive, and taken the Hummer. Barely a minute after I got outside, she came racing around the curve from the street, pulled up, and made a u-turn.

"Why don't you get your own SUV?" I grouched, getting in and slamming the door.

"Why, when you have one?" She pointed to the coffee cup in the holder.

I recognized the logo. "Yum." I licked my lips and snapped off the lid, taking a drink. "I'm afraid to ask what's on the agenda for today, since showing up with my favorite brew feels like a bribe."

"We're going to drop in on Raul and Dickie on the off chance that they've got some information on the dead chick and, if not, get them to hit up their connection in the coroner's office."

Great! A trip to the funeral home. Just the way I liked to start the day. That was why Fab bought the extra-large coffee. "Didn't the guys tell us last night to stay away from the case? You know, those two good-looking ones we had dinner with?"

"They're going to thank us when we bring the killer to justice."

I wouldn't count on it. "Wasn't it also last night that you pitched a fit because the guys told you in explicit terms to let the cops do their job? Your husband whispered something that shut you up, but I did hear, 'We'll discuss this later.' Did that happen?"

Fab squirmed in her seat. "I told him on the way home that I was working hard on putting personal safety first."

I gagged. Fab punched me in the shoulder. "Ouch. Didier bought that?"

"This morning, when he questioned me about my day, I told him that I had a few sources I could check with, and all it will take is a phone call."

"I take it this is one of your phone calls? Except we're showing up in person."

"One thing we all agreed on last night is that the sooner this case is solved, the better. I'm doing my part."

I couldn't fault her idea. Dickie and Raul were

always eager to help us.

Fab sped across town and turned into the Tropical Slumber Funeral Home. Once a drive-thru hot dog stand, it now, after a few renovations, delivered on all your final send-off requests, no matter how weird.

Fab parked next to a Mercedes SUV with the driver leaning against the door. The hefty middle-aged man's suit jacket was open, revealing a shoulder holster. Dark glasses covered most of his face.

We got out and walked across the parking lot, but not before Fab and the driver exchanged head-to-toe once-overs. We were a foot from the door when it opened and two dark-haired, suited men walked out.

One of them turned. "We'll be in touch," he said to Raul.

They walked by us with a nod.

Raul smiled at us and held the door open. "You owe me five bucks," he said to Dickie, who stuck his head out the door. "As soon as we heard about the murder, I bet that the two of you would be by."

"Sorry we missed the grand opening," Dickie said. "We had a funeral for a local man. It was a nice turnout, and everyone was well-behaved."

Dickie and Raul couldn't be any more different. Dickie was tall and painfully thin with little skin pigmentation. Raul had a bodybuilder physique and could pose for a men's health magazine. The two men had bought out the previous owner, added a crematorium and pet cemetery, and recently started holding weddings. Raul ran the business side and was open to any suggestion that would enhance their portfolio of options. Dickie, the more laidback of the two, prettied up the dead folks in a respectful way and didn't care for new tricks.

I turned before Raul closed the door and got one last look at the two men climbing into the Mercedes. "Since when do you two do business with thugs in expensive suits?" I sat in my favorite plastic slip-covered chair inside the large entryway next to the door. In my opinion, it was ideally located for a fast getaway.

"We came highly recommended." Raul preened.

"By whom?" Fab asked, prowling over to the main viewing room and sticking her head in the door.

Raul and Dickie exchanged a look, and it was clear neither had thought to ask the question.

"Where are Astro and Necco?" I asked.

Raul crossed the entry, opened the hall door that led to the living quarters, and whistled. "Not everyone likes them. They're intimidating."

The Dobermans skidded into the big room, looked around, and ran over for a head scratch. They seemed to know when there was leftover funeral food and when there wasn't. Today was the latter. They laid down on my feet, which was one of their favorite spots.

"I've never seen the dogs be aggressive."

"Wait until you hear what those men want." Dickie threw himself in a chair outside one of the viewing rooms on the far side of the entryway. He crossed his arms, an irritated scowl on his face. "I hope you can talk sense into Raul; he's not listening to me."

Fab and I stared at Raul.

Raul's cheeks reddened. "Mr. Richie would like to have his great-grandmother mummified and heard that we accommodate special requests."

It wasn't often my mouth actually dropped open, but this was one of those moments. *Mummified!*

Fab recovered before I did. "You should check to make sure it's legal before you get their hopes up. Isn't that an extensive process that requires organ removal and that sort of thing?"

Of course, she'd want the gruesome details.

"It does." Dickie groaned and covered his face.

"How old was great-grandma—a hundred?" I asked. The men who'd just left weren't spring chickens.

"Hundred and eight. She's not dead yet, but doing poorly," Raul said.

"I don't have any experience with mummification and don't want to do it anyway." Dickie wrinkled his nose. "It requires a labor-intensive process that I'm not interested in undertaking." He chuckled. "Undertaking."

Must be funeral humor. "Free advice: The driver had a gun and I'd bet the other two were also carrying, so I'd be careful before entering into any kind of agreement with them."

"Better yet, find out who referred them and see what they have to say. Or give me their names, and I'll have a background check run," Fab offered.

Raul took out his phone. "I'll text you."

"Send it to me," I said. "Since she'll delegate it to me to do."

"You hear about the murder?" Dickie asked. A man who was usually devoid of emotion, his pale features perked up.

"How do you get your information so quickly?" Fab asked.

"The suicide was all the talk at the bakery the next morning," Raul said. "So, I called Pitch, our coroner friend, and he said not so fast. The scene was staged, but whoever it was did a good job."

"Has dead chick been claimed yet?" I asked.

Raul's brow shot up.

"Don't look at me. I can't be expected to remember names all the time. She doesn't." I stared at Fab.

"Really, Madison," Fab teased.

"Fab's been hanging out with Mother too much; she's starting to sound just like her."

The guys laughed.

"To answer your question, she hasn't been

claimed," Raul informed us. "Do you want me to let you know when she is?"

I nodded. "I know this Pitch fellow isn't supposed to be blabbing about the dead folks in his care, but any time we can repay the favors, let us know."

Fab stood. Apparently, she'd just remembered that she hadn't made the rounds of the viewing rooms. She crossed the room, opening each door and peeking inside. When she'd finished, she said, "You've got a full house."

The guys smiled ear-to-ear.

Not wanting to know where the conversation would go next, I stood. Sensing the movement, the dogs jumped to their feet. "Almost forgot. We have another appointment." I gave the dogs one last pat and turned to the door.

"We'll be in touch," Fab said, and didn't waste time catching up to me.

The guys stood in the doorway and waved as Fab cut out the rear exit.

"As often as we've been here, you're still squeamish over a nicely dressed dead person." Fab smirked.

"Stop. There's not enough coffee for this conversation, and besides, I'm out." I picked up the cup and shook it.

Chapter Seven

Fab took one of her shortcuts to the office, whipping through a residential area and down a street clearly marked "Dead End," except the driveway that was really an alley dumped out where we needed to be.

"You need to feed me," I told her.

"We're not going to be here long. I need to pick up a file I forgot." Fab pulled up to the security gate as it rolled open. "What's that?" She hit the brakes just inside the fence and peered out the driver's side window.

I scooted up so I could see over her shoulder, but still had no clue what she was talking about.

Fab put the SUV in park and jumped out. "It's a baby," she yelled.

"A real one?"

The baby answered by unleashing an ear-piercing scream.

I got out and rounded the front of the Hummer. Sure enough, Fab was staring down at a crying baby in a car seat.

Fab picked up the seat and wrinkled her nose. "It smells."

"Probably needs changing." I scanned every

inch of the lot, shrugging off Fab's attempt to hand the baby off to me. "Finders keepers. Until we locate the mother. Where is she, by the way?" I walked to the open gate and stood in the driveway, checking out the street. Not a person or car in sight. I stepped out into the middle of the street for a second look and scanned both sides.

"I don't know anything about babies, and you probably babysat as a teenager."

I maneuvered around her and reached inside the SUV to close the gate. "I did. But I'm not going to deprive myself of the amusement of watching you muddle your way through."

"This is a helpless child."

"Yep. About six months old." I got behind the wheel. "I'll park the car." I shut the door on her response, which, judging by the glare, wasn't very nice. I chuckled and pulled into the garage.

"You could be more helpful." Fab had followed on foot, baby carrier in hand, and was now shooting me daggers and, at the same time, cooing at the baby.

"I don't even need to use my premonition skills to tell you that the baby needs a diaper change and we don't have any." I grabbed our bags out of the back, turned, and went up the stairs.

"You could improvise while I check the neighborhood for the mother."

"Good one. This is a commercial area, and

there are few places to hide. And why hide? A baby and no mother worries me. We should be reporting this to the police."

The door flew open, Xander on the threshold. "You missed the excitement." His gaze went past me. "Where did you get that?"

I breezed by him.

Fab attempted to pass the baby off to Xander, who backed up and almost tripped. "Before you ask, I don't know jack about babies and don't want to learn at my young age."

I tried not to laugh, I really did, but it escaped anyway and earned me another burning glare. "Take the baby into the bathroom and wash it off in the shower. Xander, you come up with something to fashion a diaper with."

"What are you going to do?" Fab sniffed.

"Take pics." I whipped out my phone. "Hold on." I stopped and turned my attention to Xander. "What excitement?"

His brown eyes danced. "The cops were in chase mode when I came to work and had swarmed the area. I was lucky to get through the gate. I raced upstairs and had a great view from the window. By that time, they'd blocked off the street and started a search."

"Did they catch anyone? A woman, perhaps? Minus a baby. It came from somewhere," I responded to Fab's huff.

"No woman." He shook his head. "It didn't take long before they had a thirty-something man face down on the ground and cuffed, and after a couple of minutes, they shoved him in the back of a cruiser and drove off."

"Wonder what that was about?" Fab made clucking noises to the baby, who'd quieted momentarily but now started fussing again. "There's bound to be a write-up on the local news site. Forward it to me," she instructed Xander.

"While you're doing that, look for any reports of a missing baby." I followed Fab into the bathroom and opened a cupboard, removing a stack of towels and placing one on the floor of the walk-in shower.

The first surprise came when Fab lifted the baby out of the carrier. Lying underneath it was a Smith and Wesson. What the heck? The baby had been sitting on it the whole time.

The second was that, when the diaper was removed, a good-sized baggie of white powder fell out. The only expected item was a baby bottle that had been tucked into one side.

"Bring a couple of trash bags," Fab yelled to Xander.

He came back with them in hand, and she picked up the gun with the corner of a towel and put it in one of the bags, then the drugs in the other, careful not to leave fingerprints or smudge any that might've been left behind.

The baby turned out to be a boy.

I turned on the shower and fiddled with the

temperature until I was certain it wouldn't burn his skin.

Fab gave him a good rinse, then covered him in soapy bubbles, which made him laugh. Once she had him smelling good, she sat on the bathroom rug and wrapped him in a bath towel.

I sat next to them and watched with amusement. "I'm going out on a limb here. Gun, drugs—I'm going to take a guess that if the man who was arrested was the dad, he shouldn't be babysitting."

"You think the guy who was apprehended and the baby are related?"

I gave her a *what else?* look. There hadn't been anyone else lurking around, at least none that we saw.

"If so, how was he able to leave the baby here without anyone noticing?" Fab asked, turning to Xander, who stood in the doorway, phone in hand, not paying attention to either of us. "It had to have happened when you came in the gate."

"Or the baby's appearance isn't related in any way, and that makes it weirder," I said.

Fab rolled the baby on his back and clapped his feet together; he waved his arms and gurgled happily. "What now?" The baby reached out and grasped one of her fingers.

"Nothing on the internet… yet." Xander was still focused on his screen. Under his other arm was a roll of paper towels. He pulled them out and tossed them to me. "I'm thinking these can double as a diaper."

"Any clue how the baby got here?" I asked Xander, now that he was done with his search.

"Probably my fault." He shifted uncomfortably. "I think it's cool to trigger the gate from down the street so I don't have to wait for it to open."

"That sounds like Fab." I half-laughed.

"I got held up by a cop for several minutes. He'd seen me open the gate and asked if that was where I was going. Told him I worked here. He let me through with the admonition not to leave until they apprehended the suspect."

"I'm surprised they didn't want to search the property," I said.

"They probably would have if they hadn't got their man," Fab said.

"After I got up here, I didn't leave the window. I swear I didn't see a baby or anyone lurking around. It wasn't more than fifteen minutes before they had the guy in custody. Nabbed him half a block away on the other side of the street."

I slid my phone out of my pocket and made a call, happy that I'd recently been given a direct number. "We need legal advice about what's best for this little guy and what to do next," I told Fab, who nodded. When Emerson answered, I said, "Remember when you said I could call anytime if I needed legal assistance?"

Emerson Grace, who was dating my brother,

was a family law lawyer who'd helped my brother get custody of his daughter and get her out of foster care.

"I'm so excited. I hope it's not a dead body or anything," Emerson said in mock horror.

I told her about finding the baby and everything Xander had witnessed.

"I've got some time right now. I'll make the calls for you, come to your office, and see that everything goes smoothly. I've got a good friend who's a case worker, and I'll give her a call. Once you report what happened to the cops, their first call will be to Social Services to take custody until they get everything sorted out and find a relative."

"We could come to you, if that would be easier," I said, thinking we could seatbelt the carrier into the back of the Hummer.

Xander had taken out the seat cushion and was washing it as we spoke.

"It would be better if I came to you," Emerson said. "The cops will want to check out the property and surrounding area."

"Fab will so owe you for this."

"I'm on my way." Emerson hung up.

"Little Dude just pooped on the towel." Fab jumped up. "Your turn to shower him, and I'll get another towel." She threw his onesie in the washing machine and grabbed a couple of towels before sitting back down.

I held on tightly as I washed him. It had been a

long time since my babysitting days, and I didn't think I'd ever looked after someone so young. I managed to get him showered with no mishaps, and he laughed when the water rolled down his body. Fab had snuck out of the bathroom while my attention was otherwise engaged. I wrapped him in another towel and carried him out to her desk. "I think we should keep him wrapped in towels. We have a large stack to go through." I handed the baby to Fab, who took him without complaint, and sat across from her. "You need the practice."

"I didn't drop him, so that's good."

I laughed, thinking, *me either*, then sobered. "What's going to happen to him?"

"Let's hope he's got someone better to look after him than the person who left him with a gun and drugs," Fab said.

I had snapped a couple of pics of the baby in the bathroom and now stood and took a couple more.

"You get anything on the dead chick?" I asked Xander.

"Rebecca Herd? So far, just boring background." Xander was on his phone again and running his finger over the screen. "Not much to snoop into. Nothing on her credit report. She doesn't even have a credit card. The car left at the motel was registered to one of those rent-by-the-week places. Only people with really bad credit do that—car loans are easy to get if you're willing to pay through the nose on the interest rate."

Fab's phone beeped, and she smiled at the screen. Didier. Only he garnered that reaction. After a short exchange, she hung up. "What did you do?" she shouted at me.

Xander jerked in surprise and sent me a questioning look.

"I texted Didier a pic of her and the baby. Didn't take him long to call." I laughed along with Xander.

The gate buzzer rang. Fab eyed the monitor. "It's Emerson."

Xander jumped up and raced across the room. "I'll go get her." He opened the door and ran down the steps.

The baby had made himself comfortable in Fab's lap, head leaning back against her chest, sound asleep.

"He looks comfortable." I smiled at his sleeping innocence, wanting to cover him in kisses. "I hope everything works out for him and he's got a loving family waiting for his return."

"Hi," Emerson called out, coming through the door. "Love the offices." She stopped in the middle of the space and spun around, checking everything out. "You did a great job," she said to Fab.

"Let me take you on a tour." I showed her around the office and gave her an exaggerated version of showering the baby, then led her through my office and out to the deck.

She looked over the railing. "Any water view is a good one." We agreed on that and went back inside. "So cute," Emerson sighed, fingering the baby's cheek lightly before taking a seat in front of Fab's desk.

I took the chair next to her.

"Drinks?" Xander called. We all chose water, and he got out the bottles and set them in front of us, then took his favorite seat on the couch.

"I called my friend who works at Social Services, and she's on the way over." Emerson smiled at the baby. "She's already called in a report to the cops, so they should be arriving at any time. She'll be taking him with her, and I told her to bring some baby supplies. She'll know what he needs."

The baby's eyes popped open and he began to whimper. I stood and got the bottle that had been left in the baby carrier from the kitchen counter. I unscrewed it and smelled it; it had no odor. "Is room temp okay?"

"You're going to find out." Emerson laughed.

I ripped paper towels off the roll, crossed to Fab, and handed her everything.

The buzzer rang for the second time that day.

"That was well-timed." I motioned to Xander. "You've got door duty today."

Fab had buzzed whoever it was inside and kept her eyes glued to the monitor. "Kevin drew the short card."

It didn't take long for him to clomp up the stairs. Xander stayed downstairs for the next arrival, or at least, I was sure that was his excuse. He'd told me once that Kevin made him nervous. Kevin had approached Xander during one of his visits to The Cottages and said he'd heard an interesting story about him, but didn't have the opportunity to elaborate because Crum, who was standing close by and eavesdropping, had taken over the conversation, saying, "You don't have carte blanche to question people. It's rude and not the least bit professional."

Xander told me he'd breathed a huge sigh of relief and toughed it out, tamping down his inclination to cut and run. Good thing, too, since that would only make Kevin more suspicious, and the last thing any of us wanted was for him to find out about the attempted purse-snatching which is how we'd first met the young man. Shortly after he decided a life of crime wasn't for him.

"The professor should know all about the rude part," I'd said. But Crum had accomplished what he wanted when Kevin stomped off, and I was happy for Xander. I'd suggested that he throw out an offer to fix Kevin's computer for free should he ever need it, which would earn him some brownie points.

"Nice offices." Kevin checked every corner. "This is my first invite." He made a sad face.

I replaced the waters and threw the empties at

the trash can one at time, practicing my shooting, then grabbed a Coke for Kevin. Not wanting to drag furniture around, I took up my usual seat in the far corner now that the chairs were full, and listened while Fab told Kevin about how she'd spotted the baby as soon as she drove in.

The gate buzzed again.

Kevin turned his attention to me.

Before he could ask, I said, "My story is the same as hers."

Minutes later, a middle-aged woman came up the stairs, followed by Xander. A tote bag over her arm, she greeted Emerson with a friendly, "Hello."

While Emerson was making the introductions, I noticed Xander disappearing around the corner into the office space we shared. I followed him—I'd get the good parts from Fab later.

"You know what's weird," Xander said, looking over his laptop. "No Amber Alert and not a single report about a missing baby."

"You'd have thought that if it was the dad who got arrested, he'd have said something by now and the cops would've been back. Apparently not, since Kevin was hearing the baby side of the story for the first time. You'd think that a man's son would take priority over any additional felony charges he might incur."

"A father of the year wouldn't use his baby to hide a gun and drugs, then ditch the kid. Whoever left the baby had to have noticed that this place has a barbed wire-topped gate. How were they planning on getting back in?" Xander shook his head in disgust. "If I come across anything, I'll forward it."

Fab joined us. "The other three are in conference. I let them use my desk." She sat down in one of the new chairs she'd ordered after complaining that when she deigned to visit my office, she didn't want to have to drag a chair along.

"You were great with the baby." I smiled at her.

"I managed to send a text to Didier once I got over the initial fear and was sure that I hadn't made any glaring errors."

"Let me guess: he sent a coo-y face emoji?"

Fab glared at me.

"Aww." I pouted. "That was my way of saying, 'How sweet.'"

Xander looked down and laughed.

"I hate the idea that the baby is headed to foster care," Fab said. "I thought earlier that we should've just kept him and located the parents ourselves. But then we'd be in big trouble."

"Jail trouble," I reinforced.

"Emerson told the social worker that she'd volunteer to be guardian ad litem, subject to approval of the court. Since she has a good reputation, it will probably happen. I told her we'd cover her fee to represent Baby Dude."

"Tell her we want a family discount." I

laughed at Fab's look of chagrin, knowing she'd never ask.

"Don't we have another appointment?" Fab smirked.

"You know I made that up. I can only hang out at the funeral home for so long, and then I need to get the heck out of there." I whipped out my phone and sent Xander a text. "I almost forgot. Check this guy out, and that includes a criminal background check." To Fab's raised eyebrow, I said, "I'm having Xander run the name of one of the gunned-up thugs we saw at the funeral home."

"I hope this one's more interesting than the last one." Xander flipped open his laptop, ready to ferret out yet another person's past.

"When can we leave?" I asked Fab. "I do need to make one more stop." I turned slightly to make sure that Xander's attention was diverted and mouthed, *Crum*. "After that, I want to sneak over to my neighbor's. They've got a floating dock, and I thought I'd sip something cold and enjoy the view."

"Aren't you worried you'll get shot for trespassing?" Fab made a trigger finger.

Emerson poked her head around the corner. "Kevin and the social worker are getting ready to leave."

We followed her to where the social worker was strapping the baby into his carrier. Both Fab and I kissed the baby's cheek and watched as the woman carried him out.

"I've got to get back to the office." Emerson checked her watch. "Don't worry, the baby will get good care and I'll keep you updated."

"I'll be calling to set up a date for dinner at Fab's," I said.

"I'd love that." Emerson followed the other two out the door.

"I'm certain it's okay for me to set up social events at your house without asking." I winked at Fab.

"The husbands can cook."

Chapter Eight

Fab cut around the corner to The Cottages and backed into the driveway across the street from the ten-unit property. The property belonged to Mac, but she didn't care if we used it for parking.

"Five minutes," I said to Fab, and held up my fingers, as if she wouldn't know what I meant. It annoyed her, as I knew it would. "Try to behave. If you do, iced coffee on me." I shut the door of the SUV and cut across the street. I heard the sound of the other door closing and knew Fab wasn't far behind. For all her complaining, she hated being left out of even the most mundane of activities. It would be nice to place a wager on a trip to my property being uneventful, but I knew that would be money down the drain.

At first glance, the property appeared quiet, no one passed out on their porch or craning their head through the slats in the blinds. As we moved closer, Fab and I exchanged glances at the sounds of music drifting from the pool area, followed by laughter, voices, and splashing water.

"Party?" Fab smirked.

"Wonder where Mac is. She usually meets us

in the driveway." I hesitated to round the corner, but what was the worst that could... "Stop," I reprimanded myself and moved forward. "Just great." I took a quick headcount of those in the pool—six, with another dozen filling the chaises and chairs in various states of barely covered. A couple of that lot were year-round tenants; the others, I didn't recognize and hoped were registered guests, though it would be unusual for all of them to be out and mingling at the same time. Hopefully, none had wandered in off the street.

"Whatever they're barbequing, it smells good and I'm hungry," Fab said.

"If you'd said something, we could've stopped at Greasy Burger and I'd have treated."

Fab made a retching noise.

What did the woman have against hamburgers—the staple of life after tacos?

The stools at the tiki bar had all been claimed, probably due to their proximity to several large buckets that sat on the countertop, beer cans sticking out of the top. The pool gate was open, despite the sign warning against it. Just inside was my missing manager, Mac, kicking back on a chaise, sunhat pulled down over her face.

I kicked her foot, and she jumped up, her hat toppling to the ground. "No sleeping on the job."

"You're about to fall out." Fab pointed to her chest.

"Lordee, you know how to scare a woman."

Mac huffed and readjusted her bathing suit. There wasn't really enough material in her bikini top to corral the pair, but she made it work, and as long as she didn't breathe too deeply, she'd be fine. She'd hiked her skirt up around her waist and now tugged it down.

"What the heck is going on?" I asked as she continued to fiddle with her top.

"Pool party for the new guests." Mac looked supremely proud of her idea.

"A great way to meet and greet. Make new friends."

"Where's my invitation?" Fab kicked her chair.

"Stop it, you two," I admonished the pair, neither of whom bothered to back off from their staredown lest the other claim a win. "I'm here to talk to Crum."

Mac unleashed an ear-splitting whistle, finger-pointed, and motioned the big man over. That brought all conversation to a halt, and those that hadn't yet noticed our arrival did so now. "Hey, Prof, over here," she bellowed, so loud that people passing by in the street could hear.

Crum disentangled himself from charming two giggling women whose husbands, I presumed, straddled a chaise nearby, playing cards, not caring that they were flirting with the old codger.

I flinched when he stood up in a pair of turquoise men's speedos. It wasn't uncommon to see older men strutting the beaches of Florida in the briefest of swimwear, but Crum really took it to an extreme. I'd banned him from wearing his tighty-whities outside his cottage and once suggested he might want to consider a pair of board shorts, which earned me a snort.

Crum's bare feet slapped the concrete as he made his way over. He bowed. "Ladies, how may I be of service?" He flashed a toothy grin, one of the few men living at The Cottages to have all his teeth.

"You and I need to talk." My brow shot up, daring him to argue differently. "Privately."

"Come into my office." He waved for me to follow.

I thought we'd be going to his cottage, but I was wrong. He led me over to the bar and grabbed a stool, placing it at the far end, then went behind the bar. "Beer or beer?"

I turned up my nose, which he rightly understood as a *no thanks*.

"You're looking haggard," he said with a smile that made me want to kick him. But I'd have to climb over the bartop or go around, and neither was happening.

"You need to keep this conversation between the two of us, or I'll make good on my threat to kick your butt out into the street."

"Can't we have a civilized conversation without you attempting to intimidate me?"

"No. The reason being I enjoy it. Setting

niceties aside, this is about Xander. He doesn't know that I'm here or what I'm about to ask and doesn't need to. You're not to embarrass him in any way."

"I like the kid, even though he's wasting his talents." Crum popped the top on a can of beer and took a long drink. "I don't suppose you're here to tell me that you're going to encourage him to step up his game."

"I understand you've worked your magic, getting him into a university in California to finish up his degree." That piqued his interest. "I'm asking you to find a college closer to the Keys. University of Miami, perhaps."

"Why would I do that?" He peered down his nose at me.

"You know Xander lost his father and doesn't have anyone except this motley group that we've introduced him into. Although he'd never tell you, lest you name-call, he doesn't want to go off by himself."

"Why not just speak up?"

"Because he respects you and doesn't want to appear ungrateful."

"You expect me to whip pixie dust out of my pocket, sprinkle it about, and produce an acceptance letter to another stellar university?"

"Pretty much." I flashed a cheeky smile. "If you can't do it, fine. I know it's nervy to ask, but let's face it, I have nerve a-plenty."

"Don't know," Crum said, lost in thought,

suddenly oblivious to me sitting there, staring him down. "I'll get with my connections and see what I can make happen and get back to you."

"Not necessary. You need to hear the next part of my plan." I ignored his groan. "You're going to pitch the change of plans as your idea. His hero worship of you will only grow." I emphasized the point by throwing out my hands.

Fab came up behind me and put her chin on my shoulder. "You going to do it or not?" she barked at Crum.

"I'm going to try, and if I'm successful, I'm going to take all the credit." Crum puffed up. "So much for a secret, since she knows," he said snootily.

"No worries about her. Fab's tight-lipped. When she wants to be." She poked me in the back. "One more thing before I go. Can you refrain from getting involved with the guests, especially those that have husbands?"

"No worries." Crum shook his head with a dramatic sigh. "Mac already threatened my manliness if a fight breaks out over a female guest. I can't help that women are drawn to me." He puffed out his chest.

I had to restrain myself from gagging. "I imagine it's difficult for you." Sometimes, even when I tried, sincerity escaped me. I slid off the stool.

"How many of those IOUs do I get if I make this miracle happen?" Crum smiled craftily.

"One."

"That's it?"

I nodded and held his stare.

"We've got another appointment." Fab grabbed my arm. "Try not to get your butt kicked," she said to Crum, and pulled me away.

"We have to stop using that excuse," I whispered, pasting on a lame smile as we weaved around sunbathers who didn't bother to hide that they were checking us out.

"Why? It's a good one. We're busy women, so it only makes sense we've got places to go."

I forced Fab to come to a stop in front of Mac. "If this—" I waved my arm around. "—shindig of yours gets out of hand, I'm holding you responsible."

"Yeah, yeah." Mac snorted, followed by a different noise. "Try not to suck the fun out of our little afternoon soiree." She flashed a phony smile. "You do know that some kind of ruckus is always a good thing, right? If not, never mind."

"Where are the normal people? How about attracting them?"

"This is Florida." Mac rolled her eyes. "Normal is on back order."

Chapter Nine

The next morning, I called Fab early, reminding her that I needed to go to Jake's for a meeting. I'd insisted on being in on the hiring process for a new bartender.

She laughed and made some unidentifiable noise. "Have fun. I'm meeting my security guy to install more cameras at Beachside."

Instead of my usual table out on the deck, I sat at the bar, armed with a notepad. "You handle the interviews, and I'll interrupt if I have any questions. I'm here to learn from the master." I smiled cheekily. "It would please me if you decided to hire someone normalish."

Doodad snorted. "Whatever that means. Someone who starches their underwear?"

My manager, Doodad—aka Charles Wingate III—who sported a "fell out of bed, hit the floor hard" look, stood behind the bar, irritated that he had another job opening. We had a tendency to fill jobs with Cook's multitude of relatives, but he had exhausted that list of possibilities.

"How many eager applicants do we have?"

"Stop with the cheerful; it's hurting my head." Doodad grasped it between his hands and rocked back and forth, a stupid smile on his face. "Three. Sort of. The first one is late and no-call." He tapped his non-existent watch. "So, two."

A thirty-something, dark-haired man poked his head through the door, gave the interior a once-over, and sneered before stepping inside. His blue cotton suit was ill-fitting, the pants too big and the jacket two sizes too small. "This dump needs to be bulldozed," he said in a snotty tone.

"If that's an applicant, no way." I drew my finger across my neck.

The man sauntered over and stuck his hand out to Doodad without a glance in my direction.

Doodad ignored his hand. "The job's been filled."

"Asshole."

I giggled as the man stomped out. He'd barely cleared the entrance when Kelpie came in with a youngish woman in tow. The woman had on baggy black scrubs that matched part of her hair. On the other half, she sported a man's blond toupee with a piece of netting pinned to the top.

"This is Lizzie." Kelpie made the introductions. Lizzie nodded, her lips pulled tight.

"Interview three," Doodad whispered. Why he bothered, I wasn't sure, since we all heard him. "Why do you want to work here?" he asked in the surliest of tones.

Lizzie glared at him.

"Because I told her what a great place this is, and it beats the taco joint where she works now," Kelpie answered for her.

"I like tacos." I licked my lips.

Doodad frowned at me, reminiscent of Mother's *behave* look. "You have any bartending experience?" he asked. "You didn't fill out the whole online application."

"I did it." Kelpie grinned. "Wasn't sure what to put, so I left most of it empty. Figured you could ask."

"That's what I'm trying to do," Doodad huffed. "Do you think you can contain yourself long enough for her to answer? I'd like your friend Lizzie Borden here to answer for herself."

"Ha," Lizzie snapped. "You think I haven't heard that before? We're not kin, in case you want to know. And no, I've never killed anyone."

"Can you mix a drink or not?"

Kelpie only followed directions when she was so inclined, and this wasn't one of those times. She opened her mouth to answer and got cut off by a loud explosion.

"Call 911," I yelled, and slid off my stool, racing to the front door. I'd just poked my head out when another boom half-deafened me, and I saw flames leap into the air. "Twinkie Princesses just blew sky-high." I ran out into the parking lot. "Let's hope the fire doesn't spread," I said to Doodad, who'd followed on my heels.

Sirens wailed into life in the distance. Two

trucks rolled up within minutes, and it didn't take them long to get the flames out. The pink-and-lime coach had lost all resemblance to its previous incarnation, turned into a burned-out jumble of aluminum.

I pulled out my phone and called the owners. I had only talked to one or the other a handful of times in the years that I'd owned the block. Their "we'll fry anything" business had come with the property and, in all that time, had never been open. Besides being a fun eyesore, I liked it because the rent was always on time. The phone rang and rang. If they didn't answer, I'd have to contact them via email. They needed to get this smoky mess hauled out of here ASAP.

"This is Madison," I said, when one of them finally answered, and got dead silence. "I'm sorry to call with bad news, but your roach coach blew up." I gave her what few details I knew.

"We never had roach one in all the years we owned it," she said stonily.

Oops! "I thought you'd want to know ASAP. Who am I speaking with?"

"Yes, well, that's too bad, but that problem doesn't affect us one way or the other, as we sold it over a month ago. You'll need to talk to the new owner—Werner Titan."

It wasn't lost on me that she hadn't offered her name. "New owner? This is the first I'm hearing of it. I specifically informed you via email that I had to approve any change of management."

"What's the difference? We got a new opportunity, and you can't blame us for wanting to take it."

"Let's hope that you didn't lead Werner to believe that the space came with the coach."

"Could you be a bigger bitch?"

Actually, I could, but didn't think now was a good time to boast. "I'd like contact information for Werner."

"You know how the Cove is—word of the explosion will spread fast, and I'm sure he'll be showing up. Since we're no longer involved with Princesses, don't bother us. Take it up with Werner." The line went dead.

I checked the screen to verify that the call had been disconnected, and sure enough. "That was a weird call," I said to Kelpie, who was standing close enough to eavesdrop. "Did you know the coach had a new owner?"

"That's odd." Kelpie shook her head. "You'd think we would've seen someone hanging around."

"Ever heard of Werner Titan?" I asked Doodad, who'd gone to talk to one of the firemen and was back.

He answered with a "What are you talking about?" look.

I told him about the phone call. Kelpie hadn't budged; her attitude was everything was her business. "Ask around and see if anyone knows him. He shows up here, get contact information; I want to talk to him. This thing needs to be moved out of here, and pronto."

"This might be good for business." Kelpie made cha-ching noises. "It's not a fight, our number one crowd-pleaser, but we can't always have them or folks will think we stage them."

Except we had. She had!

Doodad sucked in a deep breath and blew it out, screwing up his nose. "Or drive away customers not wanting to suck in the smoke smell."

"Wasn't Lizzie great?" Kelpie jumped up and down. "She had to get to work, but if you have any more questions, you can ask me."

Doodad snorted. "In case you don't know, applicants answer for themselves in an interview."

I cut in on their staredown. "Lizzie's not quite right for the job. Too timid, for one thing."

"What do you mean?" Kelpie thrust her chest in my face.

"You hit me with those and you're fired," I snapped back.

Kelpie roared with laughter. "My tips would go through the roof if I could get these babies trained."

I waited for her to catch her breath. "We need someone more outgoing, personable. She let you take charge. We need someone who can handle the likes of you to work here. She didn't strike me as being able to deal with our more raucous customers. If you could clone yourself, that would get my approval."

"I thought you said you wanted someone normal," Doodad reminded me in exasperation.

"You know, buddy, I can kick your butt." Kelpie's leg shot out.

"Only because I've never hit a woman and I'm not starting now," Doodad grumbled.

"Would you take pics of the remains of the coach and forward them to Fab?" I said to Kelpie to change the subject. "Take one of the lighthouse too, so she can see that there's no damage."

"What about the bruiser that rents office space?"

Gunz! If the place had needed any repairs, and it didn't, he'd have waved his magic wand and it would have been done. "With his connections, he probably already knows. Speaking of…" I took out my phone and called Creole; it went straight to voicemail.

A couple of regulars drove in the side entrance, heads out their windows, and looped around for a slow crawl to check out the damage before parking. They got out and whistled for Doodad to meet them halfway so they could question him, which didn't last long, since he wasn't one to tell what he knew. The men went inside to get their morning beer. They could get all the information they'd ever want from the woman loping after them—Kelpie.

The fire inspector pulled in, and I hustled

down the driveway for a word before he got busy with official business. As it turned out, he had questions for me, which I answered in a forthright manner, being honest that I had no clue how it happened. I told him about the phone call and gave him the contact information I had. Perhaps he could get the new owner's information out of them.

Doodad dragged over a couple of chairs we had sitting outside next to a newly installed bench on the off chance we ever had a wait. Hadn't happened yet, but better to be prepared. I sat down next to him, having made the decision to hang around until the fire was deemed out and the trucks left. It was also my hope that this man Werner would show up.

"What do you want done with the coach?" Doodad asked.

"I want it out of here pronto. Let's hope the new owner has insurance. Last resort, we'll pay to remove it, but only if there are no other options."

"It's odd that there's been a new owner for a month and we've never seen anyone coming or going," Doodad said, staring down the driveway.

"The whole deal reeks of not being above board. All parties involved sneaking around. The Princesses didn't want me to know they sold the coach, guessing correctly that I wouldn't green-light the deal, and this Werner character apparently didn't want me to know that he'd taken possession. Lots of questions and no answers until we can get someone to talk to one of us."

"No one buys a business and doesn't open it." Doodad was keeping an eagle eye on the mop-up. "I smell trouble ahead. Or would've if it hadn't burned down. Be interesting to find out the cause of the explosion, since they don't typically happen on their own."

The coroner's van pulling into the driveway caught our attention.

"Don't they only show up when there's a body?" It felt like the air had been sucked out of my lungs.

"Why are you asking me?" Doodad asked indignantly.

"Because you're sitting here, and haven't you claimed a time or two to be a know-it-all?"

"Caught me." He held his hands up. "I may have exaggerated... once." He stared off in the distance, and I was afraid to look to see what had caught his attention. "Here comes the fire inspector and he appears irritated about something."

"If you leave me here by myself, you're fired."

"Please. I'm as nosy as everyone else around here."

"Excuse me, Ms. Westin." The inspector walked up.

"Madison. Before I forget..." I extended an

open offer of food and drink to him and his crew. "I've got a woman inside who'd love to serve hunky firemen."

He half-grinned. "Did you give me the right number for the previous owner? This one is disconnected."

I pulled out my phone and held up the screen.

"That's the same number," he said.

"That's odd. I talked to one of the owners just after the explosion. I guess when she said she didn't want to be involved, she wasn't kidding."

He asked questions about the new owner, to which I didn't know the answers.

He was about to walk away when Doodad stopped him. "Couldn't help but notice the coroner's van."

"Found the body of a deceased male inside."

"The new owner? Werner Titan?" Murder? But I didn't voice that question since I didn't have a good reason for asking except curiosity.

"No way to tell, given the condition of the body. Unofficially, the man did himself in cooking up something illegal... unless the coroner comes up with a different cause of death."

"That would be a good reason for him to keep a low profile," I said in disgust. "And explain the fact that no one's seen him around the property."

"I know where to find you if I have any more questions." The inspector walked back to where the trucks were being loaded.

I pulled out my phone and tapped out a message: "Run a check on a Werner Titan," adding, "Anything good, let me know." I wasn't sure what I meant by the latter; I'd leave it for Xander to figure out.

"Wouldn't it be something if the Princesses knew that he was up to something illegal and looked the other way for the money?" Doodad said.

"If there's some kind of wager in there, don't hold your breath waiting for me to put money on any of that."

Chapter Ten

I said good-bye to Doodad, adding, "No more emergencies today. Or tomorrow."

He grunted, rubbing his temples—he'd also had enough excitement for the day. I waved and got in my SUV. Perfect timing—my phone rang, Fab's face staring back at me.

"Where are you?" she demanded. "Rude was arrested for kicking the moly out of a man. And no, he wasn't a guest."

That wasn't a good start for a new employee. "Did you arrange bail?"

"Called Tank, and he's going to represent her. Gave him the bondsman's number. If you want details, you need to come by the motel."

Tank—unless he was in a courtroom; then it was Patrick Cannon—was our new lawyer and built like his moniker. Fab and he had met during a jail visit when we'd been there to see someone else. Fab always had to scope out every inch of the visitation center, and she'd found Tank waiting behind the glass panel for his visitor. She had a soft spot for people who had no-shows, so she sat down and chatted it up. Case of mistaken identity was his story, and his law license wasn't revoked, so I assumed it to be true.

"Remind me when I get there to give you the details about Twinkie Princesses blowing up." I hung up with a satisfied smile and threw my phone in the cup holder, ignoring it when it rang again, my smile only getting bigger.

When I pulled up in front of the motel and parked, Fab came through the gate and met me. "Took you long enough."

"It takes longer when one obeys all the traffic signs." I laughed at her eyeroll. "You miss me?" I reached out to hug her, and she stepped away. "So mean."

"Me first. Besides, I already know about the explosion. I called and got the details from Doodad."

"You couldn't wait five minutes so I could revel in the telling?" I frowned.

"Not everything is about you. I've got a poor cat for you to focus your attention on." Fab grabbed my arm, which I jerked back, and led the way through the gate and to the office.

What the heck? It was times like these when I wished we had a liquor license. I'd go for a margarita on the rocks by the pool, and I wasn't going to check my watch, since it didn't work anyway, and feel guilty that it still might be morning and too early to think about drinking. "Blah, blah..." was all I heard from Fab, half-listening, smiling at the two lucky guests sunning themselves in chaises and the even luckier one who was swimming and had the pool to himself.

"Are you even listening?" Fab asked indignantly, as if how dare I.

"I'm hanging on every word." I pasted on a smile. Nope, she wasn't fooled. "Let me get some water." I crossed to the far side of the lobby and grabbed two bottles from the enamelware bucket full of ice that was sitting on a table. I chose a chair that had a view of the pool, pointed to the one next to me, and handed Fab a water. "What were you saying? A cat story that has my name all over it?"

"Ernest Short. And before you ask, yes, he's short, rotund, and needs his personality reworked. I also spotted some facial hair that appeared infected."

I refrained from making a barfing noise, knowing that wouldn't please her. "Is Ernest a cat?"

The corners of her mouth curved up, but only for a nanosecond. If I hadn't been staring, I'd have missed it. "Ernest is a neighbor. So he says. A creepy one at that." Fab grimaced. "He showed up looking for his cat, swearing to everyone who'd listen that we stole it and were keeping the feline against its will."

"Got it. So, he doesn't know jack about cats. And…?"

"He, meaning Ernest, spotted Furrball stretched out on the coffee table, asleep on the magazines, and jerked it up by its neck, the cat howling and hissing its displeasure. He shook it so hard, I thought if he lost his grip, the cat would fly out into the courtyard."

"Furrball?"

"I didn't make that up. That's what Short called him, and I assume it's because he has fifty pounds of fur."

"How does Rude fit into your story?"

"If you'd let me finish…"

Okay.

"Rude, an animal lover, came around the front desk and planted her foot in Short's butt."

Ouch.

"He dropped Furrball, and it raced off. Short couldn't get to his feet fast enough to grab it again and was livid. Even more so when Rude ordered him off the property while threatening to kick his butt out to the alley."

"That's not an arrestable offense. You said he wasn't a guest, so he was trespassing."

"Short's not the brightest fellow. He sized up Rude, figured he could take her, and was wrong. Not sure how he came to that conclusion. He laughed and took a swing, which Rude intercepted, twisting his arm behind his back and throwing him to the ground." Fab relished the retelling, clearly proud of the takedown. "Short started yelling for help like a girl, and unfortunately, that's when one of the guests called 911 and the cops showed up."

"He died."

"You're annoying. Although he *was* transported to the hospital. After reporting that Rude stole his cat and attacked him despite his warning her of his heart condition."

"This has been quite the day. One dead. One in the hospital. Unless Short dies. Then two dead."

Fab snorted. "I'd put cash on his faking it."

"If he's gone to all this trouble, he's probably going to sue. I'm hiring you to scare him out of that idea."

"Really, Madison. That wouldn't be professional of me."

I glared at her until she laughed. "Fine. I'll do it, and by myself."

"You're not leaving me out of all the fun."

Cootie ran in from the parking lot, fast enough that one would think his pants were on fire. "I'm so sorry," he panted.

"Short swung first," I said. "All niceties are off at that point. I'm surprised Rude was arrested."

"You know…" He stared down at his dirty tennis shoes. "That's her fault. Getting all mouthy to the cop. I tried to tell her to dial it back, but she ignored me." Cootie's phone dinged. He fished it out of his pocket and breathed a sigh at the screen. "Tank sprung her."

"That Short fellow is banned from the property," I said. "He comes back, neither of you are to confront him. Call the cops. If necessary,

Tank can get a restraining order."

"Short will be back," Fab said. "Furrball changed his address and left no forwarding, but unfortunately, Short tracked him down and is obsessed with getting the cat back, even though he doesn't give a flip for the feline and the feeling is mutual." She flashed her secretive smile.

I knew she was tallying up how much more she knew than me.

Just then, an enormous grey Maine Coon came strolling into the office like he owned the place, and I'd bet it was Furrball. I wasn't sure if the cat had heard its name or what, but he jumped up on the counter and stretched out, leaving minimal space to conduct a transaction. My cat Jazz was twenty pounds of black fur, and this one looked twice the size. I couldn't resist walking over and sticking my hand out. He rubbed his face against my fingers.

"I'm surprised that Short lets him out of the house," I said.

"Furrball showed up as soon as construction was completed and has been a constant visitor. He disappeared for a while, then recently reappeared, made himself comfortable, and hasn't left." Cootie went behind the desk and fed him a cat treat. "It took Rude about a minute to get attached. He's also a guest favorite."

"The cat appears to have made his decision. Short is going to be a problem, and one that needs to be turned over to Fab. Everyone in agreement, raise your hand." Mine shot in the air.

Cootie's hand shot halfway up, then came down when he caught the glare Fab leveled.

"That's settled," I said and tried not to laugh. "I'm afraid to ask if there's anything else that requires our attention."

"The murder room has been cleaned and is ready for guests," Cootie said. "I've had calls specifically asking for that room. I tripled the price and still got takers. There were two supposed sightings of Isabella, but neither of them was by me or Rude, much to Rude's disgust. I'm not vouching for it until I see the lady for myself."

"That's annoying." I pouted. "If Isabella was going to make an appearance, I think I should've been the first to see her."

"As though people don't think you're a big enough nutjob, you want to boast about seeing ghosts now?"

I laughed at Fab, not about to admit she was right. "What have you got?" I asked her.

"My guy installed new security cameras. We've got all the corners covered, so there shouldn't be any problem getting the next murder on tape, unless it happens inside a room. There, we wouldn't have a ringside seat, but we'd know who came and went."

"It's better not to advertise the added security, or the next murderer will choose a motel in the next block down. There goes the extra business." I tried to tone down the sarcasm.

"Why pay for advertising when word of mouth works just as good, if not better?" Cootie said.

"I'm assuming there's nothing else?" Neither of them said anything. "I'm so ready to go home and ignore the rest of the day."

Chapter Eleven

It was early, too early, and so, when my phone rang, l let it go to voicemail after glancing at the screen. Chatting before coffee was highly overrated, and I doubted it was an emergency. Then Creole's phone rang. I groaned.

Creole reached over me and wolfed a laugh, picking up his phone off the beside table. "You so owe me." After a very short conversation that elicited a few laughs, he hung up, then withheld tidbits as to what was so funny, why Mother was calling, and what could be so important since she had to know we'd still be in bed. "Time to hit the shower." He slapped me on the butt.

"Nooo…" I grabbed the sheet, tucked it around the two of us, and gave him a wink.

"Here's some cold water for whatever plans you've got brewing—your mother wants to meet for breakfast in one hour. And I agreed."

I sighed. "Call her back and tell her two hours."

"Yeah, right. And you're not going to call either."

"You're no fun." I frowned at him.

"Raincheck on the fun business."

"I feel bad for not going to see Mother before now. If she didn't know when she left the property, I'm sure she's heard since that the woman found in her room was murdered and it wasn't a case of drunkenness, as I first thought." I rolled out of bed.

We shared the shower to save on time, and I congratulated myself for getting ready to leave in record time and with no coffee. The outside doorbell rang as I slipped into a pair of wedge slip-ons. I grabbed my tennis shoes and stuffed them in my bag, just in case.

"You answer it," I told Creole, "while I get in some last-second practice at a surprised face on seeing Fab and Didier."

Creole laughed, hooked my tote over my shoulder, and grabbed my hand, pulling me outside and opening the gate. To my surprise, Didier was behind the wheel of his Mercedes, window down, grinning, Fab next to him. Creole walked over, exchanged a few words, then waved him off. We got in the Hummer and followed them to the Bakery Café.

We pulled up in front and got the last two parking spaces. Mother and Spoon had already arrived, along with Emerson and Brad, and they were all sitting at two outside tables pushed together.

I got out and joined Fab, who was rocking a sleeveless black dress and sandals. "Breakfast is a new one. Do you think Mother thinks we'll be better behaved when we barely have our eyes open, as opposed to at dinner when we've knocked back a few?"

Fab surveyed the people at the nearby tables, performing her usual perp search. It made one wonder if she got wanted posters delivered to the office. "Madeline's up to something,"

"Probably."

I enveloped Mother, who'd stood as we approached, in a hug. "This is a great idea," I said, and traded a smile with Fab over her shoulder. I stepped back and gave her a once-over. "You look cute. As always." We were almost twins in skirts and tops. Before sitting, I walked around and kissed everyone's cheek, then took the chair next to Creole.

We sat around the table, taking our usual seating arrangement no matter where we ended up. Spoon filled our glasses with orange juice from the pitcher that sat on ice in the middle.

"Thank you all for coming on such short notice." Mother held up her glass and tipped it. "I have an ulterior motive."

Fab kicked me under the table. *Told you so.*

A server showed up with a large tray and stand, setting it down and putting two platters in the middle of the table—egg soufflés and fresh fruit on one and assorted danishes on the other.

"I'm calling dibs on leftovers," I said.

"Too late." Brad smirked. "They're mine."

The table got quiet as we filled our plates.

"Before either of you—" Mother flitted her eyes between me and Fab. "—think about weaseling out, I have a pile of IOUs, but as the matriarch, I shouldn't have to pull those out." She sipped her juice, gauging the response. Good luck. We were all poker-faced. "Now that Brad has Mila enrolled in pre-school, I've got free time, so I thought my amazing husband and I would buy breakfast." She winked at Spoon, and he smiled wolfishly back at her. "Afterwards, I'll tag along with you girls."

"You're going to have to settle for shopping." I made an exaggerated sad face that made Creole laugh. "There's no excitement scheduled for today."

"That's hard to believe," Didier said with a smirk.

"Not so fast." Fab's hand shot in the air and waved wildly.

She wouldn't think she was so amusing when she clipped someone in the head, and if it were me, the fight would be on. I almost laughed at how badly that would end.

"A client called and wants me to check out the security system I had installed at his house. The alarm keeps going off, but when security shows up, they find it's a false alarm. To quote him, 'It must be your shoddy work.'" She growled out the last part.

"Did you bring a handgun?" I asked Mother.

She beamed and lifted her top, showing her

waist holster.

A chorus of male groans went around the table.

"Once again, I'm missing out on all the fun." Emerson pouted. "I don't carry, so I wouldn't be much help."

"Then you'd be recruited to drive the getaway car." I grinned.

"Anytime you want to learn, I'll take you to the range." Brad put his arm around her and tugged her to his side. "I taught Madison. Behind Mother's back."

"Those two were a handful." Mother shook her head. "I'm going to enjoy the payback of watching you two deal with your own children."

"Guns, getaway cars… let's hope this job doesn't require either one," Creole said, and the guys all nodded in agreement.

In an attempt to change the subject and avoid a safety lecture, I turned to Emerson. I'd been meaning to call her and hadn't followed up. "Happy you're here. Do you have an update on Dude Baby?"

"I heard about that," Mother said. "I would've wanted to keep him."

"I'm happy to say that he fared well in our care, and it wasn't an issue when the cops and Social Services showed up," Fab said. "I did wonder what to expect, but everything went smoothly. Lucky us that Emerson was there to take charge."

"Thomas is his name, and he's currently in foster care while other living arrangements are being checked out. As you're aware, first choice is always a family member."

"The parents?" Mother asked.

"The father was arrested on an outstanding warrant that same day, not far from your office." Emerson nodded at Fab and Didier. "My source says he's denying having anything to do with the gun and drugs. Claims they were planted. He won't be getting custody anytime soon, if ever. The mother is nowhere to be found. No one in the family has any contact information, and they don't seem to be concerned about her disappearance."

"Hopefully, she hasn't met with foul play," Fab said. "We'd be happy to run a check on the woman and see what we can find out."

"I'm sure that Social Services already did that. If they don't come up with anything, I'll get back to you."

"Keep us updated. We'd both like to know that Thomas is well taken care of," I said.

"I'll keep bugging my friend to let me know if anything changes."

"Heard the Twinkie coach exploded yesterday," Didier said.

"I can send a couple of guys over and have what's left towed away in a matter of hours," Spoon offered.

"I'll get back to you on your offer once I talk to

the new owner. Hopefully, he has insurance that will foot the bill. Insurance or not, no one's going to be able to move the coach until the cops finish their investigation regarding the body found inside."

"Any word on what caused the explosion?" Creole asked.

"Not yet," I said. "Part of our day is going to include a quick stop to see our funeral friends and ask them nicely to put the squeeze on their coroner connection as to the identity of the body, the cause of death, and any other snoopy details he's willing to part with."

Mother tsked and made a face."You can drop me off before you make that stop."

"Oh, okay." Not happening. "If you're really good, Fab can give you a tour and get you a nice close-up look at the recently dead—one of her favorite things to do. And she looks so normal." That garnered laughter.

"What do you do while Fab's making the rounds?" Brad asked, a pinched expression on his face as he did his best to block the vivid imagery.

"If I'm lucky, there's leftover funeral food and I share it with the dogs, which makes me the favorite." I grinned at Fab.

"One of these days, I'll get animal rapport and surprise... well, shock everyone here."

More laughter.

"I hate to be the one to break this up," Fab

said. "But I need to go check out my client's house so I can report back that he's being girly."

"I dare you to say those exact words to him," Creole teased.

Fab shot him the stink eye and turned away. She would never admit that she went out of her way for her clients, often giving better than she got in return. It was only lately that she was less willing to straddle the grey line for them. "I've got it covered," she said to me. "You can spend the day with Madeline."

"Not happening," I said. "You know the rules. No traipsing off on a job by yourself."

"Yay." Didier grinned at her.

"We'll deputize Mother as sidekick number two. Besides, three guns are better than one." I enhanced my comment with shooting sound effects that got me a couple of eyerolls and turned heads at a nearby table.

"If there's trouble, give me a call," Spoon grouched and kissed his wife.

Chapter Twelve

"Pay attention to the speed limit." Mother tapped Fab on the shoulder, followed by a glaredown between the two. "Eyes on the road."

We were headed south, to where, I wasn't exactly sure, as Mother was in charge of the GPS and ignored me when I asked.

Fab growled and Mother growled back.

I stretched out in the backseat and put my hand over my mouth to keep from laughing. "You learn that from your husband?" I asked Mother.

"I had him teach me." Mother beamed.

"So, what's the job really about?" I asked.

"It's exactly as I described." Fab's voice was tinged with frustration. "Monty should be arriving any minute. I thought it would be a good idea if the two of us went over the entire system together. I haven't had any issue thus far with any other installation and don't understand why there's one now."

Aww... the elusive Monty Round, her security installer. She held any information about the man as a closely guarded secret.

It was a short drive from Tarpon Cove. Fab turned off the highway and into a residential zone of newer homes, where her client's two-story house backed up to the water. She pulled into the circular driveway and parked behind a truck that I recognized as belonging to Monty. All seemed quiet.

"You want us to wait in the car?" I asked, hiding my smirk.

"You can forget that," Mother answered in disgust. "I didn't come down here to sit in the dumb car."

"Mother, I know it seems like it, but not every case of Fab's ends in gunfire." I winked at Fab, who stared at me in the rearview mirror. "You can take my role as sidekick, but know that means you have to do everything Fab says. If not, she gets grumpy. Then the threats fly. Such as getting a new sidekick, as though it's that easy." I tossed Mother a pair of latex gloves. "You don't want to leave your fingerprints anywhere."

"You hear a gunshot, hit the floor," Fab ordered. "Now out, so we can get this done and go do some shopping."

Mother and I followed Fab and Monty up the steps to the front door, where Fab entered the code and opened the door. "Anyone home?" she yelled as she stepped over to the pad, set her bag down, and entered another code.

"I can't believe they didn't change their codes after the system was installed," I said.

"They did, and they'll have to do it again, which is a good thing because I don't want to be at the top of the list of suspects if something should happen." Fab and Monty traded a smirk.

"I brought a new set of instructions, knowing they probably can't find the first set… if they even kept them." Monty reached down and pulled them out of his bag, handing them to Fab. "Saves me or you another trip out here."

"I'll sit in the living room and enjoy the view while you and Monty go to work." I grabbed Mother's arm. "Something tells me I need to keep an eye on you. No getting into trouble." I shook my finger at her.

Fab and Monty dismantled the security box and spoke in low tones as he went to work and she watched, eagle-eyed. She'd told me once that they worked well together, and she wasn't exaggerating. It took about fifteen minutes to run a check.

"There's nothing wrong here," Monty assessed. "You sure the maid or someone isn't tripping the alarm?"

"Mr. Douglas swears there's no one living here full-time," Fab said.

The two turned away and lowered their voices again.

"That's annoying," Mother said, not bothering to lower her voice. "Can't hear a thing over here."

"I think that's the point." I gave her a stern look.

"If you're mimicking me, you're not very good. Faced with that paltry look, neither you nor Brad would've ever behaved. I'd have had to back it up with detailed threats."

"We weren't all that bad."

"There's no doubt in my mind that you got in the most trouble but had the ability to cover your tracks better and avoid getting caught. Most of the time, anyway."

"There's that." I laughed.

Mother nudged me. "Something's happening."

Monty had gone outside, but I knew he'd be back since he left his bag on the floor.

Fab walked over and sat down. "Monty's going to replace the main pad to be on the safe side. Fingers crossed that fixes the problem, if there was one, and I won't be getting any more calls. It sounds better when I can tell the client that changes were made to the system."

Monty sailed back through the door and went to work. It didn't take him long to install the new equipment and run it through several checks. "I'll email you the invoice." He waved and left.

"That was sure a lot of fun." Mother sniffed.

"I'll treat for lunch. Will that improve your day?" Fab engaged in another staredown with her.

All our heads snapped around at the sound of a door closing.

"It came from that direction." Fab inclined her head toward the south end of the house and drew her Walther. She turned to Mother. "You need to go back to the car until we figure out what we're dealing with."

"Fat chance. I can hardly be helpful from the car."

"That way, we wouldn't have to worry about you getting hurt." I knew that getting her to wait outside wouldn't happen. At least, I could say I tried.

"Pish." Mother drew her weapon.

"You keep an eye on your mother." Fab let out a frustrated sigh. "I'll check out the noise." She strode down the hall towards what I assumed was the kitchen.

I followed, my Glock out. For all her bravado, Mother stayed in the living room, for which I was thankful.

Fab stuck her head in every room before entering. There wasn't much to search. The dining room was an open space, and no one was crouched under the table. The large kitchen was easy to search, and there wasn't much going on inside the walk-in pantry except shelves stocked with household supplies. Very few food items. Both rooms had sliding glass doors that faced the back patio and were locked. The laundry room was the only one with a closet. Fab yanked open the door, revealing that it was filled with cleaning equipment.

"That's odd. We all heard the same noise." Fab walked over and opened the back door, where a path led to the driveway and enclosed trash area.

I reholstered my gun and returned to the living room, Fab not far behind.

Mother confronted her and peered over her shoulder. "What if it was a rat and it's hiding under something?"

Rats don't usually close doors. "Last time we had a rodent case, it turned out to be some dude living in the attic." I looked up. "I didn't sign up to be a rodent catcher. Especially the six-foot-tall, two-footed ones."

"My client is going to think I've lost my mind if I try to pitch a rat as the reason for the alarm going off. I'd need proof, as in a bucket-full."

"Bucket of rats. I'm going home." I grabbed Mother's arm.

Mother jerked back. "Except the noise came from the kitchen, not from overhead." Mother's tone suggested I was a nitwit.

I needed to remind her she started it. "Hear that bus coming?" I said to Mother. "It's the one that's going to be rolling over you when I retell this story at the next family get-together."

"I'm going to catch the thing with my bare hands, so at least your story will have an exciting ending." Mother stomped toward the kitchen.

"Love your mother." Fab laughed.

"Me too. I'm happy she came along. It's been a while since she was the hot gossip in the family."

We were interrupted by a sudden ruckus from the kitchen and the sound of Mother screaming, "Hurry!"

Fab barreled down the hallway with me hot on her heels. Mother had her back to the pantry door, trying to hold it closed while something pushed from the inside. It was definitely not a rat.

Fab pulled her Walther and called out, "Step away."

Mother moved, and the door flew open.

Out stumbled a rumpled thirty-something man, barefoot in dirty shorts and a shirt, who looked like he'd just walked off the beach. He unleashed a string of foul language, his wild eyes scanning the three of us, zeroing in on the muzzle of Fab's gun.

"Hands in the air," Fab barked.

He backed into the closet and tried to close the door, but Mother hadn't let go of the knob and struggled with him.

I ran around Fab and pulled Mother away.

"What are you going to do? Shoot me?" the man bellowed.

Fab cocked her gun.

I tugged on Fab's top. "It's not worth a trip in a cop car."

The man flung himself forward and out of the pantry. Fab stuck out her foot and tripped him, and he landed face down. He rolled over and grabbed her leg. She managed to disengage and give him a couple of kicks, which stopped his struggles but left him still cursing.

"Grab my cuffs out of the car," Fab said to Mother. "I'll call Mr. Douglas and see what he wants done."

"You don't have to call anyone." The man held up his hands in surrender. "I'll leave and won't come back. This is your fault anyway. If you'd locked your door, you wouldn't have guests."

I searched the pantry closet again. The first time, there'd been no sign of the intruder. In the far back corner was a closet that was only noticeable this time because the door stood open. It was a large walk-in, and the only things inside were a stool and the man's backpack, which was open and held a few pieces of silver that I'd bet didn't belong to him. Plenty of room for him to hide out and go unnoticed. The closet was a clever place to hide, since it appeared to be part of the paneling and didn't have a knob.

"I found his hiding place," I said over my shoulder.

He was attempting to scoot out of range of Fab's gun, crawling toward the back door.

Fab pulled out her phone and called her client, and when he answered, she explained the situation. She disconnected and took a couple of pics of the intruder, then called 911, sticking her foot in the middle of his butt, which he shook off.

"Oh come on, give a guy a break. Let me go," he whined.

"I might have agreed if you hadn't looted the place, which makes me wonder if you already fenced a couple of pieces. There's plenty of quick cash around here, and you took advantage."

I surveyed the room and took note of the television and laptop that were both visible in a work station at the far end.

Mother came back swinging the cuffs on her finger. "I better not have missed anything good."

Fab took the cuffs and turned to the intruder. "You're already looking at breaking and entering. Give me the pawn receipts, and I'll put in a good word about not pressing theft charges."

"Go f— yourself." He bounced to his feet and raced for the back door.

"I'm not chasing him down." I didn't move from where I was standing.

"Neither am I. It's unclear whether or not I'm getting paid, since Douglas copped a 'tude on the phone. He had the gall to blame me, even though intruder dude claims the door was left unlocked. I can't be held responsible for that kind of stupid. Let the cops handle it."

"Your client has to blame someone. He's too rich to take responsibility," I said. "My guess is that he'll go after the security response company next."

"You should've shot him in the butt," Mother

said. She'd run to the door and poked her head out when she realized we weren't going to pursue the man. "He just ran out to the road," she informed us, conveying her disgust when we still didn't fly into action.

"If you felt that strongly, you should've shot him yourself." I bit back a smirk. "That way, you could've enjoyed the ride to the police station in the back of a squad car. Cuffed. Behind your back. And damn uncomfortable." I didn't flinch under her glare. "Because I'm a good daughter, I'd have had to call Spoon to post your bail."

"It's not right that that man gets away," Mother fumed.

"It's better than Madison adopting him." Fab snickered.

"Just when I was going to offer my collection services and make sure your client ponied up. Oh well."

"You don't do that kind of work," Mother huffed.

I flexed my muscles. "Wouldn't you pay up if I showed up at your door?"

"No." Mother rolled her eyes.

"Don't be doing that," Fab lectured. "You'll get big eyeballs."

I laughed at the stupidity and then at Mother's "are you sure" expression. "Fab's like you; she makes stuff up."

The doorbell rang.

"Put your guns away," Fab ordered on her

way to the front door.

Mother and I followed. I tugged on her arm and motioned to the living room. "The cops are going to have questions for us. Answer them truthfully; keep it short and to the point. This isn't the time to offer up an opinion or go off into the weeds with details."

"I wish you didn't know these things."

Two cops entered and stood in the entry, questioning Fab. She took them on a big-ticket tour, highlighting the salient details.

One came back and motioned to Mother, who crossed the room and answered his questions. When he was done with her, he came over and sat down next to me. "So, what's your version of events?" he asked with a big grin. He looked so young, I'd bet he was a new addition to the force.

I filled him in on the events since we arrived. "You get a lot of crime down here?"

He shook his head. "It's pretty quiet. When we do, it's petty crime or drunk-related. Your partner gave us your contact information."

"I own Jake's in Tarpon Cove. Cop discount. Stop by sometime. I hope to read in the weekly that you caught the guy."

"Won't be too difficult. He left his ID in his backpack." The cop chuckled.

Fab joined us, claiming the last of the uncomfortable chairs. "A fingerprint technician is on the way over. We have to hang out until the cops are finished and I can lock up."

"Or Mother and I can leave you here, and when you're done, you can catch the bus back to town."

If looks could kill…

Chapter Thirteen

By the time the technician was done processing the pantry closet, the cops had the intruder in custody. One of the cops had called in the runner's description, and it hadn't taken long for them to find him, since he stuck out, walking barefoot along the busy highway and fit the report to a tee.

The three of us exited the house when a third police car pulled into the driveway with the intruder cuffed in the back. Fab easily identified the man.

"Your client must be happy," I said when Fab slid behind the wheel.

"They never are. I didn't tell him about the items that were taken by the cops as evidence of theft. Let him be surprised. He blabbered on about damage, as though I could've prevented it. I passed along that the intruder said he entered through an unlocked door. The client didn't call me a liar but came close."

"I'll add extra to his bill for rudeness." I cuffed the back of her head. "Don't forget to stop at the funeral home."

"Call them on the phone." Mother sniffed.

"Then you'd miss out on a tour of the new museum that doubles as a…" Not sure what. "…showroom to display all the available options once you've croaked."

Fab coughed.

"What the h… heck are you talking about?" Mother demanded.

"Did you almost say hell?" I asked indignantly.

"You make my head ache."

"Better you than me," Fab said to Mother, which earned her a glare.

"Put your party face on. This is an honor. You'll be one of the first to tour the new building they had built across from the front entrance. It's my understanding they've designed vignettes to show their wares, so to speak. Themes, oddities, that sort of thing. Fab would know, since she's up on all things ghoulish."

"Eee," Fab yelled, mimicking squealing brakes. "Almost run over by a bus."

"You two stop. Take me home. Now."

I shot up and stuck my head between the seats. "Don't think so. You signed up for all the excitement this day could dish out, and you're staying until the end."

"It's hard to believe we're related." Mother sniffed.

"No, it's not." I kissed her cheek and leaned back against the seat.

Fab took a shortcut off the highway that really

wasn't one unless you knew the side streets to shoot down and flew into the driveway of Tropical Slumber.

I peered out the window. "Isn't that the Mercedes SUV from the other day? And the bodyguard to the two thugs who wanted to wrap Granny in gauze?"

Mother turned. "You need to behave."

"You got your pocket rocket on you?" I asked her. At her confusion, I made a gun finger accompanied by a couple of poofs of air, then got out of the SUV and opened her door.

"I'm waiting here. That way, you'll hurry."

"Next family to-do, I'm going to announce that you pussied out." I felt a poke in my back, my cue that Fab was right behind me.

"This is what I get for rescuing you off that doorstep."

"Yep… no good deed." I grinned and linked my arm through Mother's. "In case you think about running."

"There've been a lot of improvements since you were here for your sister's funeral," Fab said. "You'll like the new wedding venue."

I didn't have to be a mind reader to know that Mother thought Fab had lost her mind. Fab grabbed her other arm, and we walked down the red carpet. Fab turned the knob. Locked. She knocked on the door.

"This is the first time we've been here that they haven't already had the door open," I said.

"They're busy... Probably doing... Let's go." Mother tugged on my arm.

"I guess I'll use my key." Fab whipped out her lockpick.

"Fabiana Merceau," Mother gasped.

Fab opened the door and stuck her head inside. "Raul," she bellowed and stepped inside.

I gave Mother a push, and she followed. I directed her to my chair by the door. "This is the best one for a fast getaway," I whispered.

Raul came from the hallway, one of the suited thugs at his side. "What are you two doing here again?" the thug demanded.

"I could ask you the same question. Granny die already?" I asked.

Fab raised her eyebrow. "You okay?" She nodded to Raul, who didn't say anything.

Red flag!

The thug clapped him on the back. "Yeah, fine," Raul coughed.

"We're early for our appointment," I said. "We can wait here in the entry until you're finished."

"You two can hit the road now." The thug started to reach inside his jacket.

This scene felt like déjà vu. In an instant, Fab and I had our guns out and pointed at him.

"We're not leaving until Raul tells us to, and not even then without seeing Dickie," Fab said.

"You don't know who you're messing with." The man's bushy eyebrows knitted together.

Mother stood and made her presence known. "A quick hello, and we'll be on our way." She smiled. I recognized it as pasted on, but no one else would.

"Dickie, come out here," Raul yelled.

Dickie poked his head out from the hallway, then stumbled through the doorway, joined by the second thug, who had a gun pointed at us. "We get into a shootout, and three bodies will be conveniently located for their final services," the man threatened.

"Shoot to kill or nick them? Your call, Fab." I wagged the muzzle of my Glock.

"Nooo," Dickie moaned, trembling slightly. He was in a black rubber apron and gloves, his usual pallor turned translucent, a vein bulging on the side of his head. "These men want me to work on their great-grandmother, and I'm not qualified, but they won't take no for an answer."

"Shut up," thug number two snapped.

"She wasn't dead a couple of days ago. What happened?" I asked.

Mother tugged on my top, as though I needed to be reminded that it was none of my business.

"Actually, she was. They were reluctant to let us know that she's been dead for a while," Raul said. "They had her at another home, which wasn't qualified to do the job *either,* but kept her refrigerated as a courtesy."

"Why can't you just agree on a service that they do offer?" Fab said in a conciliatory tone, singling out thug number one, who appeared to be the lead. "I know they can flood the woman with embalming fluid, and that lasts for a while."

Dickie squealed. The man beside him had poked him with his gun.

Mother stepped forward. "If you hurt one person here, my husband will hunt your ass down and feed you through a crusher a piece at a time. I'm married to Jimmy Spoon."

Recognition of the name registered in their eyes.

You go, Mother.

"Let's not overreact," I said in a conciliatory tone. "I'm certain your dearly beloved great-grandmother wouldn't want you acting like hooligans over her remains."

"Pick another service," Fab said. "Or if you want to take her with you, I'm sure that can be arranged. Keep in mind, there's no money back guarantee with any service that you choose."

"Hurry up and make up your mind," I said. "Pointing guns at one another is so unfriendly." I refrained from rubbing my back where Mother had poked me—hard. It was going to be sore by the time I got home.

"Why don't you take a brochure and mull over your options?" Fab pointed to a rack that sat on a library table beside a photo album. "It's been updated and includes all the latest options. Once you've decided, make another appointment. In the meantime, I'm certain they can keep Granny refrigerated." She looked to Raul for confirmation, and he nodded.

That's what you get when you snoop – a knowledge of where everything can be found.

Fab waved her gun toward the entrance, signaling the meeting was over, she and the gunned thug engaging in a staredown.

The first thug stepped forward. "We'll take that brochure and be back tomorrow at three pm. You've got time to figure out if you can come through with our first choice. Keep in mind that I'm not quibbling over the price."

Raul slid away and came back with brochures in his hand, handing them to the men.

"I've been researching it since your first visit," Dickie whined. "I could get her to look decent for a while, but she would deteriorate eventually, and once the process got started, there'd be no stopping it. I wouldn't want to disrespect your great-grandmother."

"I strongly suggest you listen to Dickie about what he can and can't do. He prides himself on his work and will do the best job possible for you." Fab shot the two thugs a hard look. "And just so you know, there will be a bodyguard here tomorrow and for the foreseeable future, so bring your party manners."

"My husband won't like it if anything happens to either of these men… ever," Mother said, using her tough-girl voice as they headed to the door. "That would include anything that doesn't fall under natural causes."

The door closed behind them, and Raul locked it.

"A mere thank you seems paltry," Raul said. "But we mean it. I don't think they would've killed us. But I'm happy you showed up and even happier they're gone. Those two are the kind that want what they want and for the worst reason—to one-up their friends."

"Promise me," Dickie shouted, then lowered his voice, "from now on, if it's not in the brochure, we don't do it."

"I get it and promise no more special requests unless I discuss it with you ahead of time and you agree."

"So, you know and don't have to worry, we're going to get someone here tomorrow to act as a guard, and maybe for a couple of days more to make sure that those two behave themselves," I said.

"Thank you," Dickie said shakily.

"You remember my mother?" I made the introduction and sat down, waving Mother to sit next to me.

"Your sister's funeral was the best turnout we've ever had, and with no air conditioning in the middle of summer." Dickie beamed. "It still went well."

"You were cool under pressure." Raul shot Mother a thumbs up.

"Let's go in the kitchen and get something

cold to drink." Dickie motioned.

It dawned on Mother that they lived on site, and she grimaced, but nonetheless followed the two men down the hall.

We sat around the farm table in the corner that had a view of the driveway, where we could spot any comings and goings. Dickie pulled a pitcher of iced tea and some bottled water out of the refrigerator while Raul grabbed glasses and ice.

"What brings you by?" Raul asked.

"I've got another dead person for you to get me the skinny on." I saw Raul's brow rise and filled him in on the explosion of the coach.

"How did we miss this one?" he directed to Dickie.

"It's been a busy morning." Dickie snorted, shooting his partner a dirty look.

"I promise I'm running future requests by you." Raul held up his hands in a conciliatory gesture. "All this drama was too much, even for me."

Some of the stress drained from Dickie's face. "Pitch is probably wondering why we haven't called. We should probably introduce you to the man, but we like being the go-between for the two of you and love the impromptu visits. You two are more informative than the crime report."

"We're happy you showed up today." Raul put his head in his hands. "Mr. Richie is one of those men who snaps his fingers and isn't interested in hearing no."

"Put together a short report of what's involved in the mummification process and all the ways it's doomed to failure. Double down on the gruesome," Fab said to Dickie. "Then Raul takes over and sells them on another idea."

"Throw in how bad you'd feel if Grandma ended up looking like… well, not her best." Mother smiled at the two men.

"That's a great idea." I leaned over and kissed Mother's cheek. "Now I know where I get all my great ideas."

"Stop." Mother laughed. "I'm not taking credit for anything."

"Idea girl, who are we going to get to show up tomorrow?" Fab asked.

"It's not going to be either of you," Mother said irritably and pulled out her phone. "What time do you open in the morning?"

"We don't have regular hours," Raul said. "Appointment only. Mr. Richie isn't due here until three."

"I don't imagine that the guys have barge-in traffic except for Fab and me." I grinned at her and got the *behave* look.

"Hi, honey." Mother stood and went outside.

"Doesn't she know that she's supposed to hit the speaker button so we can listen in?" Fab asked in annoyance.

Raul laughed. Dickie looked appalled.

"You tell her," I dared.

It didn't take long before Mother came back

inside, a satisfied smile on her face. "Spoon's going to send an as… someone around noon and for a couple of days after to make sure those men don't turn out to be a problem. I'm sure they won't once it's explained that it would be in their best interest to choose one of the services provided."

"Thank you, Mrs. Spoon," Raul said. Dickie nodded.

"No need for such formality—just call me Madeline. And no thanks are necessary. I did it to keep these two from getting involved." She wagged her finger at us, as though they wouldn't know who she was talking about.

"It's a solution that will make our husbands happy as well," Fab said.

Chapter Fourteen

A whole day went by with no drama or last-minute calls about fires to put out. The following morning, I groaned when the phone rang.

"What was that about?" Creole rolled over and took me in his arms, peering over my shoulder at my phone screen. He growled at seeing that the call had already been disconnected.

"That was Cootie. Kevin showed up in his official capacity and, after grabbing a Coke, informed him that the owner of the Maine Coon called in a theft report and fingered Rude for it. He came to investigate and found the cat loitering at the motel, but he took off when Kevin attempted to pick him up."

"How did Cootie take the firing of his pretend wife?" Creole tightened his arms so I couldn't turn and face him.

"I know you're smirking. No charges were filed on the original assault. I then made an executive decision, since you guys had disappeared, and turned the file over to Fab, my sidekick for these kinds of cases. You know, when butt-kicking is involved. She taught Rude a couple of techniques in case of a next time. I never gave a thought to firing her."

"Of course, you wouldn't." He snorted in my ear, which made me jerk. "It's not that they're not a nice couple—"

I cut him off with a huff. "They've done a good job, with the exception of this small glitch, which Rude didn't instigate. If either of them leaves, know that you'll be responsible for finding me someone more appropriate to interview. By your standards, that means normal. Good luck."

"Normal." He groaned. "Whatever. While eavesdropping, I distinctly heard 'I'll take care of it.' I'm afraid to ask what that means."

"It means I'm taking my chief muscle, and we're going to return the animal and inform Mr. Short that should Furrball wander off in the future, he can retrieve the cat himself. As long as he doesn't set foot on the property." Let's hope my good idea worked. "You know what I think?"

Creole rubbed a circle in my forehead. "I feel a change of subject coming on."

"When predicting the future, you need to need rub your own head."

"Right or wrong?" He gloated.

"We need to get away for a few days." I pushed away and sat on the edge of the bed, holding out my hand. "Join me. It's good for the environment when we shower together."

* * *

Creole sat at the island, drinking coffee, while I glared at my phone screen.

Seeing he was dressed in jeans and a t-shirt, work boots parked by the door, I asked, "Didier calling in sick today?"

"We're meeting at the job site. We've got a few issues to deal with, and we need to make sure everyone's on the same page."

"Then why isn't Fab answering her phone?"

"Because she wants to be annoying. I don't want you confronting anyone on your own." He picked up his phone and, after a pause, said, "Since your wife bailed on mine, I'm going to be late."

I laughed quietly.

"Beachside business. Unless you want to handle it?" Whatever he said made Creole laugh. He shoved his phone in his pocket and pulled me to my feet.

* * *

I parked in the front, passed one man kicked back on a ring in the pool, and went directly to the office, waving to Cootie at the front desk. I perused the choices of coffee, making myself a cup.

"I hate your husband," Fab huffed as she came through the open sliding door, pausing to wave to Didier, who got behind the wheel of the Mercedes and sped off.

"That's not very nice." I wondered what he'd done and knew I'd probably soon find out.

"Creole knew that Didier and I were on the way to your house, but you two pulled a disappearing act. Then he calls to gloat and refuses to tell me where you went. Good thing I'm a darn good detective."

I grinned at her. I bet it took her all of two seconds. "There's a dark roast coffee over there for your picky tastes." I didn't tell her that Creole had told me when he walked me to the car that she'd be meeting me at the motel.

"It's not a favorite," Cootie warned. "Most people spit it out. Haven't seen anyone actually finish a cup."

Fab held up her hand. "No spit stories. What I want to know is why you can't handle a simple cat eviction without the cops getting involved?"

Before he could answer, Rude rushed in from the back, hair tousled, cheeks flushed, and out of breath. "He's after me," she shrieked.

Through the front doors rushed a middle-aged man I assumed to be Short. "There you are." He shook his fist at Rude. "And there you are," he said to Furrball, who had just strutted in and stretched out on the coffee table. Short took off his jacket and approached the animal. "You're coming home with me." He threw the jacket in an attempt to cover the animal, but the cat leapt up and hightailed it out the door.

"The cat doesn't like you," Fab said, and laughed.

The man's face turned beet red. He turned on Fab and drew his arm back. She easily caught his fist mid-swing and dumped him to the ground with the aid of her foot, then drew her Walther and stuck it in his face. "Dare you to get up."

Short struggled to sit, then gave up and instead flopped down and pulled his phone out of his shirt pocket.

With a well-place kick, Fab sent it flying. She jammed her heel down on it, splintering the screen. "Oops."

A male guest walked in and surveyed the scene, wide-eyed.

Short yelled, "Help. She's going to shoot."

With a furtive glance around, the guest darted back out.

"Help," Short yelled again.

"You're way too dramatic." I snorted. "Besides not being very good at it. If you stop whining, maybe we can broker a deal before the cops show up and haul you off."

"I'm not the one with the gun."

"You are the one who's trespassing *and* the one who attacked this woman in front of three witnesses. You should be thanking my friend here for her restraint in not shooting you."

Short held out his hands. "Let's forget this happened," he said. "I'll take the cat and go."

"If you kept Furrball in the house, you wouldn't have these problems."

"I'll never understand how my mother put up with the hair everywhere, the barfing, the howling in the middle of the night."

"Easy fix. I can easily find it a new home."

"Can't," Short whined. "Mother left her money to the cat, and in order to finance any kind of a life without having to get a job—and who'd hire me?—I have to prove I'm taking care of the thing. I get it all to do with as I please when the cat dies, but it has to be of natural causes and not because I strangled it."

"So, someone is making house calls to make sure you're living up to your part of the deal?" I asked.

"There are monthly visits to make sure I'm complying with the rules. The lawyer would love to have a reason to cut me off. You wouldn't believe the way he spoke to me at our last meeting, and I'm a client."

"Here's my free advice." I wanted to beat the smirk off his face. "Make an unholy deal with the lawyer about the care of the cat and suggest that someone else would be better suited, at your expense of course. If you do manage to get your hands on that cat, he'll claw your eyes out, since it doesn't appear that either of you can stand the sight of the other." I asked Fab, "Are you pressing charges?"

"Her?" Short sniffed. "I'm the unarmed one,

and I was maimed." Idiot.

"Get out of here," Fab told him. "We're getting a restraining order. Your cat problems are yours to figure out. Don't set foot on this property again." She waved at Rude and Cootie, who hadn't moved. Cootie had drawn his weapon after Fab and not yet holstered it. "You see him again, shoot him. The guys at the funeral home will bury him."

Short jumped to his feet and ran out the door.

Chapter Fifteen

Fab, who'd had her fill of drama, stared a hole through me and jerked her head, telegraphing *let's get the heck out of here* without saying the words. Message received, but I dragged my feet for a few extra minutes. She actually sighed in relief when I stood and made our good-byes, following her out to the SUV. Before getting in, she removed an envelope from her briefcase and tossed it on the dash. "We've got a busy day." She slid behind the wheel and blew out of the parking lot of the Beachside.

"Doing what?" I pointed to the exit that would take us to the coffee drive-thru.

"Have you considered that it's all about your attitude in how you approach the job?"

"What a bunch of drivel, besides not answering the question. Don't send me a bill for that advice." I snatched up the envelope, opened it and peered inside, then upended the contents on my lap. A bunch of pawn receipts fell out. "Let me guess, rich dude wants his items redeemed and doesn't want to smudge up his hands doing it himself?" I organized them by store, and there were three locations.

"Apparently, I'm the only one of us with pawn shop experience, and I happen to know that your client couldn't even go fetch his own stuff unless he's the one who pawned it. Store rules and they're inflexible about it. Where *is* the owner? Jail?"

"My client is never going to set foot in a pawn shop," Fab said in her snootiest of tones.

I tapped her on the shoulder, and when she turned, I rolled my eyes. "So, that means there's another party involved? That special someone stole his property and pawned it? Been there. You need to find *that* person. The other option is to involve the police, but then the goods are held as evidence for who knows how long." I smiled at her disgruntlement, no easy fix within her reach. "You can thank me for saving you a trip to Miami."

"His grandson ripped him off. He doesn't want him jailed." Fab pulled up to the drive-thru window. "While I order the coffee, you come up with a plan. Then we'll go to the office."

Fab handed me my coffee, and we rode in silence to the office. Sort of. I slurped my coffee and licked the whipped cream off the inside of the lid. Since finding the baby, we always slowed and scanned the property after passing through the gate and before parking.

"You need to explain the situation to your client and that the grandson is necessary to retrieve said items." I walked up the stairs behind her. The door opened for us. "What, do you do, hang your head out the window when we're not around?" I asked Xander, who grinned.

"I've got an app on my phone that notifies me when the gates open, and I jump up for a look. I've had a surprise or two and don't want any more." He'd already stretched back out on the couch with his laptop on his lap, which he preferred over his desk or sharing mine.

"When you find out the grandson's name, give it to Xander so you know what you're dealing with," I said to Fab, who threw herself in her chair, glaring at her phone. She hated making calls to clients informing them of a glitch. They never took it well.

"I've got an update on Rebecca Herd. The dead chick," Xander reminded us, as though we might have forgotten. "Turns out she's not actually this Rebecca chick. The identification found on her was phony. The fingerprints on file with motor vehicles don't match. She's been relabeled a Jane Doe."

I sat in a chair in front of Fab's desk and shoved it around to face Xander. "So, there's no real Rebecca?"

"If there is, she hasn't been located. I ran a check myself and hit a dead end. But I'll keep looking."

"You're telling us that someone lured Jane to opening night and murdered her, leaving behind a fake ID and thinking that would go unnoticed?" Fab suggested in a tone that implied he was making it up.

"I'm just updating you. End of my job."

"And a good one at that." I winked at him.

"I'm no cop, but wouldn't that put the real Rebecca at the top of the suspect list?"

"I'm certain the cops wish it was always that easy," I said.

"If it is, she's really stupid." Fab jerked her phone off the desk.

I looked at Xander and put my finger to my lips. "We want to listen in. To her side anyway." I twisted back around so I could hang on every word.

Fab explained the situation in the patient tone that she reserved for clients and, after a moment of silence, frowned at the phone, taking a notepad out of her drawer and making a few notes. "I'll keep you updated." She hung up and said to Xander, "Charles Frank III, Grandpa's namesake."

"Put a rush on it," I said. "Other than a few yeses and noes, you didn't have anything to say. That's unusual."

"That's because he didn't take a breath. How do people do that? He rambled on, and even if I'd wanted to cut in for something other than to end the call, there was no opportunity," Fab said in disgust. "Mr. Frank is adamant that the Third needs to be escorted to the pawn shops, where

I'm to pay and take control of the items. He repeated it five times, in case I didn't get it all the other times."

"Would your client be Frank One?" I asked, and Fab nodded. "No tantrum over your not being able to get the things yourself? I'd guess he knew that Third's presence would be required all along, since he acquiesced so quickly. What did he think, you'd shoot these places up to retrieve his family's silver?"

"You're right. Mr. Frank didn't seem all that surprised by the change in plans." Fab picked up her phone again. "I'm going to arrange a time tomorrow to meet with the Third and get this done."

"I'll be shocked if he's cooperative. Good luck." I flashed her a smile. "Go all sexy girl and he'll agree, thinking with his... whatever."

Xander laughed.

"That's not professional," Fab said sternly.

She got Third on the phone and explained the situation. "He hung up." She growled at the screen and hit redial. "No answer." She left a message for him to call back and that if he didn't, she'd call his grandfather and report his uncooperativeness. "I've got his address."

"You can't drive him around town with a gun in his back. If he won't cooperate, call Grandpa back and suggest he threaten to press charges."

Before Fab could answer, Xander piped up, "I figured you didn't need a credit report, so I opted for a criminal background check, and according to his extensive record, Third stays busy breaking the law—misdemeanor stuff." He scanned his computer screen for additional information.

I walked over and leaned over Xander's shoulder, perusing the report. "Breaking and entering, shoplifting, burglary, and resisting arrest. That's nice. Grandpa isn't doing this guy any favors."

"I'm surprised he's not in prison." Fab tried calling him again. "Turned off."

"He will be when a judge gets tired of his repeat performances," I said. "Once Didier hears about his rap sheet, he's going to flip, and if you plan to omit that part, remember that he'll figure it out when he hears I'm not going. In the spirit of friendship," I said hurriedly to ward off her tirade, "I suggest you foist the job off on Toady and bill triple."

Toady was a neighbor of Brad's other property out in Alligator Alley. Who buys a second house out there? We'd met the man when visiting the property; turned out he was caretaker in Brad's absence. One look at the sexy French woman, and the man was smitten. Toady exuded menace and was the self-appointed muscle for any of her dirty jobs. He never said no to any of Fab's requests and had been known to deliver a well-placed threat on his own without any prodding. Unless this Third character was on drugs, he'd do as he was told or find the necessary persuasion painful.

"Hey VP, get me a current address on this guy. I'm texting over what Grandpa gave me." Fab was either fast or had it typed out already, as Xander's phone pinged immediately. "I need to call Toady. Mr. Franks wants this job done ASAP."

"When don't they?" I sighed.

Before Fab could reach for her phone, the door blew open and the man himself strode in, smiling broadly, his single gold tooth glinting in the overhead light. "Hey." Toady acknowledged everyone with a sweeping wave.

At Fab's suggestion, the old reptile had upgraded his old uniform of wife-beater and stained jeans to tropical shirts and crisp jeans, but today had opted for shorts and cowboy boots. I'd bet that holstered under his shirt was a badass weapon. He favored the Smith & Wesson.

"Just the man I want to see." Fab motioned him over, pointing to a chair.

He detoured by the refrigerator first, helping himself to a soda.

I clipped Xander in the head and motioned for him to follow me into our shared office space, where I slid into my chair. "You got anything for me?"

"It's official—the Werner guy was the one that died in the roach coach. The explosion was caused by a propane leak. Cause of death: heart attack, maybe from fright." Xander shuddered. "Another one with a rap sheet. He liked to defraud old people with one scam or another. A few of his victims filed lawsuits and won. The folks that sued aren't getting anything, as Werner had zero financial net worth."

"And the Princesses?" After our phone conversation, I'd dug through some old paperwork that I'd moved from Jake's into my office, found the women's names on a crude agreement with the former owner of the bar, and given Xander the information.

"The names you gave me were bogus. The Princesses don't exist, at least, not under those names. The driver's license you had a picture of was forged, and not a very good one if you look closely."

"That doesn't make any sense." I picked up his report and flicked through it. Thorough, as always. "They paid their rent every month and on time for years. I'll be honest, I was in over my head when I first came to town, so I took the rent money, always put in the mailbox in an envelope, and didn't ask any questions. After a while, I accepted it as the norm, with the added draw that the cops never showed up asking questions."

"Werner didn't appear to be doing anything illegal. At least, nothing was discovered by the cops. No drugs or anything like that. Could he have been living there? He had enough collectors on his tail." Xander gave me a copy of the man's credit report, and his score was close to rock bottom.

"I've been wanting the coach gone for a while, but not like this. Certainly not by leaving behind a dead body and a multitude of unanswered questions. It wouldn't surprise me if the cops had a few questions, and they'll probably ask me, since there isn't anyone else around to ask. I hate either giving or receiving the answer, 'I don't know.'" I rolled over to the half-refrigerator, grabbed a water, and held it up. Xander nodded, so I grabbed two.

"The phone number you gave me for the Princesses goes to a burner phone. A little investigation, and I was able to uncover that it was on a pay-by-the-minute plan, and though they've had the number for years, they never signed up for an account. It's not required, so nothing shifty there. You want my advice?"

I watched as he guzzled his water. That would give me a stomachache, and I'd probably end up spitting it all over everywhere. "I probably shouldn't pass; it might be good."

Xander pushed out his chest on a long exhale and grinned. "Don't go looking for trouble. There's a lot of unanswered questions, and I don't see them leading anywhere good. Besides, you're an innocent party. Don't give anyone any reason to think otherwise." His brow went up, as though I was about to ask a question. "So, don't get yourself mired in something and wish later that you'd listened to my virgin attempt at giving advice."

I laughed. "For your first time, you did good."

"Need a place to hang while my girl is on the phone," Toady announced, coming around the corner. He set some papers in front of Xander. "Got you a client. Dude's a dick, but he pays. Told him your name was VP, and so you know, no need to meet in person. All business can be conducted by phone."

"It better be legal business," I said.

"Repos cars. Clint's always tracking someone. He's gotten in a few skirmishes, but they were self-defense." Toady air-boxed, then threw himself in a chair. He was about to put his feet on the desk but thought better of it.

That's what they all say. "Anyone die?"

"You're a suspicious one." Toady squinted. "And no."

"I'm finding I'm not suspicious enough, but that's about to change," I said.

Before Toady could shoot any more questions my way, Fab breezed in and took a seat.

"This is a first, a meeting in my office. And all of the chairs are filled." I managed a friendly welcome smile.

Fab leveled a 'don't get used to it' stare. "Gunz has an emergency job that takes top priority."

I covered my face with my hands. "I'm afraid to ask," I said through my fingers.

"His cousin's daughter has set out to avenge the death of her brother by shooting the man that killed him, and he wants us to stop her. I know what you're thinking—oh well, to him. But she's young and will end up in prison, and the brother's not really dead. The mother made up a fatal shooting and staged the funeral so he could leave behind a messy life and relocate to California."

It took a minute to digest that story. "The mother couldn't come clean before her daughter turned vigilante?"

"The mother is of the school that says tell one person and it's no longer a secret. Brother in question has gotten his act together and is living a decent, non-criminal life, and she doesn't want that to change."

"How happy is he going to be when his sister is doing life in prison or worse?" I asked. "This whole messy drama comes to light, and Gunz's first thought is for you to track down a gun-toting would-be killer who probably won't believe a word we say? We'll end up facing her wrath ourselves."

Toady rolled to the refrigerator and opened the door to help himself. "Water or water, anyone? Not much choice here."

Xander held out his hand.

Fab and I shook our heads.

"Gunz isn't certain whether she's acquired a gun or not. Her mother doesn't know either. If she has, then it's illegal, because she's only eighteen. Gunz wants credit for imparting the dirty details up front."

"That's nice." I snorted.

"The girl have a name, credit card? Maybe I can track her." Xander was poised at his laptop, ready to go hunting. "If she hasn't located the supposed shooter, that buys you time."

"Gunz says she procured a couple of addresses for him—from where he didn't say—and is in the process of tracking them down. So, we need to get on it."

"Where are the cops in this story?" Toady asked. "The supposed shooter takes the rap for murdering someone he didn't kill, because why? I'm surprised he's not still being housed by the state."

"There were rumors at the time, but nothing came of it—no body or witnesses or evidence of any kind, and now we know why. The supposed shooter had his life trashed by the mother of the so-called victim. She apparently didn't think twice about how the false allegations would affect the other man's life."

"She's an enterprising woman." My words dripped with sarcasm. "Why, instead of turning to Gunz, didn't she tell her daughter the truth the second she got wind of the plan?"

"She did. The daughter thought she was lying." Fab sighed.

"The simple solution would be to get the

brother on the phone for a reunion chat with his sister. Or send her on a vacation to California." Toady tossed his water bottle across the room, missing the trash, which earned him a glare from Fab. He grinned.

"Gunz talked the mother into that very idea and offered to pay for it, but before she could make it happen, the daughter disappeared. There's one thing I haven't mentioned." Fab paused. "The supposed shooter is back in town to renew old acquaintances. It's unclear how many people still remember that he was labeled a murderer or if they'd take any vigilante action."

"Folks have long memories." Toady snorted, a loud honking noise. "Big town or small one, there's always one person around who never forgets and is more than willing to stir the pot. No 'old lady of the year' award for this woman."

I flapped my hand around just to be annoying and succeeded, judging by the irritated look Fab sent my way. "The supposed shooter needs to stay gone—have Gunz pack him off to Disneyworld or wherever—until the daughter can be found. Then the mother needs to straighten out the mess she made."

"If the two women were sharing the same house, how did the mother not know her daughter was harboring revenge fantasies?" Xander threw out.

Fab radiated her exasperation at each of us. "We have to find her before she kills an innocent man." She pushed back her chair. "We need to get going."

"Hold your horses." I didn't shout, but close.

Xander snickered.

Fab turned a hair-raising glare on him. "You might want to remember that you also work for me and I can shoot you out the door."

"Ignore her," I said. "She's annoyed that I didn't jump right up." I flicked my finger at Fab. "Sit. Before you go running out of here chasing a woman bent on revenge, you might want to give Didier a call and run it past him. Tell him I'm sitting this job out and you'll be on your own. I've got a good idea how that will go over."

Fab, who'd ignored my order to sit, leaned forward. "We don't know that it's going to be a dangerous job."

"Yeah, right. What could go wrong when hunting down and trying to stop a gunned-up woman bent on revenge? But if you insist... I suggest that you hire other muscle." I pointed at Toady.

He wagged his head at us. "I volunteer."

"There you go." I dusted my hands together. "Didn't you tell me once that you're a chick magnet, that women fall all over you?"

"I'm pretty popular with the ladies." Toady puffed up. "They assess my suavo exterior and flock to me when I hit the bars." It'd shocked me the first time I heard that, and my reaction hadn't changed at any point since.

Fab stood and flounced over to her desk without a word, beckoning to Toady. After a short conversation, she strutted to the door, Toady following in her wake.

"You better call Didier," I yelled. "And I mean before you hit the highway."

Fab responded by slamming the door.

Chapter Sixteen

"You want to make a wager?" I said to Xander. I leaned down, pulled a dollar out of my bag, and slapped it on the desk between us.

Xander clearly wondered what I was up to. "Depends. On what?"

"The bet is that Fab took my SUV for her adventure, leaving me here to get a ride home from you or, in the event you refuse, walk."

"Hmm... no thanks. There's a slight chance they took whatever ride Toady showed up in, as long as she got to drive." He got up and walked over to the window. "If we'd had a bet, I'd owe you a dollar."

"Almost forgot my backup ride downstairs." A beater truck that ran like a charm and had come in handy a time or two. "It needs to be driven anyway. I've got some paperwork to shuffle, and then I'll be going home. You can cut out early."

"I've got a project I'm working on and like hanging out here; besides, I've got room to spread out." He slapped down a couple of files. "I *am* leaving a little early today, though; the professor invited me to dinner."

"If there's any chance he's going to stick you with the check, go eat at Jake's." Though I didn't think Crum would run out on the bill because he had to know I'd kill him. "Remind him to wear pants."

"All the restaurants in the Keys require a person to wear clothes." Xander laughed. "Crum says it's good for me to spend time with people who aren't mentally deficient."

There was nothing more that man enjoyed than flaunting his high IQ. "He's got some nerve. One look at him, and most people think he just escaped from a locked ward. Have a good time."

"Should be an interesting dinner. Crum's got an agenda, but wouldn't say what exactly. I heard the excitement in his voice and questioned him, with no luck."

I opened my laptop and stared at the screen, trying to figure out where I'd left off while thinking about Crum and hoping that he'd been able to pull strings with the University of Miami. Xander and I worked in friendly silence, and it didn't take long to update the few files that the CPA had requested and get them sent back. I wanted to pack up and leave before Didier decided to drop by the office and started asking about the whereabouts of his wife.

The door flew open. I looked at the clock. Thirty minutes.

Fab stormed in, bypassing her desk and throwing herself in a chair across from me.

"Toady assured me he could handle the case without me, so I gave him all the information I had on the woman, and he's headed into Miami now." She pulled out her phone and sent a text, then told Xander, "Find out anything you can and forward it to Toady. I called Gunz with your Disneyworld suggestion. If the niece can't find the man, she can't kill him."

"How did that conversation go?"

"Gunz was one step ahead. He'd already contacted the man for a sit-down and worked out a more permanent solution. Everything Gunz offered, the man jumped at, and I know it included that he move out of state."

"What brought you back?" I asked.

"Toady. He asked me, 'How mad is the old man going to be with you traipsing off?' After answering honestly that Didier would probably divorce me, I made an illegal u-turn."

Xander had done a poor job of pretending he wasn't listening and totally gave himself away when he lowered his head and his shoulders shook. He was behind Fab, and it was fortunate she couldn't see him.

"I'm happy you're back." I smiled at Fab. "It's a long walk home."

Fab rolled her eyes. "I'm certain Toady will find whack-job. Once she's found, he'll deliver her to Gunz and suggest that he send her to California for a reunion with her brother and advise her to get some sunshine and mental health rest while she's out there."

"We have plenty of sun here, and some folks think that's part of the reason we have so many crazies."

"I told Toady to call if he needs your help," Fab said to Xander.

"No ride-alongs." I arched my brow.

"Don't need to worry about me," Xander said. "I don't need firsthand experience."

"Free advice, which I know you love," I said to Fab. "Tell Didier about your day. All of it. He'll be pleased that you made the decision to turn around."

"I'll have to wait for the right time," Fab hedged.

I tapped my cheek. "When you're all snuggly under the sheets and he's already half-asleep."

Xander blushed.

"That's the perfect time."

"I'm going to tell Creole at the same time."

We both laughed.

"Are you ready to leave?" Fab asked.

I shut off my laptop. "Can you guarantee that we'll make it home drama-free?"

"Oh, heck no."

Chapter Seventeen

I beat Creole home by a few minutes. Hearing his truck drive up, I got a beer out of the refrigerator and handed it to him with a kiss when he walked in the door.

"Must have been a heck of a day." He twirled me around, running his hands down my body.

"Not even a scratch." I grabbed his hand and pulled him to the couch, tugging him down beside me. I leaned in and kissed him.

"You're here, so you don't need bail."

"You're killing the romance."

"I know how to get it back. Now tell me about your day, *dear*."

I hit the highlights of the day, during which he groaned a couple of times. When I got to Fab's latest case, I hesitated to mention Gunz's name, as he knew the man from his unsavory days. The last time his name came up, Creole had been skeptical of his makeover.

"This Gunz cretin has to know that sending you two to track down one of his relatives intent on murder instead of calling the cops could land you in jail if she did succeed. You could wave out your cell window to him if the facilities were adjoining."

My stomach twisted at the thought of even one second behind bars.

"You do you know that well-intentioned jobs almost always blow up into a bigger mess?" Since he was waiting for a response and I didn't have one, I smiled weakly. "Is Fab going to tell Didier, or am I going to have to plead ignorance when he confronts me? Because he will find out."

"Fab's going to come squeaky clean." Probably an exaggeration, and I knew Creole agreed, since he snorted.

My phone rang. He reached around me and picked it up off the table, making a face at the screen. "Hopefully, the whole place didn't blow up." He handed it to me.

"Hey, boss," Doodad said when I answered. "The code guy came by today and wants to know when the remains of the coach are getting hauled away. I asked him to give us a day or two."

"I'll be in tomorrow morning and deal with it then. All the information I've got on Werner, which isn't much, I forwarded to Tank, and I'll have to check with him first before we do anything. I don't want to be sued."

"I've got to go." Doodad groaned. "Got a fight to break up." He hung up.

Creole picked the phone out of my hand and set it back on the table. "I don't know what you're planning, and I hope that it's not taking care of the problem yourself. That's why you have a lawyer. My unlawyerly advice is that you can have it hauled off, but hang onto it in case there's some sort of claim."

* * *

I'd gotten up before Creole, which was unusual, and rolled out of bed quietly, not wanting to disturb him. I showered and had the coffee going before he opened his eyes and went to take a shower.

I turned at the sound of banging on the back door, wondering who on the short list had gotten through the secured gate. I opened the door, and Mila squealed, "Auntie," holding out her arms. I took her from my brother, and we traded kisses on each cheek like her French grandfather, Caspian, had taught her.

"You're here early," I said, kissing Brad before pulling him over the threshold and closing the door.

"Emerson asked last night what you were up to now, and I didn't know. So, I thought, 'why not kill all the birds at once?' and show up early with my daughter, since I know you'd never throw her out." He grinned.

I slid onto a stool, Mila on my lap.

Brad took a sippy cup out of his pocket and set it in front of his daughter. "I brought milk, since she's too young for tequila." He turned and grabbed a mug out of the cupboard for himself, filling it with coffee.

"Very funny. Isn't Miss Mila supposed to be at pre-school?" The two of us rubbed noses, which made her laugh.

"Another surprise." Brad claimed a stool across from me. "Mother will be here any minute to pick Mila up. I enrolled her in a new school after she came home using the "F" word in a variety of ways." He whispered the last part. "Cook referred me to a place that's well-respected. They stress making learning fun. She's got a couple of days before she starts, and she's spending them with Mother."

"This is what you meant by birds. Are there any more?"

Brad flashed me an innocent face.

Mila spied Jazz and Snow sleeping next to the patio door and wanted down. She ran over and plunked herself down, combing their fur with her fingers.

"Since you're here for an update..." I gave him a rundown, and when I got to Gunz, he rolled his eyes. "The more of his cases you can farm out, the better."

Agreed. But how to convince Fab? "Anything new on the baby?"

"Father of the year is still in jail. No word on the mother, and that's not a red flag for her family. When interviewed, they blew it off as 'she likes to visit friends.' They said they saw no reason to file a missing person's report, figuring she'd turn up."

"If that's true, she's a crappy mom, going off and leaving her baby with a man with a long rap sheet. I hope she's not dead."

"Emerson shares your sentiments. She was ecstatic when you called and asked for her help."

"I mean, who else? She acted like the pro she is, called all the right people, and handled the situation efficiently."

Creole came out of the bathroom, and Mila jumped up and ran to him. He crouched with open arms, and she slammed into him, hugging him tightly. He scooped her off her feet and spun her around, eliciting squeals, then set her down, and she ran back to the cats.

I got up, poured a cup of coffee, and handed it to Creole, offering Brad a refill.

"You making sure I'm going to get to the meeting on time?" Creole greeted my brother.

"Barged in, knowing early is a good time to catch my sister and get caught up. Let someone else in the family have the title of 'last to know.'"

The gate buzzer sounded.

"That's how it's done." I wagged my finger at Brad. "You ring and wait patiently for someone to open it for you."

"Then why give me a key?" He opened the door and went outside, yelling, "Who's there?"

"Brad Westin, the neighbors will hear you," Mother admonished.

Creole and I laughed.

"There aren't any neighbors." He opened the gate, sticking his head out. "You only get in if you have a pink box in your hand."

"I've got two." Mother held out the boxes, which he took, kissing her cheek.

"You're the best, and not just because you come bearing sweets." Brad followed her into the house.

Mother hugged Creole and me and held out her arms for Mila, who came running. She picked her up, and they sat on a stool. "You need to get out the other coffee pot. I called Fab and told her I was stopping at the bakery and she and Didier should finagle an invitation."

"Fab saw that as an invite and should be here any minute." Creole got out the dark roast they liked.

He called it. A few minutes later, the twosome showed up and banged on the back door. No ringing the bell for them. Brad scooted back and opened the door, and Fab blew in ahead of Didier and plucked Mila out of Mother's arms. They exchanged some unintelligible talk.

"If you're here to take my SUV for your own use," I said to Fab, "you're out of luck. I need it for business. You're welcome to tag along if you like."

Fab whispered to Mila, and they both growled at me. Except Mila followed hers up with a huge grin.

The guys laughed.

"Where's your hunky husband, Spoon?" I asked Mother.

"I know who my husband is," she huffed. "Some big deal is bringing in his Bugatti and will only deal with the owner, not an underling. His exact words."

"Hmm… I could use his help. I'll run the job by you first, and you can call him and give your okay," I teased, then reminded her of his offer to rid my property of the burned-out coach.

Mother groaned. "Don't say it like he needs my permission. That'll just remind him how annoyed he was with me the last time I interfered. When he got wind that he missed out on some chaos, I got the 'I'm a grown man' lecture again. I just worry."

Brad made an unintelligible noise, though it came out loud.

"Whatever that was supposed to be, it needs some work." I laughed.

"You have a daughter to set an example for," Fab said in her snooty tone.

"Yeah, Brad." Didier winked at Fab.

"Hate to break this up, but we've got a meeting." Creole stood and wrapped his arms around Mother. "Thanks for the breakfast."

Brad lifted Mila into his arms and, after hugs all around, walked Mother out to her car.

"Do you think you two can have an uneventful day?" Didier cocked a brow.

Fab and I shrugged.

"I'll go out on a limb and give you a definite maybe," I said.

Chapter Eighteen

Fab slid behind the wheel of the SUV and gunned it out to the main highway at a breakneck speed, laughing at herself as she slowed to almost the speed limit before hitting the side streets for a quick trip across town.

"Broke my record," she boasted, pulling into the driveway of JS Auto Body and parking.

I got out, grabbing the breakfast leftovers, and marched over to the entrance. "Stand back, I'm going to beat the door down." I raised my fist.

Fab snickered from behind me.

The door opened before I could carry through with my threat. Spoon filled the doorway, glaring in a way meant to be intimidating. Someone who didn't know him would have hit the road with some speed.

"Come in, you two." Spoon reached out and took the pink box.

"Your wife knows how to buy out the bakery." I stood on tiptoes and kissed his cheek. "I came to hit Step-daddy up for a favor."

Fab made a retching noise and earned herself another glare from the big man.

"Come in and tell Daddy what you're up to now." His lips curved slightly, humor in his eyes.

"If anyone overheard you two, they'd think other things besides that you think you're funny when you're not," Fab said in a huff.

I turned to her. "Not even a little." I claimed a chair in front of Spoon's desk.

He took his power seat and peered in the bakery box. "I'll share these with the guys in the shop, which will make Madeline more popular than she already is."

Fab lurked around the office, going to stand in front of the only item of interest—the standing safe. The door was closed, and I'd bet she was debating seeing if it was unlocked. Deciding against it, she moved to the door that led out to the bays.

"Don't even think about making a run for it," I told Fab. "You do, and I'll come after you and drag you back. By the hair," I added cheekily.

"No more coffee for you." Fab flounced over to a chair next to me and sat down.

"Back to my favor." I turned my attention to Spoon when he returned, and whose patience was dwindling. "I'm taking you up on your offer to have the roach coach hauled away. I told Mother. She didn't squawk and said you could make up your own mind. That last part is a secret." I went on to relay the details of the explosion, punctuated it by throwing my hands in the air and blowing out a popping noise.

Spoon stared, shaking his head. "What do you want done?"

"I want whatever's expedient, but according to my lawyer, the law says not so fast. I need owner permission, but that's not going to be easy because nothing ever is." I sighed, thinking about how many calls I'd made in that vein without getting any answers. "A quick check showed that dead dude didn't transfer the title into his name. The original owners—legally still the owners, aka the Princesses—have gone incommunicado and hightailed it out of town. Xander to the rescue. He is in the process of tracking down the pair and forwarding the info to my lawyer. I've already instructed him to forgo any niceties and play hardball to get the mess cleaned up."

"So, your best tenants don't bother with a good-bye and the ratty coach blows sky-high." Spoon chuckled. "I've dealt with shifty folks my entire life, and they're coming not back. Fake names means they've got something to hide, and the last thing they're going to do is raise a ruckus over a burned-out shell that will leave them answering questions they'd rather not, and they know that."

"Your advice would be?" I asked.

"We're all ears." Fab yawned.

I shot her the stink eye, which she ignored.

"One of these days, young lady—" Spoon glared at Fab. "—you're going to need a favor, and I'm going to relish saying N. O."

"Do it, and I'll tell Madeline on you."

"Okay, you two." I clapped my hands. "Back to biz." However much the man maintained an irritated expression, I knew he was amused by our antics.

"I'll go check it out and make arrangements to have it hauled away." Spoon slid a notepad across his desk and made a few notes. "I've got a friend that owns a junkyard who can store it, and I'll incentivize him to keep his mewling to a minimum. He's a dramatic fellow for someone who looks like he's lived in the woods his whole life and only talks to animals that he claims talk back. I'll suggest that, after the paperwork is in order, he salvage what's left in lieu of any fees. That okay with you?"

"Perfect." Fab stood. "Ready to go?"

"You're annoying," I said, and stood.

"It's like a Zen moment for me—makes me feel whole."

I followed with an "ommm…" noise.

Spoon laughed. "You headed there now?"

I turned to Fab, and she nodded. "We can meet you there."

I hugged Spoon and followed Fab to the door.

She paused and yelled over her shoulder, "See you soon." Out she went and didn't waste time hopping behind the wheel.

I turned back to Spoon. "I appreciate that you're willing to work your magic on this problem. It's not going to be long before it stops attracting lookie-loos wanting a picture and instead is labeled an eyesore." He laughed and waved me out the door. I walked out and got into the passenger side. Fab tapped her foot on the accelerator, racing the motor. "Could you be more annoying?"

"We both know the answer is yes." Fab waved through the windshield. "Spoon loves it when you bring problems to him."

"You couldn't be nicer?"

"Not unless you want him suspecting I'm up to something." She backed out of the driveway and, for once, took the direct route to Jake's.

Fab slowed, turning into the driveway, and checked out the lighthouse and Junker's. No one was around, which wasn't a surprise. She cut around the back and parked next to the kitchen door, and we trooped inside.

I turned and took one last look at two cars parked on the far side of the lot under a tree, neither of which I recognized. It surprised me we had early arrivals, as we weren't open to customers yet.

Cook was behind the grill. "I'm whipping up a new special," he yelled.

I smiled lamely, and my stomach lurched as I remembered a couple of the recent specials. Not a one of them was something I'd touch with a ten-foot fork, no matter that a couple had turned out to be popular. Fab led the way down the hall, then turned with a raised brow and a jerk of her shoulder.

I followed her gaze to the large, curvy woman with fluorescent red hair who sat on a barstool. One look at us headed her way, and she snapped her fingers at Kelpie, who appeared annoyed with the two men at the far end of the bar, not her usual sparkly self.

"Hey, Bossaroo," Kelpie said evenly. "These gents are here to see you. Lucky them, you showed up just when I was telling them 'fat chance' and to give it up or I'd throw them out."

The two skinny, hard-faced men slid off their stools and stood. Their appearance screamed unsavory. "How about we talk over here?" One pointed to a table.

Fab nudged me in the small of the back, tapping my Glock.

"The bar works for me. Have a seat, gentleman." I pointed to the stools they'd just vacated. "No secrets here. My bartender will grumble if she's not kept in the loop, and I can't take the whining today." I gave the redheaded woman, who was the picture of serene, a closer look. "You look familiar."

"Lizzie." She stuck out her hand.

I responded with my knuckles, which didn't faze her.

"I interviewed for a job and didn't hear back. I know you haven't hired anyone, so I'm back for a second shot. Your manager dubbed me Lizzie Borden."

Gone were the oversized scrubs and man's toupee. Today, she sported a red tartan schoolgirl skirt that skimmed the tops of her thigh tattoos, a black sports bra that didn't suck the life out of her overly large breasts, and calf-length fishnet stockings stuffed into motorcycle boots. Her makeover could be summed up in one word: Kelpie.

"If you don't mind waiting…" I wracked my brain and vaguely remembered that she had no experience.

Lizzie nodded and moved to a stool next to where Fab stood at the end of the bar, her Walther in her hand but out of sight.

"What can I help you with?" As I walked behind the bar, I split my gaze between the two men, unsure who was going to take the lead.

"Werner Titan owed us money, and we're here to collect." The squinty faced man pushed a piece of paper at Kelpie, who stood in front of the two. She picked it up, glanced at it, and whistled, handing it to me.

Without looking, I wadded it up and tossed it toward the trash, missing by a foot. "I'm not responsible for Werner's debts. I'm not any relation and, furthermore, never met the man. It's unfortunate he blew himself to bits." An exaggeration, but he was still dead. "Had I known he was out there, I'd have run him off.

Sorry for your wasted trip." It was probably a stretch that they'd get up and go, since they appeared ready to start trouble, but one could hope.

"It would be in your best interest to pay up. If you do, we'll go away quietly and stay away," the other one growled.

"Until the next time you're in the mood to scare money out of a woman."

He bristled and took a step forward.

Fab didn't hesitate, pointing her Walther at them. "Hit the door."

Squinty reached for his weapon, Fab pulled the trigger, and he yelped, holding the side of his head. "You coulda killed me!" His fingers came away covered in blood.

The other man, not a quick learner, was clearly about to duplicate the failed move. Lizzie leaped from her stool and, in a whirl, grabbed the stool next to her and clocked him in the side of the head with a resounding whack. He crumpled to the floor. Kelpie roared, reminiscent of a wild animal, and jumped around the bar ninja-style.

"I'm bleeding to death," Squinty whined.

Spoon roared through the entrance, his weapon in plain sight, and skidded to a stop. "What the hell is going on?" He quickly took in the situation. "You call the cops?"

"It's up to Fab; she shot him. Protecting me." I beamed at her.

Fab shrugged.

Spoon bent down to the man "bleeding to death" and, after a quick once-over, held a one-sided conversation with him. "Now, repeat what I just told you." Spoon grasped him by the scruff of the neck, bringing him to his feet with a hard shake.

"You'll never see either of us again," the man whined.

"Better not, or it will be grisly. I'll be back for the other one," Spoon called before hauling him out the door.

The man who still lay on the floor was coming around, judging by the moaning sounds, and Lizzie fisted the back of his shirt and dragged him out the front door.

A couple of minutes later, Lizzie and Spoon came back inside. "Those two won't be back," Spoon said. "I had a chat with the one, and he's going to convey my wishes to his friend when he's fully awake." He said to Fab, "Surprised you didn't kill him. You did a good job; only took a small piece off the rim of his ear."

"Too much paperwork."

I turned and enveloped her in a hug. "I know you hate this, but get over it. Are you okay?" She nodded.

"The dumbass told me that Werner owed money all around South Florida and beyond and that there were folks looking for him. So, don't be surprised if more *collectors* show up. It came as a surprise to them to learn that Werner had been holed up in the coach, or trouble would've arrived sooner. I didn't mince words about what would happen if I saw them around here again. They're not locals, so I made it clear that there was no need for them to come back."

"You scaring the devil out of those two is probably the only thing that will keep them from planning a sneak attack."

"Called my friend on the way over. The coach will be hauled off today." Spoon brushed his hands together.

"You're hired on a probationary basis," I told Lizzie. "Kelpie needs to train you, and you should know that Doodad has the final say. You proved that you can handle the customers today, and I want to thank you for your part in that."

I hustled after Spoon, who'd motioned to me and was headed outside. "I'm going to hang around until Sergeant shows up for the coach. He's an odd one and lacks social skills."

"I have expertise with those kinds of people," I joked.

"Yes… well… I don't mind. Alert your staff to be on the lookout for any copycats of those two that show up. After my short exchange with them, it's my opinion that this could've gone a lot worse."

Fab appeared at my side in time to hear his comments. "What happens when the one I shot shows up at the hospital?"

"My guess is that he won't want the scrutiny

and will turn up at the office of a doctor who takes cash and doesn't ask questions. He can always say he shot himself. He can easily pull off being a dumbass."

A truck rumbled into the driveway and parked beside what was left of the coach. An older man in a flannel shirt and shorts, with a beard to his waist, climbed out.

I didn't know how his truck was going to accomplish the haul-away. There must be a Plan B.

"Keep me updated." Spoon waved to his friend and closed the distance between the two.

"Are we done here?" Fab asked. "It's quiet inside. I told Kelpie to update Doodad and Cook to stop with the exotic foods. Whatever he was cooking smelled." She turned up her nose. "He was about ready to take my head off when I reminded him of his stellar rep as the best cook in town. That worked so well, I'll be sure to trot it out again."

Me too.

Chapter Nineteen

"Where are we going?" I asked when Fab turned onto the main highway. My phone rang, interrupting her response. I picked it up and looked at the screen.

"Throw that thing out the window." Fab made a tossing motion.

"It's Liam," I told her before answering the phone. "This is a pleasure."

"Can we meet up today?"

I heard the sounds of traffic in the background and knew he was in his truck. "When? Where?"

"I just drove past the Tarpon Cove city limit sign. I could come to your office."

"How about I have pizza delivered, and we can eat and talk?"

"That sounds good."

We hung up, and I called in the order and texted Xander to alert him to the delivery.

"If Liam drove down here to talk to you; it must be important," Fab said. "You know, he could call me once in a while; I'd never turn him down."

"He knows he's getting both of us to help with any problem he brings to me."

"Let's hope it's nothing serious."

"I need to update Creole." I continued to stare at my phone.

"I called Didier, and he didn't answer, but texted that they were in a meeting and would call later. I texted back, 'More drama today, no one hurt.'"

"Except for the earless guy."

"It wasn't the whole ear. So, Creole got his update."

"Thank you again. I knew when you tapped me on the back that whatever went down, you had it handled."

"If you're really thankful, I'll take a fistful of favors."

"Like you need them." I humphed.

Partway down the block, Fab hit the gate opener for the office so she wouldn't have to wait several seconds to drive in. She parked next to Liam's truck, got out, and flew up the stairs and through the open door. I trudged behind her and walked into a welcoming hug from Liam.

"You know you don't need a reason to stop by," I said. "VP is almost always here." I waved to Xander.

"Xander told me you aren't around a lot to annoy him."

"He did not," I said in mock annoyance.

Liam laughed.

"Pizza here?" I asked over his shoulder.

"Not yet," Xander yelled back from where he

lay stretched out on the couch.

I linked my arm in Liam's. "Is this a private conversation?"

Fab dumped her bag on the floor and yelled from behind her desk, "It better not be. Another thing—I don't know why you don't call me once in a while. Tell him how I saved your life today."

I took a step back, made a gun finger, blew out loud bursts of air, then grabbed the side of my head. "She shot the guy's ear off." I dissolved into laughter and threw myself in a chair. "Fab can tell the rest."

Fab held court, giving an animated retelling of the morning's events. When she was finished, she stood and took a bow. She'd managed a fun and exciting version of events much better than reality and far more gruesome, which the guys saw through.

It made all of us laugh.

"You might as well air your problems to us all—get them out in the open," Fab said to Liam. "I need to know, for my sidekick status, if it's something serious that I should take the lead on."

"I've got any background checks handled," Xander offered.

"I can't believe you used the word sidekick to refer to yourself. Was that painful?" I smirked.

"See what I have to put up with?" Fab huffed. "Ignore her."

"My story isn't going to be as exciting as

Fab's." Liam smiled at her and took a seat in front of her desk, turning sideways. "This past weekend, there was a blowout party not far from school. A ton of kids showed, even those that hadn't been invited. Word travels. A friend snorted a few lines of cocaine." He reached out and grabbed my hand. "Promise I don't do drugs. I'm into craft beer."

"Your friend?" I asked.

"Damn near died. He was hitting on a girl when he passed out, and her screams could be heard throughout the house. 911 got called, and he was rushed to the hospital. Tests showed that the cocaine was laced with fentanyl. After doing some research, I found out that he was lucky to survive. A lot don't. In fact, people of all ages are dying in record numbers after using the stuff."

"He's going to be okay?" I asked. Liam nodded.

"What do you want us to do?" Fab asked.

"Put the dealer out of business," Liam said adamantly. "The cops interviewed my friend in the hospital, but he pled ignorance. Some contrived story that it was his first time experimenting and he didn't know where the drugs came from—they magically appeared or some such nonsense. His evasive answer probably had a lot to do with the fact that his parents had shown up by then."

"The cops aren't stupid; they know they got half the story," I said.

"You know the dealer?" Fab asked.

"Never met him. I got the contact info from another friend and was informed that he delivers."

"How considerate."

"My friend is scared to give the dealer's name to the cops for fear he'll be killed. I'm thinking it's probably not much of an exaggeration."

"Give all the information you have on the dealer to Xander for him to check out," I said.

"I know I'm asking a lot. I thought you two could come up with a way to stop the guy without anyone else ending up in the hospital or the morgue."

"In order for us to put this guy out of business, the cops will have to be involved," Fab said. "Anonymous tip maybe. Creole is the one with the law enforcement contacts; it makes sense to get his advice first. Or better yet, make it his problem." She shot me a sneaky smile.

"Curious question. Is there a way to tell that the drug has been tampered with before snorting it?"

Liam shook his head. "The university is trying to get the word out to just not do it, since there's no way of telling. Some kids will listen and stop, and others will think they're invincible."

"I remember the days when I didn't think much about consequences." Xander grimaced. "Bad way to live."

The gate buzzer rang. Fab checked the monitor

and opened it. She handed money to Xander, who jumped up and ran downstairs to meet the delivery man. He came back with two pizza boxes in hand, setting them on the kitchen table.

Liam pulled sodas and waters out of the refrigerator.

"Don't worry," I said to him as we all took seats at the table. "I'm working on putting together a plan that doesn't include our involvement." I waved a finger between Fab and me. "Once I get it worked out, I'll send a text telling you it's done."

"Madison's better at coming up with plans than I am. My first choice would be to shoot him and rid the streets of the vermin."

"Except that would bring his dealer friends down on us." I reached for a slice of pizza. "So happy we're using the everyday china." I ripped a paper towel off the roll, then nudged Fab under the table and mouthed, *Crum*.

"How did dinner with the arrogant professor go?" Fab asked. "Did you have to remind him to put on pants?"

Xander laughed. "He wore a suit of sorts. A bit mismatched—the jacket doubled as a shirt and his bare chest showed. The pants would've been good if we'd walked through a puddle—the cuffs wouldn't have gotten wet."

I bit back a laugh at the look on Fab's face, knowing she'd have a hard time getting rid of that visual.

"You need a strong stomach to drive with him, as he only uses one hand and doesn't always keep his eyes on the road." Xander made a shocked face. "The restaurant wasn't far but still a remote location. It was a dump that leaned to one side, but the food was excellent. Surprised me to learn that he knew the owner, and they had a regular conversation—none of his usual snarky comments."

"He can do normal, and I missed it?" I pouted. "So, you had a good time?"

"Crum and I always got along good," Liam interjected. "When I lived at The Cottages, he helped me with my homework when I got stuck. He'd check it over; said there was no excuse for handing in schlock. Because of him, I got in the habit of double-checking everything. He never took me to a restaurant, though. Hot dogs, that was it. I'm going to have to talk to him about that."

Xander laughed. "Crum would love that. I've got some good news. So far, the only person I've shared it with is my roommate."

"We like good news," Fab said.

"Crum is working on getting me into the University of Miami next semester on a scholarship. His first idea was a California university, but he thought I'd like it better if I could stay close to people I know. I was relieved not to have to move across the country. My plan is to keep my job and drive back and forth, so don't go replacing me."

"No chance of that," Fab said. "The pickings around here are slim, as most exaggerate their abilities."

"Plus, we like you." I glared at Fab.

"Oh yeah. Sure we do." Fab and Xander made eye contact, then laughed.

"That awkwardness didn't last long," I said.

"I'll show you around campus and introduce you to 'those of your ilk,'" Liam said, mimicking Crum.

Fab and I each had one slice of pizza, and the guys devoured the rest.

Just as we finished, Creole and Didier clumped up the stairs. They walked in sporting well-fitting jeans and work boots. After a quick kiss, they traded stories with Liam.

After a few minutes, Liam and Xander left to go have coffee and talk about school, and Fab rehashed the details of the morning before the guys could ask.

Then I told them why Liam had visited. "I've whipped up a half-baked plan. I vote that we turn this information over to Chief Harder and let him sic his drug unit or whoever on this guy."

"What are you going to say when he has more questions than you have answers?" Creole asked.

I sighed. "Thought of that. I'm going to ask for another favor and informant protection." I smiled lamely. "Or—"

"Oh no," Creole cut me off. "I've never had

the sway with my old boss that you do. I'm fairly certain he'll get it worked out for you, since he's never turned you down before. If I was a petty man, that would irk me."

"Make the call now, so I can listen in," Fab said.

Didier shook his head. "You don't need to listen in."

"Second-hand sucks."

"Don't you think he's going to notice that he's on speaker when his voice is echoing about?" I pointed out.

"You'll think of something," Fab said smugly.

Creole laughed. "Knowing Madison, she probably will."

I fished my phone out of my pocket and called Chief Harder.

"A call in the middle of the day," he greeted me. "You must be up to something."

"So suspicious. Before you ask, I'm not in need of bail money." That was usually the man's first question.

He laughed.

"Would you mind if I put you on speakerphone? Fab's head is sure to explode in flames if she can't listen in, and the husbands are here."

"Go ahead."

I hit the button.

"That means I'll have witnesses to whatever felonies you're about to cop to. Hello, everyone."

Everyone called out hellos.

"About that. I'm going to need immunity." I tried not to come off as weaselly and barely succeeded.

Harder groaned. "What is it this time?"

I told him about my conversation with Liam, leaving out the names.

"How reliable is your source?" Harder's interest had perked up and could be heard in his tone.

"Very. He was at the party and is a friend of the victim. That kid didn't come clean because he didn't want to be a murder victim."

"Dealers don't take kindly to being ratted out to the cops." Harder was silent, papers rustling in the background. "Fentanyl-laced cocaine is a big problem. Too many people die every day from the drug. Text me the info, and I'll turn it over to one of my men."

I snapped my fingers at Fab and handed her my phone. Doing two things at once when one of them involved electronics wasn't my strong suit. "I've got my guy doing a background check, if you want that forwarded."

"Big outfit like the one I work for, we can do our own." Harder laughed. "In all seriousness, it will be a pleasure to take this dealer off the street, and with any luck, we can squeeze a few more names out of him. It won't clean up the problem, but it's a good thing to make a dent, regardless of how large or small."

"The thought of more college kids dying makes me sick."

"Same here. We've been trying to get the word out about the dangers of these drugs. Hopefully, more will heed it. Now, what do I get for being willing to help without an unkind word?"

Creole laughed.

"I heard that, Detective."

"Name it and it's yours. Unless, of course, it's illegal." I laughed.

"I'll make a note in my book. One more IOU for me. Two, actually. Since your friend is listening in, I get one from her."

"Agreed," Fab said. "And I'll try not to complain."

"With any luck, you'll be reading about a big bust soon."

Chapter Twenty

Creole had planned an early morning surprise—coffee on the beach. He poured our favorite blends into two thermoses, grabbed a blanket, and we headed barefoot down to the sand. We sat and faced the shore, his arm looped around my shoulders, and watched as the small waves rolled in.

It surprised me to hear his phone ringing in his pocket, as I thought he'd left it behind as I had mine. He pulled it out, glanced at the screen, and laughed. "It's for you."

Judging by his sneaky grin, whatever the problem was had just been shuffled off onto me. "Since it's not polite to call at this hour, it better be good," I said upon answering.

There was a long pause. "You weren't answering your phone," Cootie accused.

"And? You might want to keep in mind that I'm short on morning personality today." I poked Creole, who'd leaned over to listen, in the ribs.

"I've got that problem every morning." Cootie humphed. "You find a cure, let me know."

"Coffee's the closest I've got. It's certainly my drug of choice."

"Bad news, bad news, and good news. That bartender chick tipped me off that you like good news," he said, his laugh letting me know he found himself amusing.

"Kelpie?" Easy guess, since the new one hadn't been on the job long enough to dispense advice about my preferences.

Creole covered his laugh.

"Bad news: break-in into Isabella's room. You know, the haunted room."

"Got it." My eyeroll was lost on him, since he couldn't see me. "Someone who couldn't afford to pay? Any damage?"

"Here's the deal—the woman didn't stay long; just long enough to rip the bed apart and ransack the room, although there wasn't much to sack." He made a sucking noise. I didn't bother to ask what he was drinking. "Wouldn't have known until I went to check in a guest, except that the broad left the door ajar when she split. You want to know how I know it was a woman?" he asked, clearly proud of himself. "I checked the security tape. Clever of me, huh?"

I nudged Creole away as he started to laugh. "Did she steal anything?"

"Nope. Even that smelly soap is accounted for."

"Get a good look at her face so we can call it into the cops?"

"Nopers. Got a quick look, long enough to know it was a chick. She'd wrapped herself in a coat that dragged the ground. It had a hood, but strands of her long dark hair stuck out on the sides. Must have been sweating like a pig with the humidity off the charts."

Creole rolled away, and I slapped his butt.

"So… the woman was looking for something," I said. "I wonder what. If she'd been a guest and left something behind, she could have gotten a key at the desk. I need to have a chat with Isabella and have her run off any future interlopers. Scaring them would be ideal. Boo…"

Cootie laughed. "Rude said the same thing. I know she's been in the room to talk to our resident ghost, but pretty sure there hasn't been any reciprocal chitchat cuz I'd never hear the end of it if there was."

"Tell Rude that during her next visit with Isabella, she needs to tell the ghost to step it up and scare the heck out of any trespassers. Nobody stays for free," I said. "Keep an eye out. We have two choices: wait for it to happen again, although I'm hoping it's a one-off, or hire a night guard."

"I'll put that on the agenda for the next meeting; maybe I'll have more info for you by then. The last bit of bad news—cat guy, aka Short, was back last night. Had the hissing feline corralled inside a pillow case and was inches from the gate when Rude jumped on his back and wrestled him to the ground. The cat escaped. Rude told Short to git. Then proceeded to detail how she'd rearrange his body parts and where she'd put them if he told anyone. He hightailed it off the property," Cootie relayed with pride.

Creole winced.

I smothered a laugh.

"One more thing. Rude told me to relay that you're not to worry your curls—she's got a plan for dealing with Short, which she augmented with sound effects. But mine aren't as good as hers, so you'll have to take my word for it. If her plan goes south, I'm thinking you could get Frenchie to pay him a visit and kick the tar out of him. He'd think twice about where he set his squatty feet then."

"I'm more than happy to send Fab out to hunt the man down." I was tired of hearing about the man and wanted him gone. Hearing Creole's groan, I added, "Rude isn't to get hurt."

"Da-da-da."

I imagined him throwing his hands in the air, as though he'd scored a touchdown but didn't ask.

"Now for the good news: it's a beautiful day outside."

That's it? "This has been fun. Call me if anything else happens." I hung up and rolled over. "I'm happy that you found the conversation amusing," I said sarcastically.

Creole pulled me into his arms. "I'll take care of that stupid cat man."

"Don't think so." I shook my head. "Problems

are my domain, thanks to the almost unanimous vote. Besides, my money's on Rude. She's a tough old bird. If not, there's my backup problem solver—Toady."

"I imagine the wildlife around his house eat well."

Creole's phone rang again. I looked at the screen and handed it back to him with a laugh. *Fab!*

"Good morning," he said in a saccharine tone. After a brief pause, he said, "She's busy for the next two hours."

Chapter Twenty-One

Not having spoken to Fab and with no clue what the plan was for the day, I dressed in my usual work outfit of skirt and top, sliding into sandals and shoving a pair of flip-flops in my bag. I was holding my phone when it beeped. "Meet me outside" was the text I got. I went outside and slid into the passenger seat.

"Your husband is annoying." Fab rocketed down the street.

"Don't expect me to apologize for the delay, since I was about to get lucky."

Fab's eyebrows shot up so high, they almost disappeared into her hairline. "La, la, la, I don't want to hear that, and besides, you sound like you're sixteen."

"You ought to be thanking him for reversing my earlier 'tudiness. I'm thinking a caramel latte will be just the jack I need for the rest of the day. If we're headed to a shootout, make sure you order me the ginormous size."

"We're meeting Gunz. He says discretion is of the utmost importance in this next case."

I groaned. "After we're done with his highness, I need to hit The Cottages. The mental patients have been quiet of late, and I need to check to make sure my property is still standing."

"Really, Madison. They're folks, just like you and… not me, but other people. You could be a little nicer."

"Coffee," I bellowed and turned toward the window, smiling at my reflection and how much fun it was to annoy Fab some days. "I got a call on the trouble hotline this morning…" I related the conversation with Cootie. "You should be proud, when he thought butt-kicker, your name topped his list."

Fab sped through the coffee drive-thru and placed our order, remembering the extra whipped cream. Then raced over to the office, pulling through the gate and parking next to Gunz's SUV.

"Gunz better not be attempting to lure Xander away to work for one of his other enterprises. You need to make it clear—no poaching."

"We're not a career choice." Fab got out, ran up the stairs, and breezed through the open door. One would almost think she didn't want to listen to me grumbling all the way up the steps, since she hadn't paused to acknowledge my grievance.

I entered the office and set a cup of coffee in front of Xander, who sat at the kitchen table, absorbed in whatever was on the screen of his laptop. He glanced up and smirked.

Gunz had made himself comfortable behind

Fab's desk and was talking on his phone. At the sight of her, he cut it short. "Hello, hun."

Looking at Xander, I rolled my eyes; he tried to hide a grin. I sat on the couch, knowing it was a good location for eavesdropping.

"You were instrumental in dealing with my cousin, and I'm happy that no one ended up dead." Gunz winked at Fab. "Relocating the man has worked out, and he didn't squawk, since he has no family and few friends around here anymore."

"It's always good to have a satisfied client," Fab said. I wondered if, like me, she was wondering what he was doing here and suspected it had nothing to do with delivering a thank you.

"Can't quite close that case." Gunz flashed his signature smarmy smile.

Here it comes!

"Anything we can do to help," Fab said.

"Happy to hear that. My cousin wants to see her brother in person. A phone call isn't enough, in her words. So, I'm sending her to California for a week or so. I'd like the two of you to escort her, make sure everything goes okay."

"How old is she?" I tried to ratchet down the sarcasm, knowing full well she was just barely legal.

Gunz kept his back turned, not acknowledging me. "Nola has never traveled before. The fellow you sent to find her, although he did a good job, isn't suitable as an escort."

"His name is Toady." I sniffed. "He was good enough to track down her out-of-control ass and keep her out of prison. Oh yeah, and keep the family secrets buried. And now you have a problem with him?"

"I can make the arrangements, and you can leave tomorrow." Gunz tapped out something on his phone, as though it was a done deal.

I waved my hand, which he couldn't see, but I amused Xander. "Not going. I can tell you now that my husband would have a flipping fit." It didn't bother me in the slightest to use him as my excuse, especially since it was true. I'd make it up to him later on the retell. "Guess what, *big guy,* Fab's not going either, and for the same reason. So, you might want to get less attitudinal regarding Toady because he'd go in a heartbeat. Guaranteed. And *nothing* would happen to her on the mean streets of Los Angeles."

How did Gunz get so lucky as to have a passel of relatives, and all of them certifiable? When he'd pitched his fixer nonsense, I never figured it would turn into a full-time gig. I was tempted to suggest that he buy acres of land, build houses, and fence them all in. Our luck, they'd escape from time to time.

"Madison's right. My husband would be like-minded on the matter," Fab said in a conciliatory tone.

"Since when do you do what someone else tell

you?" Gunz asked.

"Since she got married to the love of her life and wants to stay that way," I answered.

Gunz turned slightly. "You're making me forget that I sort of like you."

I clasped my chest. "Isn't it better to get the truth up front, rather than have your cousin waiting at the airport by herself? Move on to Plan B."

"Why not Toady?" Fab asked, then mouthed, *Be nice,* to me.

I interpreted that as "be quiet." *Fat chance.* But no way to convey that back.

"Nola developed a huge crush." Gunz snorted. "She's young. Thinks he's a knight or some such thing. She unburdened her heart, and he hung on every word. What kind of man does that? One who wants to get laid. I don't want the likes of him in the family."

"On the bright side," I said, "if they did get hitched, you wouldn't need us. Toady could keep them all rodeoed up."

Xander laughed, which started me laughing.

"He's old enough to be her granddaddy." Gunz turned and glared at me.

"If Nola's formed an attachment, Toady needs to be the one to let her down," Fab said. "Gently. You don't want her going off all gunned up again. Only this time with you in her crosshairs for standing in the way of true love."

"Toady has a way with women," Xander said.

"He manages to stay friends with all of his women, even after they're not doing it."

I wanted to tell him that he wasn't being helpful but instead choked on a laugh.

Gunz's face flushed with anger.

I stared at my feet.

Even Fab made an unintelligible noise.

Gunz whipped his designer water bottle off the desk and downed the contents, then slammed it back down. "Get the man on the phone and make it happen." He took a sheet of paper out of his pocket and slapped it down in front of Fab. "Here's the itinerary. There's a contact number on there for any changes that need to be made. Make it clear that he's to end any feelings Nola has for him, and in a nice way."

Fab perused the instructions.

"There's an extra charge for last-minute," I said. It wasn't true, but there should be.

Gunz crossed his arms in a huff while Fab stood, grabbing her phone, and went out to the deck. She pulled the slider almost, but not quite, closed to discourage eavesdropping, and leaned against the railing that overlooked the water.

"If it gives you peace of mind, I'd trust Toady with my sister," I said. "He's not a complete dick."

"That recommendation does nothing to get me past my misgivings." Gunz harrumphed.

Fab stood outside for about five minutes. I

checked the clock continuously, not making the effort for small talk, since I didn't know where to begin. "Nice weather" would only garner disgust from the big man.

"Toady's in," Fab announced, walking back inside. "He's going to call Nola and work out the details. I told him to hire a car to take them to the airport. He'll escort her wherever she wants to go, back off when she needs him to, and never be far away. Her personal bodyguard." She crossed the room and leaned against the edge of her desk in front of Gunz. "Does that meet with your approval?"

"I knew I could count on you. It's not as good as you being involved, though. Nola would do well to spend some time around your charm."

Good one!

Gunz stood and hugged her. Looping an arm around her, he walked her to the door, and they engaged in a few words before he beat it downstairs.

"He thinks you need your rough edges refined." Fab's eyes sparkled with amusement.

"Too bad he didn't say that to my face. I'd have given him the finger."

Xander laughed. "This is the best job."

Chapter Twenty-Two

"I wouldn't have gone to California even if I didn't have Didier as an excuse." Fab pulled into the u-shaped driveway of The Cottages, parking in front of the office. "I would've contracted measles or something. It would had to have been something contagious. For once, I appreciate you inserting yourself into the conversation in a brash way."

"I try to be helpful." I got out and surveyed the ten-unit property. Everything seemed quiet. One of the tourist guests was sprawled out in a chair on her porch, her butt hanging precariously off, snoring logs. Laughter and shouts could be heard coming from the pool area.

Mac's truck roared around the corner, and she parked across the street in her own driveway. It didn't bother her to live across the street from where she worked. She'd told me, "It allows me to be up in everyone's business at all hours."

She bounded out and slapped across the street in a pair of shoes shaped like unwashed men's feet with matching dirty brown laces. She saw me staring and lifted one foot and then the other, checking them out. "Aren't these the cutest? Got a deal on them from Bond at the gas station."

"I thought he was banned from selling off the back of his truck." Without a permit, anyway, and I knew he'd never get one. "Aren't you afraid the previous owner will come looking for his feet?"

"That would be something." Mac stared down at her feet. "I checked before I bought them, and they're rubber."

"What's going on at the pool?" Fab demanded.

"No clue. I've been busy all morning doing stuff." Mac thrust out her chest and swiped at the front, then pressed her ruffled skirt down.

"I don't believe that *stuff* is one of your job duties," I said.

"A lot of things aren't part of my so-called job duties, but I adapt."

I laughed. "Yes, you do. If I haven't told you lately, I appreciate you. And Fab does too." Which Fab responded to with something akin to a snort. "She knows that without you, I'd tie her to an office chair here, where she would undoubtedly create havoc, and this place would be vacant."

A burst of laughter floated across the driveway.

"Party time?" Mac craned her head.

The three of us turned towards the pool. "Let's hope not." We rounded the corner and saw that a couple of the tables had been pushed together, and an even mix of men and women, six in total, were playing cards. Each had a bottle of liquor in front of them.

They were hurling insults and cards across the table. One woman stood and made a production of taking her bathing suit top off and flinging it in one of the men's faces.

It was at that moment that I realized that two of the people were buck naked and the rest had only a piece or two of clothing left to lose. I kicked the gate the rest of the way open, whoever left it that way having ignored the sign warning users to keep it closed.

"What the heck is going on?" I demanded.

Crum looked up from his cards. "Party killjoy is here," he announced, and all eyes turned in our direction.

"Could I have a word with you?"

Crum stood up, completely naked. He picked up a skirt… no… fringed loincloth and proceeded to tie it at the waist. "Let's take this party to my cottage." None of the others were in a particular hurry to break up the shindig; they turned in their chairs as he shuffled across the concrete.

Joseph, another tenant, who was sitting on the far side, waved. He'd obviously just woken from a nap and shared a chaise with his rubber girlfriend, Svetlana.

Fab groaned and stepped behind me. "My eyes hurt."

"I know, the fun's over," Crum pronounced once he got closer.

"What the heck is going on?" I hissed.

"Strip poker," he said in a tone conveying that I couldn't be that stupid, could I? "You know, lose the hand you're dealt and pay up with a piece of clothing? I hope you're not going to yammer on about a little card game."

"I came here to thank you for helping Xander—"

A woman screaming, "Madison, Madison!" from the pool and waving frantically left me momentarily speechless until I realized it was Miss January, straddling a noodle along with her equally inebriated boyfriend.

I waved back. Not taking my eyes off her, I said to Mac, "Get those two out of the pool. New rule: Drunk swimming not allowed."

Mac kicked off her shoes and waded into the pool, not giving a thought to her attire. Her skirt floated around her waist, her pink panties on display.

The male poker players turned their attention to her.

Like Joseph, Miss January had been given a terminal diagnosis by her doctor. So far, their "screw you" attitudes had worked for them, and they were still alive. I'd be damned if she was going to drown.

"Mac needs help." I glared at Crum, daring him to say otherwise.

"You're in charge," I yelled to Mac and made a beeline for the gate, stopping just inside. "All that nakedness fried my brain cells and rendered me speechless," I said to Fab. "I don't want to, but I should help."

"Too late." Fab grabbed my arm.

I looked over, and Crum was helping Miss January out of the water.

"Look at Mac; she's not even ruffled," I said in awe.

Mac was giving what's his name, aka the boyfriend, an earful while giving the man's considerable bulk a shove. "I've got this," she yelled and waved. "I'll call you later."

"If it wasn't for Mac, I'd sell this place." I shuddered and walked with Fab back to the SUV.

Chapter Twenty-Three

Fab hadn't even made it out of the driveway when her phone rang. With a raised eyebrow, she answered. "Of course, I remember." She made a face. "You should know that if drugs are involved, which was the case the last time I was at your house, the police will be called. Not doing so would be illegal, and I need to protect myself and my people." After a pause, she said, "I'll drive down now and check it out," and hung up. I opened the door at the red light and was halfway out when Fab grabbed the back of my shirt and tugged. "What the heck are you doing?"

I wrestled away and managed to get out without tripping and falling in a heap. "I want the details before you hit the road and I'm stuck. If I don't like what I hear, I can walk home from here."

Fab sniffed in frustration and gunned the engine, pulling over to the curb and parking. I dragged my feet getting to the car, where I knocked on the passenger window.

She rolled it down. "You remember my client, Scott Knight?"

I made a face, thinking. "Ungrateful lout, as I recall. College party gone awry; party guest almost died from an overdose. That Mr. Knight?"

"You probably remember the neighbor, Marjorie Ross, since you and Didier dealt with her and I didn't. Her son had a party over the weekend, and she hasn't been able to get ahold of him and wanted Mr. Knight to go check. He thought she should handle her own problems but apparently has too big a heart to tell her so."

"Compassionate fellow. This smells like a freebie."

"Hardly. He lied and said he was out of town and that he'd send his man and she'd get a bill. Now get back in," she said in exasperation.

"From now on, there's an extra fee for my collection services." At Fab's sniff, I said, "Have you noticed how many of your cases get turned over to me for collections? I'm the one who gets it coordinated and the money collected."

"Good job."

"That didn't sound sincere." I opened the door, but remained standing on the street. "Before you blast down the highway, we need to take backup. We could be walking into anything or nothing. If you ran this jaunt by your husb before we ventured south, he'd agree."

An SUV passed us, laying on the horn, and pulled to the side of the road.

"Get in the car," Fab ordered. "You're making a scene."

"Takes one—"

"Oh, stop it and get in."

The SUV backed up and parked in front of us, and Brad opened the door and got out. "You two about to fight?" he called. "Or something less exciting? Car trouble perhaps?"

"How would you like to win the best brother award?" I asked as he approached the passenger side.

"What's the prize?"

"That joyous feeling you get from doing something nice for someone else."

"Joyous? You been drinking?"

"Maybe later."

"You coming or not?" Fab yelled across the car.

I told him about Fab's call and the last job we did for that client.

"You two are lucky. I've got the time and inclination to play backup." Brad flexed his muscles. "It will give me something to lord over the guys at the office."

"And something for Mother to take you to task for at the next family dinner."

He grinned. "Ah yes, the family get-togethers, where all the dirt comes out." He scanned the street. "I'll park at your house."

"This might be a decent idea," Fab said when I got back in. "Taking Brad along keeps us covered with the guys and out of trouble. I vote that *he* calls and updates the guys."

"That's a unanimous vote." We both laughed. "I'm hoping he doesn't regret coming along."

"What could go wrong?"

"You actually asked that with a straight face?"

Fab followed Brad to the house and parked, and he climbed in the back.

"Islamorada, here we come," he said.

"You tell him." I poked Fab's shoulder.

She favored me with a demented glare. "When we go out on a job, before we leave, one of us is technically supposed to fill in the guys. And since you're the new guy, we voted 2-0 to let you do it. Did you bring your phone?"

He snorted and took it out of his pocket. "This is going to be fun."

Fab flew down the highway, but not at her usual hair-raising speed.

"Both went to voicemail. I left a message that I was with you two. That should get a return call." Brad shoved his phone back in his pocket. "What's the plan?"

"Girlfriend here—" I poked Fab's shoulder. "—isn't one for plans. She prefers spontaneous."

"Not this time." Fab smiled smugly. "I'm going to knock on the door with the hope that I get lucky and Todd answers. I'll tell him to call his mother and mention that I think he's a dumbass."

I looked over the seat at Brad, who had a grin on his face. "Trust me, Bro, her jobs for her snooty clients never go smoothly."

He pulled his phone out again. "I'm going to have Mother pick up Mila. That will make her happy." He punched in the number. "I need you to pick up Mila, and I'll pick her up at your house. I'm on my way to one of Fab's shootouts, and I may be late." He gave her the briefest of details. Whatever Mother said in return, he laughed. "I'll tell her. And we will." He hung up. "We're supposed to be careful. She's going to organize dinner for all and is calling the guys. That's what they get for ignoring my call. I know they'd never turn down an invitation from her." Brad laughed. "Liam told me about his friend and that he approached you. Before I flipped out, thinking you'd risk facing a dealer, he said he'd gotten a text telling him to be patient, that it had been taken care of. What did you do?"

"I turned it over to Chief Harder. He was happy for the tip."

"How did you get to be friends with him, anyway?" Brad asked, more than a little surprised. "Creole?"

"Through one of Fab's clients. Did Bestie here a favor, got arrested—out in the hinterlands, I might add—and needed a ride home. And who shows up? It was the start of a rocky friendship that's smoothed out over the years."

Fab and Brad laughed.

"I'd never take advantage by trying to sneak something illegal past Harder. So, when I do call,

I'm always upfront with the facts as I know them."

"My first thought was that it was a case for the cops," Brad said. "I'm happy they're involved without some college kid getting fingered as a snitch."

Fab pulled off the highway and headed towards the water.

"Nice houses." Brad peered out the window and whistled, surveying the neighborhood.

"The client is waterfront," I said. "If the gate is closed, you're the one who's going to climb over," I warned Fab.

"I have the code," she said, with such authority that most would believe her.

I shook my head at my brother.

Chapter Twenty-Four

Fab pulled up in front of a white two-story Mediterranean house. Surprisingly, the gates stood open, a white Porsche and a faded blue Mercedes in the circular driveway.

"Someone's home," Fab said and parked, getting out.

"Party time," I said and got out, Brad behind me. "Bring a firearm?"

He lifted his shirt. "Had one locked in the car. Any chance there really will be a shootout?"

"Most likely not, but I can't say with certainty."

Fab crossed the wide porch that framed the interior windows and rang the bell. Brad and I waited at the bottom of the steps.

No response. She rang again, this time several times in a row, then beat on the door with her fist for good measure.

Finally, it opened. A young guy, well over six feet, stuck his gaunt face through the narrow opening. "What?" he said groggily. He'd spent more than one night deep in overindulgence.

"Todd Ross?" Fab asked, trying to peer around his body.

"Yeah." His hooded eyes made eye contact with the top of her head.

"Your mother is worried that she hasn't been able to reach you on the phone. She'd like you to call."

"Boring," Brad whispered in my ear.

I nudged him.

"Got it." He closed the door.

Fab beat on it again, and he opened immediately.

"I'll wait while you call."

He shut the door again.

It took several minutes before the door opened again. Todd stood on the threshold, shirtless and clad only in grubby jeans, phone against his ear. "I'll call you tomorrow. Love you." He disconnected and thrust the phone in his pocket. "Happy now?" He didn't wait for an answer and closed the door in Fab's face.

"Let's go celebrate. Our most uneventful job ever." Fab marched down the steps.

"Not so fast," I said. "That's not the Ross kid. My memory of him is that he had black hair and not greasy brown. He also had a set of well-defined abs. The guy who answered the door has never lifted a weight in his life."

"How certain?"

"Not a hundred percent. You could give Marjorie a call and see if her progeny got in touch," I said.

"Or you could leave and end up apologizing

later for being hoodwinked." Brad smiled devilishly at Fab.

"Do you even have Mrs. Ross' number?" I asked, and Fab shook her head. "Your options are call Mr. Knight or take Brad's advice and leave."

"Neither of you are helpful." Fab opened the SUV door and reached for her phone in the cup holder, leaning against the seat.

"That's so painful to hear." Brad grabbed the front of his shirt. "Erodes my confidence in billing myself as a side-chick."

"It's kick," I said.

"Inanity aside, if it turns out that grubby isn't the son in question, then what?" Brad asked.

"We blow the door off the hinges and go charging in."

Brad frowned. "You're freakin' hilarious."

I curtsied. "Remind you of our younger days?"

"I'd rather be redistributing newspapers from people with a paid subscription to people in the neighborhood who wondered where they came from."

"There's a prank that we got away with."

"What am I going to do if Mila does that?"

"You're going to pretend that you don't know who she is or what's going on. Like Mother did sometimes." I laughed at his scowl. "Keep her busy, like you do now, and she won't have time to go looking for adventure."

Brad hugged me.

Fab stomped over to us. "Knight's having a fit. He tried to patch Marjorie Ross in on a conference call, and her phone's turned off. He got in a snit and said I'm the investigator and should do my job."

"Dude is looking out the glass panel next to the door," Brad said, keeping an eye on the house.

"Let's pile back in the SUV and go next door," I said. I turned to Brad and explained, "The houses are connected by a private beach, and one can gain access to the patio of this house very easily from there. After that, I don't know, because Didier and I didn't go any farther." I called Xander. "I need you to pull up a picture of Todd Ross, a college-age kid from Islamorada—I'll text you the family's home address. I need it five minutes ago." I hung up. "We'll know in a few minutes if my memory isn't all that great."

Fab pulled out of the driveway and headed in the opposite direction from Knight's house, pulling around the block and into the driveway of Knight's seldom-used vacation home. She flicked through her phone, then reached her hand out and entered a code. "Good thing I never delete anything."

It took about a half-hour before the picture came through, and my memory wasn't failing me, at least according to Todd Ross's Florida driver's license picture. Not by any stretch of the imagination could the two men be one and the same. I showed it to Fab and Brad.

"I could go in the back way and pass myself off as a neighbor, but then what?" Brad suggested.

"I'm fairly certain the 'welcome to the neighborhood' speech or its equivalent isn't going to work on that lying toad," I said.

"I'll go," Fab said. "Threaten to kick his ass, and if he doesn't cough up the whereabouts of Todd, I'll hold calling the cops over his head."

I hated that idea. Especially if her plan was to go by herself.

"How about Madison shows you which way to go?" Brad said. "When you're ready to make your move, text me, and I'll knock on the front door."

Fab and Brad knuckle-bumped. We split up and carried out Brad's plan. Fab and I skirted down the side of the house and crossed the patio. I led the way down the sand and showed her how accessible the neighboring properties were.

"I realize that this is a private beach, but I wouldn't like this," Fab said.

"Me neither, but I don't imagine this neighborhood sees much action, except from their own family members."

"Why do you suppose he lied?" Fab asked.

"Because he's up to something. In addition to being hungover from hard partying. Could be he's covering for his friend."

The Ross pool area was quiet. "This is a change from the last time I was here, when it was littered with passed-out college kids." We walked across the patio, where the television could be heard through the open doors.

Fab texted. Seconds later, the doorbell rang. Twice.

The same guy rolled off the couch, lurched to his feet, and trudged to the door.

Fab crept inside while I hung out at the patio door and surveyed the open floor plan—the living room and dining room easily accessible, kitchen around the corner. The coffee table was piled with food containers and empty beer and liquor bottles. Furniture cushions were strewn around the floor. It appeared that there'd been a party recently, and most of the guests had lain on the floor.

Fake Todd opened the door just enough to stick his head out again. "Yeah?"

Brad pushed the door in, and the guy went tumbling to the floor. Brad stood over him. "Answer her questions—" He pointed to Fab. "—if you know what's good for you. Hurry it up; I'm hungry."

The guy's mouth dropped open as he spotted Fab, gun pointed at him.

"Who are you?" Fab demanded. "Don't bother with the lie that you're Todd Ross. We've verified that you're not."

For once, I was the lurker and skirted around

the room. I started by poking my head into the kitchen, which overflowed with trash, including a garbage sack of beer cans that had fallen over and were now spread out across the floor and an overflowing sink of dishes, despite the fact that there was a dishwasher.

"Look, I came for a party this weekend and overstayed. I'll be leaving."

Brad kicked him in the butt with his tennis shoe. It couldn't have been very hard, as the guy jerked more from surprise than pain. "Pay attention to the questions. Name?"

He hesitated. "George," he said, but sounded like he wasn't sure.

I spotted a duffle bag peeking out from behind a chair on the far side of the room and made my way over. I bent down, tugged my sleeve down over my fingers, and pulled it open. It looked like a pharmacy inside, with an assortment of pill bottles. I picked one up. It didn't have a printed label, but was, instead, labeled with black marker, the shorthand indecipherable to me. No wonder this George fellow wasn't forthcoming with his name.

"Where's your host?" Fab asked.

"Todd and his girlfriend talked about some alone time and mentioned the beach."

"When everyone else left, why didn't you?" Brad asked.

"Nice house, why not hang out?"

I lifted the bag. "Yours?"

His eyes bugged. "Never seen it before."

"We're here to have a short discussion with Todd." Fab gestured with the muzzle of her gun.

"Like I said… you can have the house. I'll go." George stood.

I set the bag down on a chair and went through the side pockets, finding a wallet. According to the driver's license, George's real name was Robert Dobbs.

"If this isn't yours, why is your wallet in here?" I held it up. "Before you say it's not yours, it has your ID in it. Meet Robert Dobbs," I introduced. "Lots of cash." I flicked through the thick stash of twenties.

"I can't believe someone would steal my wallet. I'll have to be more careful," Robert said with a straight face and turned toward the door. *Cause it wasn't the least bit suspicious to try to leave without your wallet.*

Fab took three steps and kicked his feet out from under him, landing him on his butt. "You're not going anywhere. Since you're so friendly with the host, get him on the phone."

Robert held up his hands in a defensive pose. "Don't know where my phone went. Too much drinking, that's for sure."

Or something!

I pulled a phone out of the other pocket of the bag. "Is this yours, by chance?"

He squinted. "They all look the same."

Brad took the phone from me, knowing that I

was inept with most electronics, and opened the screen. He scrolled through it. "I'll try this one. First name Todd, with the last name R." He held the phone to his ear.

Ringing could be heard coming from another room.

Brad and I exchanged a look of surprise.

"Fab." Brad pulled his weapon, nodded to Robert as if to say, "you watch him," and took off in the direction of the ringing.

Not about to be left out of the drama, Fab marched over to Robert and whipped off her belt, rolling him onto his stomach—which wasn't hard, since he was already cowering—and securing his hands behind his back.

Brad reappeared. "You're going to want see this," he said to Fab. "Not sure what you want to do."

Lying sideways on the bed in the first bedroom was Todd, in a pair of boxers, his arms tied to the bedpost. It appeared that Brad had removed his gag.

"Untie me," Todd pleaded. "I'll pay you whatever you want. I need to get out of here."

"Does this have to do with your friend Robert?" Fab asked.

That shook Todd and fear filled his face. "He still here? I thought he left."

I hung out in the hall, expecting Robert to somehow stumble to his feet and make an attempt at a getaway.

While untying Todd, Fab explained to him what she was doing at the house.

"I'll pay your bill," he blurted. "No matter the cost. Not one word to my mom or anyone else."

Once free, he jumped up and went running for the bathroom. After expelling the contents of his stomach, he came out, retrieved a t-shirt, and jerked it over his head.

Back in the living room, Robert was spitting mad, swearing at the floor and rolling from side to side. "You can't let that bastard go. He's mine, and I get to decide what happens to him. Besides, I haven't been paid."

Todd stormed out of the bathroom and into the living room. "Crazy bastard. I didn't know Lanie was your girlfriend. Or anyone else's, for that matter. It was just sex. I don't do relationships. You can have her back."

Robert rolled on his side and hawked spit in Todd's direction, but it fell short of its mark.

"This… whatever it is—" Brad waved his arm. "—is about a girl? If she is your girlfriend, then she knew she was in a relationship and chose to do him anyway," he said to Robert. "If it's true that Todd didn't know, you can hardly blame him. If he did, then he's a dick."

"Your services are no longer required," Todd said in a snotty tone to rival Fab's own. "If you take credit cards, we can settle this now."

"Not so fast." Fab mimicked his tone. "I'm not going anywhere until I get the whole story, and it better be truthful. Trust me, I can sniff out a big fat lie."

Brad jerked Robert to his feet and shoved him down in a chair. "This guy belongs in jail."

"Let sleeping dogs and all that," Todd said. "Walk away, and we'll put this unfortunate incident behind us."

"Why don't I call the police?" I threw out to get a reaction.

"No," they both said at the same time.

"Start talking," Fab said. They stayed silent. "How long have you been tied up?"

"Overnight." Todd sighed, finally figuring out we weren't leaving without an explanation. "We were working out our differences."

"If that were the case, we wouldn't have found you in your underwear," Fab said. "This has to be about the money. How much?"

"Why can't you women mind your own business?" Robert demanded, full of arrogance for someone still tied up. "Call whoever you want; I don't give a damn. If you think you're going to pin the duffel bag contents on me, think again. There had to be a hundred people at the party; could've belonged to any of them. I'll just tell the cops you're framing me."

"They won't believe you," I said.

Robert ignored me, glaring at Todd and growling, "You don't do a man's girlfriend and walk with no consequences." He jerked his arms. "Untie me," he bellowed.

Brad walked over and stood next to me. I didn't have to look at him to know we were both wondering what Fab was going to do.

"How did you get the black eye?" Fab asked Todd.

He shrugged it off. "Difference of opinion."

"Fab." I motioned her over. "Robert is a drug dealer. The contents of his duffel are proof, and so you know what you're dealing with, there's a handgun in the bag."

She signaled Todd, and they walked over to the patio doors.

Brad and I moved close enough to hear every word.

"I'm a Ross," Todd said. "I can't be a headline in the local news and expect to have a future where it won't come back to haunt me. Mom understands an impromptu party, which is what I'm going to tell her happened, and that you found me sleeping it off. When she gets back, I'll meet her at the airport with flowers, and all will be forgiven. Now, all I need is for you to leave and forget all about this incident and, of course, keep your sexy mouth closed." He winked.

"Calm down," Fab said, her tone conveying *not interested*. "You have a clue what you're dealing with where Robert is concerned? You're taking a big chance, assuming that he won't come back and kill you. Are you aware he brought a gun to your little bash?"

"It was just a miscommunication. I'll throw

cash at him, a threat or two, and suggest that he not show his face down here. He's a businessman; he'll see the benefits of my advice."

"Stupid," Brad whispered.

Fab shared Brad's sentiment, and it showed on her face. "Robert's a bad guy, and they never go away because you ask nicely. I've known a few drug dealers, and it wouldn't come as a shock if he took your money and then you disappeared, not a morsel to be found. The oversized rodents around here eat well."

Todd grimaced.

"It's your choice. Hope you don't regret it. Robert's not leaving with his drug store, and don't bother to fight me on it; you won't win. I'm not going to stand by while he makes money getting the town high." Fab walked to the duffel bag, jerked it up, and headed to the kitchen.

She was halfway there when Robert yelled, "Hey. Let's talk before you do anything stupid."

Fab didn't slow her stride. Not bothering with gloves, she upended the duffel, and the bottles rolled out on the counter. She unscrewed the tops and tossed the contents in the sink until they were all empty, then turned on the garbage disposal until it stopped the grinding noise, and finally, opened the trash compactor, brushed the bottles and lids in, closed it, and turned it on. "You're going to want to put the bag out for the trash man," she told Todd. She flicked through the rest of Robert's personal effects, then tossed his wallet back inside the bag and zipped it up. Sticking his gun in her waistband, she marched over to Robert and dropped it at his feet.

"Stupid, stupid," Robert mumbled.

Fab stood in front of him and stared him down. "Don't ever come back to this town. If you do, I'll give a heads up to every cop on the force, most of whom I know personally, and you'll enjoy a nice long stay in a cell. That's if you ever get out, and chances are slim if you're caught with the same quantity that just went down the drain."

Judging from the fear that filled Robert's face, the threat was effective. At least, for now.

Fab jerked him around and undid the belt.

Robert shook his arms.

"Hit the road." Fab pointed to the front door. "Consider yourself very lucky that you're not in the back of a patrol car."

Robert grabbed his bag and ran to the door, pausing with his hand on the doorknob. "Todd and I have unfinished business."

"You're slow," Fab said with a shake of her head. "If you haven't cleared the driveway in one minute, I'll call the cops regardless of what Todd wants."

Shooting daggers at all of us, he banged the door behind him.

"If I were you, I'd watch my back," Fab said over the roar of the old Mercedes, which needed a muffler. "Where's your phone?" she asked Todd, who shook his head.

Brad handed it to her.

Fab called herself and then texted him. "Pay that amount to the email listed, and I'll consider the case closed," she said, and handed him back his phone.

Todd looked at the screen and didn't register a reaction, cool customer that he was. "You'll have it tonight. I'll keep your number, in case I need your services again."

"It better be business," I said. "Her husband will shoot you."

"I can vouch for that." Brad leveled a glare at him.

We left and didn't speak until we were back in the SUV.

As Fab pulled out of the driveway, she said, "Keep your eyes open for Robert. He comes sniffing around any of us, you know he's looking for trouble. I don't want us to end up in the middle of anything if Todd should end up dead."

"Robert has the look of someone bent on revenge. If he had a Jones for me, I'd be watching my back." I kept my eyes peeled, watching the side of the road and hoping he hadn't pulled a u-turn.

"Nice lie about knowing all the cops," Brad said. "Since Madison is buddies with the Chief of Police, I suggest that you turn over info on Robert to him; he can decide what to do with it.

With the drug cache he had on him, it won't be long before he's refilled and open for business."

Chapter Twenty-Five

Mother thrived on last-minute tasks and easily put together an impromptu family dinner party at the Crab Shack, a family favorite. Added incentive for her was that she wanted to know firsthand what the three of us had been up to today. If she hadn't been taking care of Mila, she would've wanted to go along.

The restaurant was located off the main highway and overlooked the deeper blue waters of the Atlantic. It was low-key, decorated in nautical décor, and served award-winning seafood. Mother always booked a water-view table.

Creole turned down ride-sharing with Fab and Didier, telling the duo he wanted to be alone with me. What he really wanted was to hear about our adventurous day before we arrived. "I'm going to beat the hell out of Brad for hanging up before I got all my questions asked. When I'm done, I'm breaking a limb for ignoring the rest of my calls."

I scrunched up my nose. "That's a bad plan. Sucks for family relations. You do that, and you'll have to watch your back. Mother will flip out on you." I told him about our road trip and stressed that having Brad ride along had been fortuitous.

"Sounds to me like Todd's lucky you got there before he ended up dead." He turned and glared at me. "Where do you find these cases?"

"Me?" I pointed to myself in mock innocence. "You need to ask Fab, and if the answer is plausible, then I'll second it."

Creole laughed. He drove into the parking lot of the restaurant and honked at Harder, who'd just gotten out of his car. I'd called Mother and asked her to invite the man. Last minute could be awkward, but Mother would smooth it over. Harder came over, opened my door, and held out his hand to help me out.

"I'm happy you could join us." I smiled at him.

"Yeah." He squinted. "It was an interesting invitation. It sounded more like your mother was ordering my appearance, reminiscent of a court judge, and giving me no opportunity to turn her down. She could teach my seasoned detectives a thing or two."

"That sounds like Madeline," Creole groused.

I nudged him in the side and told Harder, "Mother likes you or she would've accepted a flimsy excuse and hung up."

Creole and Harder shook hands.

"Thanks for the tip on the college dealer. He's in custody."

Wait until he found out I had another one for him.

"It went down during a traffic stop. He went peacefully, although he could have started a shoot-out, as he had several weapons on him. Thankfully, he didn't choose that route. I'm always happy when they make good decisions. You won't be hearing anything on the news, as he's being quite cooperative."

"He drugs up college kids and gets a sweet deal," Creole said, frustration in his voice. "Hope he takes the opportunity to go legit."

"As you know, I'm not fond of deals where the dirtball goes scot-free, especially since the one kid almost died. If we'd been able to link him to a death, he wouldn't have seen the light of day. But it's hard to pass up information when a suspect is willing to spill their guts and hand over bigger names."

"I share your frustration on that score," Creole said.

"My guess is I wasn't invited for my charm and wit. Do I get a heads up before we sit down?" Harder asked as we walked in the front door.

The interior was decorated with fake palm trees, fish mounted on the walls, and lights strung along the ceiling from one end to the other.

"You're so suspicious." I laughed. "Mother reserved a table out on the deck," I said to the hostess. We paused at the bar and ordered drinks.

The whole family was in attendance, minus Liam, all seated around a large table. Mila, who sat between Emerson and Brad, waved with both hands. Caspian and Harder were seated across from Mother and Spoon. Creole and I took seats at the opposite end, next to Fab and Didier.

Once our drinks arrived, Fab gave a spirited rendition of the day. "I want to toast Brad for stepping up to help us at the last minute and actually being helpful."

"Sounds like she's surprised you weren't a slug." I grinned at Brad.

"Brad? Never." Emerson leaned in and kissed his cheek.

Harder laughed, having figured out why he was invited. "I should put you in touch with our drug unit if you're going to catch dealers on a regular basis."

No one was happy with that, and everyone except Fab and I made faces to show their displeasure over the comment.

"Big milestone today." Brad beamed and helped Mila to stand on her chair. "Go," he whispered to her, and she proceeded to count to ten in English and Spanish. When she finished, everyone clapped.

Mila curtseyed.

Menus were passed out, and Mother made a few recommendations.

My phone rang, and Creole and I traded a "what now?" look. He and I both knew from the ringtone that it was Beachside, and Cootie didn't call unless it was an emergency.

"This better be good," I said quietly into the phone. "Mother is giving me hate stares for answering."

"Another dead body in the woo-woo room," Cootie grumped. "Cops are here. Thought a timely phone call to them first was in order and didn't think you wanted to find out via the late newscast."

"You did the right thing. I'm on my way." I gave a brief thought to whispering the news to Creole and decided why bother. "Dead body at the motel," I announced. "Would you order my favorite and have Fab drop it off at the house?" I swept my gaze over Fab and Didier.

"Another one?" Mother shrieked. "You need to sell. Make a deal on both the motel *and* cottages, since they attract the same kinds of people."

"Thank you for that encouragement."

"Let that Cootie fellow handle the investigation," Spoon said. "Why have a manager if he can't handle a dead body?"

I glared at the man, conveying, *thanks for the support*. He shrugged. I looked at Creole, who sighed and stood, pulling out my chair.

"Order me something and deliver both dinners, will you?" he said to Didier. "We'll arrange another get-together. I'll call with an update."

I walked around the table, kissing everyone on the cheek, and we left.

"What did Cootie say?" Creole asked, helping me into the truck.

I repeated the short conversation.

"You'd think that if that room really was inhabited by a ghost, this would be annoying the heck out of Isabella. Personally, I wouldn't want my afterlife disturbed by dead bodies."

"Not sure what Isabella thinks, since we haven't engaged in conversation. I wouldn't be adverse if I didn't think it would scare the dickens out of me. And I wouldn't dare brag." I laughed. Creole didn't see the humor. "People already think I'm C-crazy."

"That makes me crazy woman's husband?" He laughed.

"This conversation could really devolve into what you were thinking with when we hooked up. Why go there?"

"Why indeed."

The traffic was light, and Creole blew around a couple of slow-movers, so it didn't take long to get to the motel. Several cop cars were parked in front. Creole circled the block and parked in the back. Walking into the courtyard, I was surprised to see that a lot of the guests were seated around the pool. It never failed to amaze me what a party-like atmosphere a dead body could generate. On the upside, the guests were easily accessible for the cops to question.

"Another young woman," Rude said when she spotted us walking into the office. "She was similar to the last one—close in age, with the only difference the hair color."

"Was she a registered guest?" Creole asked.

"Cathy Swan checked into the ghost room for one night and paid cash," Cootie said. "I checked the security feed, just to make sure, and it's the same woman. So, no switcharoo."

I plopped down in a chair while Creole went in search of the investigating officers. "I realize this kind of activity doesn't put a dent in our business, but we need to make it stop. To that end, be as helpful as you can to the cops."

"Gotcha, girlie," Rude said.

"Not sure what we'd do different," Cootie said. "Put a guard inside the room?" He smiled at that absurd suggestion. "Why do you suppose we're so popular?"

"A grudge-holder?" I mused. "Against the motel seems a stretch."

"People are crazy." Rude gyrated around in a circle, arms waving in the air. Cootie ducked.

"They certainly are," I said.

Cootie grinned.

"Creole and the cop are headed this way." Rude pointed out the window. "Good news before they get here—Gunz graced us with his presence, picked up his grandma, aunt, cousin, whatever... neither seemed to know. He paid the bill without a flinch, and I padded it a bit. He wanted it reported immediately to Fab. His smile when he said her name made me want to wash up."

I couldn't wait to report that bit of gossipy news.

Creole and Kevin walked into the office.

"I'd like the security tape," Kevin said to Cootie. "We'll be done here in about an hour, and then the room is all yours. I'm going to be here questioning guests. So far, no one saw anything out of the ordinary."

"You can use the lobby," I suggested.

Creole slid into a chair next to me. "We don't have to stay. I can get a copy of the report."

"Did you get a look at the deceased?" I asked.

"No one we know."

"That's good. Sucks for her family."

Creole pulled me to my feet. "Don't call unless another body turns up," he told Cootie.

Chapter Twenty-Six

The following morning, Fab enticed me out of the house with the offer of coffee. What she failed to mention was that she wanted company at the office, since Xander had the day off. She took the opportunity to question me about the events of the night before. Once I related everything, she declared it, "Boring."

We'd just gotten settled in when Fab picked up her ringing phone, glanced at the screen with a lift of her brow, and answered. "I think this is the first call I've gotten from you. Hope it's not life and death." After a couple of laughs and ignoring my hand-waves trying to get her to put it on speaker, she hung up, saying, "We'll see you in a few." She ignored my glare. "That was Emerson."

"I'm the almost-sister-in-law, and she calls you?"

Fab grinned. "At first, I thought she misdialed. Turns out, a man called her regarding custody of the baby we found. Something about the call made her uncomfortable, but she couldn't quite put her finger on it and hasn't been able to shake off a sense of foreboding. She agreed to the appointment, having forgotten her assistant had the day off, so she'd like us to stop by. Of course, she'd owe us."

"No, she would not."

"She didn't sound like her usual calm self. More harried. I suppose lawyers have radar, and it went off for whatever reason."

"We can stop by her office and do friendly. I can. You can watch and learn." I smiled at her annoyance.

"I'm happy she called. If trouble walks into her office, it's too late to call 911." Fab grabbed the car keys and started for the door. "This plan-making isn't so difficult—I just threw one together. Are you coming to my adoption appointment or what?"

"I'm looking forward to being an aunt again." I followed her downstairs, and we got in the car. "Since you've got this all thought out, what's your plan once we get there?"

"Sarcasm is unattractive."

"Yes, Mother." I turned and smile out the window. "I'd suggest a low-key approach. In other words, don't go barging into her offices."

"I'll drive around the building, scope out the property."

"Your need for excitement…" I shook my head. "I can see it radiating through your body. Hope you're not disappointed."

Fab ignored me, which meant I was right.

"Don't forget the option of peeking in the

windows. When she catches us and laughs, we wave and invite her for dinner at your house."

"And if someone's there?" Fab asked.

"We go in shooting." Duh.

"You're on a roll today with your helpfulness."

"That's why you let me tag along—to share my level-headedness."

Fab pulled into the parking lot and around the back; all the offices had industrial back doors with peepholes. She curved back around to the front and parked. "I'm going to take your suggestion and look in the window to see if it's all clear. Then we'll go in and lecture her about not scheduling appointments when she's by herself."

"You're not going anywhere by *yourself.*" I climbed out of the car and started to follow her across the gravel parking lot.

"You wait here." Fab held out her hand.

"I'll lurk at the corner and learn a trick or two from the master." We passed the large picture window in the front that opened into the reception area, and all was clear.

Fab turned down the side of the building and slowed at the window that looked into Emerson's office. She leaned against the side of the building, stuck her head forward, and glanced in the window, stepped back, looked again, then ran back. "There's a grimy-looking fellow sitting in her office holding a gun on her."

"I don't believe you." I swept past her and went to look in the window for myself. *Sure enough.* I met Fab halfway, ignoring her *I told you so* look. "Now what?" I grabbed her arm, giving it a shake before she answered. "Didier will kill you if you're planning on kicking down the door."

"It might be unlocked."

"We need to call the cops."

"And if we do, what if their arrival sets this guy off and he shoots her?"

"So, your big idea is to barge in, and then he shoots you both?"

"I've got a plan."

I groaned so loudly, passersby on the highway could hear.

"I'll go in and talk trigger-happy out of whatever his plan is because mine is better—"

"That isn't a plan," I cut her off. "That is called going off half-cocked."

"Where was I before I was interrupted? Oh yes, and while I negotiate a happy ending, you call 911."

"I'll call now, while you wait, and then go with you, because that's what backups do," I said, knowing two things—my idea was a bad one and Fab wouldn't wait for the cops. "If there's no one in the reception area, trigger-happy won't even know I'm there unless I have to shoot him."

"You stay out here and answer 911's

questions, which there will be many of and they'll want you to stay on the line. In the meantime, Emerson's facing down a gun."

I sighed with relief when Fab pulled out her phone, thinking she was going to involve the cops after all. My phone rang instead. I fished it out of my pocket and stared at her face on the screen. "What?"

"Ouch." She rubbed her ear. "You call the cops. I'm going in and leave the line open, so you can hear every word."

"I want it on the record that I object to this idea." For all the good that would do, I thought as I watched her creep over to the front door.

Fab burst into the reception area, calling out, "Miss Emerson?" and leaving the door cracked.

I called 911 and, in a low tone, relayed what was happening. After making sure the operator had the correct address, I switched to the other line and moved closer to the building.

"I was so looking forward to our appointment," Fab gushed, standing in the doorway of Emerson's office.

"Have a seat," a male voice growled.

"What's with the gun?" Fab asked.

"This is Thomas' father, Charles May," Emerson introduced. "He has a few questions."

"You should've come to my office, then, since I'm the one that found the baby," Fab said, abandoning the pretense of being a client.

There was a long pause before May answered.

"There was an envelope in the baby carrier. I want it back."

"When I found him, I set your son's car seat on the work table in the garage, as all my attention was focused on getting him upstairs to clean him up. If the cops didn't log it in as evidence, then it's still sitting there." Fab sold her lies well, especially as there was no envelope and no work table.

"Then we need to take a trip to your office. You better not be wasting my time."

"Since no one is disputing your right to said envelope, why not put the gun away?"

He laughed, ignoring Fab's question. "Okay, ladies, let's get going." His tone indicated he thought they were both idiots. "Play ball and you'll both walk away in one piece."

Yeah, sure.

A cop car pulled into the driveway, and I hustled over. Maybe not for the first time, but close, I was happy to see Kevin to step out. Another car rolled in behind him.

"You're the hostage?" Kevin asked, getting out of his car. His partner joined him.

"They're in Emerson's office." I gave him a quick rundown and held out my phone so he could listen in.

"Stand back." Kevin motioned to his partner. "They're headed out."

He and the other cop, guns pulled, ran over to the side of the building.

What went down was rather anti-climactic. Fab and Emerson walked out the front door, May behind them, not paying a whit of attention to his surroundings.

Upon seeing Kevin, Fab grabbed Emerson's arm and dragged her to the ground.

"Hands up," Kevin yelled.

May offered no resistance and dropped his gun. The other cop cuffed him and shoved him into the back seat of his car, reading him his rights.

Emerson stood with Fab's help and threw her arms around her. "Thank you," she babbled. "Facing down a gun was a first for me, and I didn't know what to do. Knowing that the two of you were on your way was the only thing that kept me from a total freak-out."

Kevin came over and asked Emerson, "You okay?"

She nodded and, without being asked, told him about the envelope that May was frantic to get his hands on and, as far as she knew, no one had seen.

Kevin turned to Fab and me. "Any clue what was in the envelope?"

"Since drugs and a gun were found in the baby carrier, that leaves money," Fab answered. "Or more drugs."

"How the heck did he get bail?" Kevin radiated irritation. "It won't happen a second time."

"The appointment raised a red flag, but I never thought it would end like this," Emerson explained.

"May's lucky we showed up. I have no doubt Madison would've shot him before he got you two in the car. Less paperwork this way." Kevin eyed Fab. "The better idea would've been for you to wait for us to show up. We're trained for these situations."

Fab bristled but didn't contradict him.

Kevin whispered something to Emerson, and the two headed to her office. "I know where to find you if I have any questions," he called over his shoulder.

"That was fearless of you." And foolhardy. "I'm going to miss our friendship once Didier and Caspian decide which one gets to kill you."

"I'm thinking—"

"I know exactly what you're going to say… don't tell them. Except Emerson will tell Brad and gush to the family about how amazing you are."

"I like amazing."

"It's true." I hugged her hard until she growled and pushed me away.

Chapter Twenty-Seven

How Didier had found out about Fab's most recent adventure was unclear, but when he did, he swept her out of town for a couple of days. She announced her return by calling a meeting at the office for the four of us regarding the latest murder at Beachside. Once we were assembled and had our drinks of choice, she asked, "Since the cops don't have a lead, do any of you have any new ideas to contribute?"

I told them that I had Xander researching the history of the property from day one, although I wasn't sure that it would yield anything useful. I also suggested that we hold the next meeting at the Bakery Café.

Once the short meeting concluded, we split up. The guys left for a meeting at the Boardwalk, and Fab and I were headed home.

The Boardwalk was a family joint venture focusing on a collection of rides, attractions, shops, and a hundred-slip marina. Creole, Didier, and Brad dealt with the day-to-day management and oversaw new construction. The rest of us were silent investors, emphasis on the silent—we only added our two cents when an issue came up that needed our attention, and that was a rare occasion.

As Fab turned on the main highway, my phone rang. It surprised me to see the funeral home pop up on the screen.

"Hello," I said tentatively, not certain which of the guys would be on the other end, since when they wanted something, they typically called Fab.

"Just wanted to give you a huge thank you," Raul gushed. "You don't know how much it means to the two of us, you helping us out this way."

What the heck was he talking about? "Hmm," I said non-committedly.

He didn't notice, since he barely took a breath. "Is there anything either of us can do to make your end go more smoothly? When I approached Fab for help, I didn't expect her to recommend you, but she assured us that you were the woman for the job and wouldn't let us down. Anything we can ever do for you in the future, you name it."

"Fab." I shot her a mean-girl stare. "I'm thinking you should go over the details with me again so I can make sure that I didn't forget anything. I apologize. It's been a hectic couple of days." I should have congratulated myself for not barking, *What the hell are you talking about?* Instead, I tried to blow out a calming breath.

"The funeral for Samuels Rice is at four."

There was a slight hesitation on Raul's part. "We'll need the guests here by three. As I explained to Fab, his representative asked that we invite people to give him the proper send-off, and the reason it's so last-minute is because he forgot. He swears he told us, but he didn't. As soon as he contacted me, I called the retirement home I rely on, but they had a field trip planned and most of the residents had already signed up."

And what?

"Ninety-eight is a ripe old age." Raul tittered. "Mr. Rice outlived all his friends, and he's the last of his family. And that's the problem."

"So, you need mourners." Breathe, I told myself. "How many again?"

"Twenty or so. That would make a nice group, don't you think?"

Twenty? I made a shocked face. "I've had so much on my mind, I'm sorry I'm sounding a bit disorganized."

"We've got so much riding on this." His worry came across the line. "Not sure if I told Fab, but we're being profiled for another senior magazine, and the piece will showcase our museum. It'll be a media event."

Twenty! Humans! In just a few hours! I'd lost the thread of the conversation.

"However many you can get to show up will be fine. A good selling point is the free food. The locals around here love it. Which reminds me, if you have a rough number, I can get that organized."

I knew Raul was fishing to see if I'd gotten anyone other than Fab and myself.

Not getting an answer, he stumbled on. "Dickie and I are doing our best to hold it together in the face of the anticipation. Once again, we can't thank you enough for your help." His excitement bubbled through the phone, like a kid at Christmas, and I didn't have the heart to tell him I was the Grinch.

I needed to woman up and dump this fiasco in Fab's lap. But I kept my lips closed. "You and Dickie don't need to worry about anything. You'd be surprised how helpful Fab's been. We'll take care of everything, and that includes the food. Fab's contribution." I managed a polite good-bye, stuffed my phone in my pocket, and turned toward Fab.

"Ouch," she yelled and hit the brakes for the red light instead of barreling through.

My fingers still entwined in her hair, I tugged again. I threw open the door and slid out, still leaning across the seat. "I'm going to beat the moly out of you." I slammed the door and stomped around to the driver's side, jerking the handle. Locked. I tugged on it a few more times, just in case I'd somehow acquired Herculean strength and could jerk it off the hinges. Oblivious to the honking horns, I marched to the front and beat on the hood, yelling more than a few filthy words.

Whatever reaction Fab was expecting—*Ohhh… I'd love to go corral twenty people to go to the funeral of a stranger*—this wasn't it. For once, she looked shocked and appalled.

At the same time, the sound of a siren penetrated my brain, I realized a couple of people had slowed to take pictures, video, whatever. If I ended up on the internet, Mother would kill me. It would make for a family story that would never die.

A cop car pulled up alongside us, and the window came down. "You need a tow truck?" Kevin yelled.

I walked over to the side of the road, and Fab took the opportunity to shoot out of traffic and let the few cars that were impatiently waiting get by. Kevin waved me back and parked behind her. He got out. "What the devil?"

"I want her arrested." I pointed to the Hummer.

"A felony? Something good like that?" He cocked his head.

I told him what had happened, and the sympathetic fellow burst out laughing and continued to laugh. Finally getting ahold of himself, he said, "The only one I have grounds to arrest is you for holding up traffic. In case you were thinking about sending me an invite, I've got to work. Thankfully."

"You could pass it around the police station—

free food. Maybe I could get a few shows that way."

"I wouldn't count on that." Kevin sounded somewhat sympathetic. "What's up with her?" He pointed to the Hummer. "Shouldn't she be over here eavesdropping?"

"I threatened to beat her up. Maybe that's a good sign she actually thinks I could do it."

"You don't have time for jail. Here's my tip: start with The Cottages. That should get you halfway to your goal. Incentivize with liquor and they'll be lined up. Make sure you've got a ride lined up for them. I wouldn't be popular if I had to arrest my neighbors."

"You're popular now?"

"Some days." He shot me a cheeky grin. "You need a ride?"

"Would you drop me at Jake's? I can get my margarita on, even though it's early, and get the guest list figured out."

He opened the back door. "Can I cuff you?"

"I'd prefer not."

It was less than a mile up the road. He dropped me off, and I cut across the parking lot. Only one of the "beer for breakfast" crowd still lingered. I waved to Kelpie, who was bartending, ordered a soda, and jammed it with cherries, thinking I needed a clear head… for now, anyway. I walked back to the office and snatched up Doodad's notepad and a troll pen with pink hair. He and Cook stood in the door of the kitchen, sizing me up and not saying a word. They weren't stupid.

I went out to the deck, closing the door, and claimed my reserved table. Then I pulled out my phone and called Mac. It was ringing when Fab burst through the door.

"I'm sorry." Fab actually sounded sincere. "They were so desperate when they called. I meant to tell you and forgot." She slid into a seat across from me.

"What's up, boss?" Mac asked when she answered.

"Big bonus if you can help me pull this off. Paid by Fab." I glared at the woman across the table, daring her to argue. One of many dares to come, I suspected.

Mac groaned. "Can I say no?"

I ignored her question, thinking a flat out "no" wouldn't get the conversation off to a congenial start. "Do we have access to that bus you talked about buying?"

"About that…"

Now what?

"It was such a good deal that I went ahead and bought it. Couldn't pass it up while you were pussyfooting making a decision. My backup plan was, if you hated the idea, I'd have Crum sell it and make a few bucks. He's good at squeezing the last nickel out of a person."

"Gas that baby up." I didn't tell her the whole story, only that I needed mourners. "Tenants, guests, anyone from the neighborhood—they're all invited. Sell it as an adventure. And free food."

"Liquor too? That'd be a sure bet."

"Open bar it is. How many takers do you think you can get?"

"At least ten."

I hung up, reached over, and opened the door, waving to Kelpie.

"Yep?" She skipped over in pink high-top tennis shoes, the toes bedazzled, her short skirt really short.

"I need a bartender for four hours, tops. This afternoon. Probably no tips, so that will be factored in, along with double pay. Got anybody who's not squeamish about bartending a funeral gig?" I picked up my phone and called Raul while Kelpie came up with someone. "I'll need you to open the bar and send the tab to Fab. She felt bad she wasn't contributing and thus volunteered. I'm also sending over a bartender."

"That's too much."

"Fab insisted. You know how she can be—so generous. I'm still working on the guest list, but don't worry, you'll have a nice turnout." I hung up and went back to my list-making.

"You're going to have to speak to me sooner or later," Fab grouched.

"I wouldn't hold my breath for sooner," I grouched back. "I need more people. It's not like you know anyone."

"Don't be mean."

"What if I trick the family and blame you?" I gave her a saccharine smile.

"Good luck pulling that off." She rolled her eyes.

"Hundred bucks and fifty favors that come with no complaining says I can get it done," I challenged.

"Two hundred. No favors."

"One hundred and make them all favors."

"No thanks. This is a trick." Fab crossed her arms.

I ignored her and scrolled through my phone, finding the person I hoped would help with my next idea.

"Yes?" Spoon said warily when he answered.

"I need a favor. An unorthodox one."

Fab stomped her foot, wanting me to put the call on speaker.

"Gone are the days when I say yes without knowing the details," Spoon answered, but he always said yes... unless Mother found out ahead of time.

"I'd like to borrow that SUV of yours that seats ten. Well, sort of. I need you to pick up the husbands, plus Mother, Brad, Billy, and Xander. I'll call the latter and tell him to hoof it over to your place of business. Your lure can be that you've got a last-minute surprise for Mother. Now, for the last part. Once you've got everyone rounded up and in the SUV, call me, and I'll give you the address for where to go. I don't want to tell you until the last minute because you'll say no. Probably hell no."

"You want me to help you trick every member in the family, do I have that right?"

The fact that he sounded somewhat amused gave me hope he'd come through. "Essentially, yes. Once I give you the backstory—at a later time—you'll be happy that you jumped to help me."

"Yeah, I'll bet."

Dead silence.

"Please. I promise it's nothing dangerous. You'd be helping one of your favorite family members, who's nice to everyone and doesn't say no often enough."

"You don't have to lay it on so thick. Is my wife—you know, one of the trickees—going to divorce me?"

"Mother? She's a better sport than that. At worst, you're running the risk of a lecture about saying no."

"I know how to cut those off—make her lose her train of thought."

My cheeks burned.

"This better not backfire."

"You're the best," I squealed. "Once I give you the address, everything will click into place and you'll realize it's relatively harmless."

"I'll get to work on getting everyone else here at my business and then pick up your mother. I'll text you when I've rounded them up, and you can send the address."

"Tons of favors. All owed by Fab. Me, you can ask anytime."

"I can't wait to hear about her role in all this. Whatever it is."

"Wow is all I can say," Fab said when I hung up. "You're quite something to watch in action."

"I'd say the same thing about you, in a different way, if I was speaking to you." I held up my phone. "One more call. This time, Emerson. You busy this afternoon?" I asked when she answered. So much for the pleasantries.

"For you, I'll make time."

"I'm collecting on one of the favors you owe Fab." She laughed. That was a good sign. "Be at my house at two, casual dress, no questions asked. You're not to tell anyone, and that includes Brad."

"Is whatever this is legal?" Emerson hedged.

"Now counselor, nothing about the rest of the day will land you in jail."

"I'm in." She laughed and hung up.

"Next time you want to run a con on me, give me a heads up." I stood up, glaring down at Fab. "I need a ride home."

Chapter Twenty-Eight

Emerson met Fab and me at Fab's house, all of us decked out in a variation of a casual short sun dress. Without a lot of time to spare, we got in the Hummer and flew out to the street. On the way to Tropical Slumber, I filled Emerson in on what was about to happen.

"So, you're telling me that, if I need a side gig, I could become a professional mourner?" Emerson asked, clearly amused by the idea.

"If you're good at eulogies, that pays extra." I told her about Liam's short stint at the job.

"Thanks for including me. This is going to be fun. I feel like a cool girl." Emerson smiled.

Fab snorted.

"Don't believe we've ever been called that before." I faux-frowned before grinning.

Fab pulled into the driveway and parked next to Lizzie's truck. Good, at least the bartender was here.

"Word of advice." Fab turned to Emerson. "Stand back. Madison thinks she's going to blame me for this… whatever it is…"

"Funeral," I supplied helpfully. "Fab isn't as innocent as she'd like you to believe. She signed me up for this gig, and, oh yeah, forgot to tell me."

"I didn't tell her to trick everyone. It's going to come crashing down on her head."

"We'll see about that." I got out and slammed the door.

Dickie and Raul stood in the doorway, Raul with a big grin on his face. Dickie smiled hesitantly.

"Mr. Edwards is on display in the main room, if you'd like the first viewing." Dickie took a step in that direction.

"Fab loves doing that." I gave Emerson a slight shove forward. "I'll go check on Lizzie before the mourners get here. You're going to have a nice turnout," I reassured Raul.

Surprisingly, Emerson tagged along with Fab with little fuss.

I went back outside and skirted around the building and over to the tiki bar, where Lizzie was setting up. I did a double-take at her black Elvira getup and long black wig. "Thank you for doing this on short notice."

"Sounds fun to me. If it doesn't turn out too creepy, I'll put up an ad on one of those online job sites that I'm available for more gigs."

A short yellow school bus rumbled into the lot. "I'll be around if you need anything." I waved and went to meet the latest arrivals.

The door opened, and I climbed the steps. I recognized most of the faces as tenants and guests, and a couple of faces from the neighborhood. Crum and Joseph were there, and even Miss January, who was passed out in the very back, snoring logs. More than likely, she'd volunteered during one of her few lucid moments of the day when she heard "open bar."

"I want to thank all of you for coming to the funeral of Mr. Edwards. It means a lot to his… family." That sounded better than lawyer. I had to take back my original assertion that most would have to be strong-armed, as they all appeared willing and excited. Except the two that were in their cups and a tad disoriented. "There will be a short service. A buffet will be served on the patio, and the bar is open. If any of you have an interest, the museum featuring burial vignettes is open for your viewing." I pointed to the recently constructed building, gave them a big smile, and refrained from jumping down to solid ground.

Mac was hot on my heels. "How did you get roped into doing this?"

"Fab," I seethed.

Mac had more questions, but had to save them as Raul ran over, greeting first her and then each person as they unloaded.

"You're the best," I told Mac. "You exceeded yourself and helped me go over my quota."

Instead of hugging Mac, which had been my first thought, I stepped back and eyed her black alligator boots, heads curved up out of the toes, shiny black eyes staring. She'd paired them with a black fringed skirt.

Noticing my attention on her feet, Mac did a little dance. "Aren't they the cutest?"

"Very cute," I lied.

Spoon's Expedition SUV rolled into the driveway and hogged a couple of parking spaces. I took a deep breath and hustled over, wishing I'd practiced an explanation about how this would be a fun adventure.

I opened the passenger door and heaved myself into Mother's arms, whispering in her ear, "Have my back. No matter what."

"Of course, dear." She patted my cheek.

I straightened as all the doors opened, the men inside ready to make a break for it. "I'd like a moment to explain what's going on," I said in an overly sweet tone.

"Soon as we pulled in the driveway, I knew this had your name on it," Creole snapped.

It was hard to tell if he was mildly irritated or had jumped to full-on mad.

"A surprise for Mother, he said." Brad, who was sitting behind Spoon, cuffed him in the head.

Spoon twisted in his seat. "You want that arm of yours ripped off and shoved up—"

"Let Madison talk," Mother interjected.

"Caspian," I acknowledged. "Almost didn't see you there."

"I knew he was in town and invited him, knowing he wouldn't want to miss out." Spoon grinned. At least one person was enjoying the ruse.

"You're all here because of Fab." I ignored Caspian's growl and gave them a version of events that sounded apocalyptic.

Didier lowered his head, shoulders shaking. *Did he know?*

"And so... you're all here to do a good deed, and I want to thank you on behalf of Tropical Slumber," I said.

"You sound like a tour guide," Billy joked.

Xander poked him.

"Where is my daughter?" Caspian asked in a snooty, irritated tone, sounding just like her.

"Fab's inside, viewing the body." I pointed to the main building. "Know this about your sweet daughter—if there's a dead body, that's where you'll find her." I pointed out the newest addition, the funeral museum, and invited them to peruse at their leisure. "One last request. Please lose your irritated faces. A camera crew has arrived, and you wouldn't want to show up in a brochure wearing a frown." I offered my hand to Mother and helped her out.

"You were a good choice to orchestrate this, since you know how to get around people saying no to you. Since Dickie and Raul are your friends, you were probably an easy choice." Mother screwed up her nose. She'd never quite understood the relationship, and to be truthful, neither did I. "I'm confident that I can turn this into a good story and be the talk around the pool, for a couple of weeks anyway." She patted my cheek.

"Thank you for not disowning me." I hugged her hard.

"The truth is my husband had such fun being in on this with you, and that makes me happy. No matter how weird it is."

The service was, for the most part, uneventful. A couple of the "mourners" even got up and, after a peek in the open casket, said a few nice words about a man they'd never met.

The preacher—who I'd never seen before, and it surprised me the guys hadn't used Crum, who was licensed to join folks in wedded bliss, though maybe his license didn't cover funerals—was about to bring the service to an end when I stood and waved my arms. All eyes turned to me. Creole slipped his hand up my dress and pinched me. I ignored him.

"Since we're here today because of Fab, I think it's only fitting that she says a few final words. I, for one, am interested to hear what she has to say, as I'm sure the rest of you are." I'd overused my sweet smile to the point where my cheeks hurt. I pointed to Fab in a dramatic fashion before sitting.

If looks could kill, what better location?

Fab stood, slipped into the main aisle, and strutted it like a fashion model, throwing insincere smiles in one direction and then the other, complete with hand flips. You'd have to know her to know she was grinding her teeth.

She wiggled up to the microphone, flicking it and sending a screeching noise echoing through the room. "Welcome, everyone." Her eyes moved slowly around the room, a trick of hers to make it appear as though she was making eye contact when she wasn't. "I want to thank you on behalf of Mr. Edwards for coming today. It would mean so much to him to see the turnout."

She remembered his name!

"Mr. Edwards was a wonderful man and loved by many." She spoke slowly. "He'll be missed by everyone who knew him. On behalf of the family, it means a lot that you could make this day so special."

She gave a slight head bow and repeated her sashay back her to seat, with one last glare for me before she sat down.

Creole squeezed my hand and leaned in, whispering, "It was nice knowing you."

Raul took the microphone, thanked everyone for coming, and invited them out to the patio for refreshments.

The guests that hot-footed it out to the patio to party split up into two distinct groups—the short bus riders, who Billy and Xander joined, and the rest. My family, huddled off to the side, wore looks that said, *Time to leave yet?*

I'd hung back, tugging on Creole's hand so he wouldn't follow. Once the main room cleared, I shared my getaway plan, to which he readily agreed. We made our way back up the aisle and out the main entrance when everyone's attention was elsewhere.

"Fab's going to be furious you left her without a ride." Creole opened the door to the SUV, and I slid inside.

Once he got behind the wheel, I said, "She'll get over it when she jumps behind the wheel of the bus, which she hasn't driven yet. I hope she doesn't leave the drunks to walk and get arrested." I pointed him to the rear exit.

Creole laughed. "How about I treat you to a burger?"

"Yum."

Chapter Twenty-Nine

It didn't surprise me that, within minutes of Creole leaving the house, Fab picked the lock and came gliding into the kitchen. I'd ignored her for a day and knew she wasn't going to tolerate much more.

"Coffee?" I held up an empty mug.

"That depends."

"Don't you worry your pretty little head." I opened the refrigerator and pulled out a bag of her swill, holding it up for her inspection. She snatched it from my hand and made her own brew. Heaven forbid it shouldn't be thick and gooey enough.

"I should apologize for leaving you stranded with your dead friends." I slid onto a stool.

"I saw you leave, and the only reason I didn't run after you cursing was that Madeline cornered me and badgered me into playing hostess to the mourners. When she had her back turned, I shoved that odious job off on Xander. He tried to weasel out by saying, 'I don't know what the heck to do.' I politely told him he'd figure it out and sealed it with a hair-raising glare, which I've been practicing and, judging by his response, got down." Fab poured herself a cup of coffee and sat across from me.

"Don't you dare scare Xander off. He's good at ferreting out the information we need."

"As a *friend,* I feel I should inform you that that new acquisition of yours... the bus—"

That one.

"—is belching black puffs of smoke. You should get it checked before you go into the tour business." Fab laughed.

"You're hilarious." I faked a laugh. My phone vibrated across the island top, and our eyes went to the screen. "Whatever it is—yes," I said when I answered.

Spoon unleashed a gravelly laugh. "You know the rule on that—you're supposed to wait for the details. Can you come to my office?"

"My cohort is sitting here, and I can bring her along." I tapped my watchless arm, and Fab nodded.

"How soon can I expect the two of you?"

"We're on our way."

"Any details?" Fab asked. I shook my head. "He probably wants to kill me, and you get to watch."

I stood. "Come on, Drama Queen. Shall we flip to see who drives?"

* * *

Fab arrived at JS Auto Body in record time,

thanks to light traffic and green lights. Spoon opened the door as we got out, flourished his hand, and ushered us inside. I took my usual chair on the other side of his desk and tugged on Fab's arm, eyeing the chair next to me, before she could stretch out on the couch.

"I've got a job for you two. Know up front that you can say no for any reason."

"Since you never ask anything of us, you can be assured that, even facts unknown, the answer is yes unless we're completely unqualified." I turned toward Fab who shook her head, *don't be weird* on her face.

"It's a relative of a friend sort of thing. Don't want to say exactly. Nice girl."

My brow went up.

"It's always about a woman," Fab said in a joking tone.

Spoon growled. "Here's the deal. The friend's daughter, Janey Kingston, recently opened a bakery in Ft. Lauderdale. Unfortunately, one of her suppliers is using her location to run drugs and money, shipping it in in crates with false bottoms. Once unloaded, they haul the crates off and no one's the wiser. The Feds and local law enforcement have had them in their sights for a while now and are just waiting until they've collected enough evidence to secure a conviction before they move in and shut everything down."

"And you want us to do what, exactly?" Cops, Feds… Fab perked right up.

"Tip her off and suggest that she change suppliers pronto." He shoved a sheet of paper across the desk. "Here's a list. The top one is highly-rated, and she'd be well taken care of."

"Is she involved?" I asked.

"Law enforcement knows she's not, but her business would be closed down while everything got sorted out, and by the time it reopened, that might be the end of her business. Not to mention the bad publicity, deserved or not. She stands to lose big."

"Why not tell her yourself?" Fab asked with suspicion. "Or how about the person you got the information from?"

"Because Janey knows me and will make the connection. She's is being watched, and if my friend makes contact with her, the Feds'll know and he could lose his job. He swears they've got a couple of other businesses under surveillance and can make their case without using her."

"So, someone with intimate knowledge of the case who's closely related to her doesn't want her caught up in this sting," I summarized.

"Exactly. I'm thinking you could present yourself as a customer with a big order and tell her, stressing that time is of the essence. Stay away from her store, as it's wired."

I looked over at Fab. "Wedding cake?"

"My friends tell me that she caters to a snooty clientele, so play the part," Spoon suggested.

"We'll contact her and tell her that we're

interviewing bakers and need her to meet with us at some restaurant," Fab said.

"If she's being tailed, then any conversation we have can be overheard in a restaurant," I said. "Another option would be renting office space for an hour, ensuring privacy."

"Any expenses you incur, I'll reimburse," Spoon said.

"We're going to meet with a total stranger, warn her her life's about to be jerked out from under her, and she's going to believe us, why?" Fab asked in disbelief.

"You two are always doing impossible s… stuff. The funeral comes to mind."

"I suppose you want this done ASAP?" I smiled at Spoon.

"Restaurant meeting is faster to set up than an office rental," Fab said. "Knowing that we'll have eyes on us, we'll have to make it look like a real business meeting. We'll also use a burner phone to set everything up."

"What about a boat? I can make that happen with very little notice." Spoon stood. "Janey will probably think you're crazy at first, but since she knows quite a few people in law enforcement, she'll see this as the opportunity it is and get the hell out." He crossed the room to the credenza, opened a cabinet door, and pulled out a phone. "It's ready for use." He set it down in front of me.

I grabbed a sticky note pad and a pen and

pushed it across the desk to him. "I'm going to need some information."

"How much lead time do you need on the boat?" Fab asked. "Write down the address."

"Snap your fingers and I'll make it happen."

"I'll call and use my society voice." Fab gave us a preview, accentuating it by looking down her nose. "Since Janey is running a business, she's going to want to schedule for early or late, since we're demanding to meet away from her location."

Spoon grinned. "You got that persona down."

Fab reached over, grabbed the notes, and picked up the phone. Taking a deep breath, she called. "May I speak with Janey Kingston?" She waited on hold. "I'm the assistant to Brenda West," she said, using the last name of a family that had recently made headlines for throwing a very successful charity fundraiser. "Your bakery is one of those chosen as a candidate to make a wedding cake for the family. We need you to come to the yacht for the interview. Tomorrow?" Fab stared at the phone in amusement. "You do realize that the publicity, if you're chosen, would be invaluable to your business?" She listened another moment. "I'll text you the information, and we'll see you tomorrow." Fab hung up with a satisfied smile. "Eight am." She grimaced. "Which means we'll be leaving here before the crack."

Chapter Thirty

I didn't think the guys were going to go for our latest job—regardless of the fact that it came at Spoon's request and the risk was supposed to be relatively low—and told Fab so on the way home.

She blew me off and dumped me at my house. "Dress boat chic," she yelled when I got out, then sped away.

I told Creole, and he didn't say anything as he jerked up his phone and went out to the deck. Coming back inside, he said, "We're leaving a half-hour earlier in the morning so we can grab food and coffee."

"We?"

"The four of us. Won't that be fun?"

Not liking that I laughed and found it difficult to stop, he tackled me and tossed me on the bed.

* * *

The next morning, we were standing outside when Fab zoomed up and squealed to a stop. Creole knocked on the driver's side window, and Fab stared, not bothering to roll it down. Creole growled and grabbed my hand, dragging me back toward the house.

Fab opened the window. "Just kidding. Hop in before we're late."

"If only she were a man, and I could beat that smirk off her face."

"You two can handle the job," I yelled at her. Another perk of not having neighbors, one could scream in the street at all hours. "Let me know how it goes." I tugged on Creole's hand.

Fab laid on the horn and yelled back, "Funny, you two. Now get in the damn car."

Creole opened the door, and I slid across the seat, meeting Didier's grin and sending one back. "We need coffee."

"Do you know where you're going?" Creole barked.

Fab peeled out without a word.

I'd check later for tire marks, and if necessary, I'd send a letter of complaint, telling her that the black streaks needed to be cleaned up. I laughed to myself—even if there weren't any, I might send an invoice anyway.

Fab drove through the coffee drive-thru and loaded up on our favorites before blowing up the Overseas to the Interstate. She took the exit to Ft. Lauderdale, following the GPS directions over to the boat marina, and we arrived with twenty minutes to spare.

"You two make yourself at home on the boat." Creole led us down the dock and climbed on board, looking around before extending a hand to help me aboard. "Didier and I will be on lookout nearby."

Fab and I settled in a couple of deck chairs.

"I say we get to the point and not bother to sugarcoat why we tricked her into meeting." Fab stretched out her legs.

"I vote that you take the lead."

Fab nodded. "In the event of an awkward silence, jump in and rescue me. Let's hope that she sees this as the gift it is and it's a quick meeting."

"I'm also hoping that it's uneventful for the guys." My phone pinged, and I looked down at where it lay in my lap. "Janey's here."

Fab stood, crossed to the railing, and waved to the woman as she came down the dock, going to meet her at the top of the steps.

The young blond woman paused to kick off her heels before climbing aboard. Her hair in a loose chignon, she was professionally dressed in a pencil skirt and blouse, portfolio in hand. "I'm the one that spoke with you yesterday." Janey Kingston took a seat on the bench across from the two of us, giving us an appraising stare.

"Something to drink?" I asked, not bothering to introduce myself, which she didn't appear to find odd.

Janey pulled a sports bottle out of her tote, along with a business card, which she handed to Fab.

"I want to apologize up front," Fab said. "We got you here under false pretenses. If you give me a chance to explain everything, you'll understand the need for a speedy meeting in an out-of-the-way location."

Fear filled Janey's face. "Okay," she stuttered.

"You've recently started using a supplier that is under investigation for running drugs," Fab blurted. "It would be a smart idea to switch to someone else."

"Are you law enforcement?"

"No, we're not. This information came to us from an anonymous tip."

"Then how can you possibly know it's true?" The fear had evaporated, a slight sneer in her tone.

"I can't give you one-hundred-percent proof. It's up to you whether you want to gamble your business that I might be... What? Drumming up business for the competition? It's an easy change, and one you can make without the slightest harm to your business." Fab pulled the list of alternate suppliers from her pocket. "If you get pulled into the middle of a drug bust, you stand to lose." She handed Janey the paper. "The advice I was asked to pass along is: stop using the company now and take yourself off the law's radar."

Janey scanned the list, her nose upturned. "This first company is the best, and they turned me down; I wasn't big enough potatoes for them."

"Call and ask for the man listed; you'll find that your delivery will be scheduled." Noting her disbelief, I said, "Here's your chance to get your first choice, and all it takes is a phone call."

"Why so clandestine?" Janey studied the paper. "Why didn't the person with the information come to me directly?"

"Honestly, neither of us knows who the informant is. But they're going way out on a limb to protect you."

"Your best course of action is to tell no one about what you've learned," I said. "Tell the company you're currently using that you got a better deal."

"The owner's a greasy fellow, and I won't be sad to stop doing business with him. If all this is true, no wonder his prices were so good." Janey stood. "As for keeping my mouth shut, I come from a long line of cops, so I know the game."

"Maybe that answers your question," Fab said. "One of them is apparently your guardian angel and doesn't want you caught up in something where you could go down as collateral damage."

Janey shoved the paper in her bag. "If this company opens an account for me, this morning won't have been a complete waste of my time. I've got cupcakes to make." She exited the boat, stopping at the bottom to put her heels back on.

I stood and leaned over the railing, watching her flounce up the dock. "Thank you, something, have a nice day." I replaced the chairs where I'd found them.

"Janey was a cool one. My guess is that she knows who sent the information her way."

My phone pinged, and I read the message. "She's left the parking lot." We locked up and walked back to the parking lot. The guys were nowhere in sight, and neither of us looked for them just in case we were being watched. We approached the SUV, and the locks shot up. Found them! Kicked back in their seats, Didier in the back and Creole behind the wheel. To my surprise, no reaction from Fab.

"Well?" I asked as soon as the doors closed.

Creole backed out and pulled out on the street.

"Boring. I had to ask myself, what would Fab do?" Didier grinned at her. "I took a picture of the plate and forwarded it to you already."

"No one tailed her," Creole updated us. "I'd say she's not a person of interest yet. Once she dumps the supplier, she'll be in the clear."

"You went the wrong way," Fab grouched.

"Creole and I picked out a restaurant on the water that's open for breakfast," Didier explained.

"You're paying," Creole said over his shoulder to Fab.

"Okay," she agreed, a little too cheerfully, which had me doing a double take.

Chapter Thirty-One

Bang!

The SUV swerved. Creole wrestled to keep control.

I covered my face with my hands to keep from squealing.

Creole slowed to the honking of horns and managed to cut diagonally across to the right side. He coasted in the emergency lane and off at the next exit, into a rest stop in the middle of nowhere.

"What the hell?" Creole threw open the door, got out, and stomped to the rear, staring at the tire.

The rest of us filed out.

Fab bent down in front of Creole and inspected the side wall. "What would make this hole?" She ran her finger around it.

"Good question." Creole cut around her and met Didier at the liftgate. Together, they unloaded the jack and spare to change the tire.

There were a handful of cars in the parking lot. Not wanting to be in the way, I walked over and checked out the selection in the vending machines. It took less than a minute to lose interest. I cut over to the playground and sat at one of the tables.

Fab joined me. "You're going to need a new tire; no fixing that one."

"I'll drop it off at Spoon's and let him deal with it. It's handy having someone in the family that deals with car issues and provides excellent service with no jerking around."

"The morning was anti-climactic." Disappointment was evident in Fab's tone. "I didn't have a good feeling about Janey Whatever. Ice-cold sums her up."

"If her name ever comes up again, we'll pass. Our best excuse is that it's way too far to drive, and that happens to be true."

"More good news." Fab waved her phone. "Guess who's been burning up the line and finally stopped calling, thank goodness?"

I shrugged in an attempt to play along.

"Gunz! You know that means one of his family members slipped their tether."

"Really, Fabiana," I mimicked Mother, including a finger shake. "That's not nice."

"Sometimes the truth isn't pretty."

"Ladies." The man was dressed in black from head to toe, a baseball cap and sunglasses covered most of his pasty, lined face. He looked like an aging gangster from a B-movie. "Hands in the air."

I gasped at the sight of the Glock pointed at

us. I was about to stand to make it easier to take him down, but he shook the gun, curtailing that idea. He didn't present as scary so much as that he didn't know what he was doing, which made him more dangerous.

Fab turned her sexy megawatt smile on him, which no man resisted for long. Unless they knew her; then they picked up their feet and beat it. "That's so unfriendly," she cooed. "You need to get back in your... uh... car and drive away, and we'll forget this happened." She'd scanned the parking lot and come to the same conclusion I did—that he owned the rusted-out wreck at the far end.

"I don't think so. I want your wallets and rings. And that fancy watch." He pointed to Fab's wrist.

"Didn't bring my purse." I held out my hands. "Car's over there." I pointed in the opposite direction of the SUV after making sure there was one over there. "I'll go get it." I stood and took a step in that direction.

"Not so fast. Hand over what you've got." He waved his gun around again. "While you're at it, give me your keys."

I made eye contact with Creole, who was on the approach with Didier, and shook my head, putting my hands in the air for him to see. I didn't want him spooking the man and getting shot. His eyes went wide, and a cold stare hardened his face.

"Let's go for a walk." The man pointed in the direction of his car.

Fab and I walked across the grass and down the slight incline, stopping at the passenger side of the dented and rusted-out Chevy sedan, which had seen better days. I knew we didn't have much time, as the two teenagers who'd parked a couple of spaces over as we approached and run for the restrooms would be returning soon.

"Slow and easy, hand over the jewelry." The man definitely wasn't in control of his gun.

"This is my wedding ring, which I've never taken off. I'm not going to now." Fab twisted it around her finger. "This is your last chance to walk away alive."

"I'm the one with the firepower, and you'll do what I tell you."

"Three?" I asked Fab. She nodded. "One..." I drew my Glock and shot the weapon out of his hand.

He grabbed his hand, shrieking and dancing around in a circle.

"Took you long enough," Creole barked. "Who is this piece of..." He kicked away the gun that had fallen to the ground. Followed by the man, who he upended in a heap.

"He's a wannabe robber and sucks at it," I said.

"I gave him the option to go home in one piece." Fab smiled moonily at Didier. "You must be a good influence on me."

I gagged.

"What are we going to do with this guy?" Didier stood over him. "911?"

"How long is that going to take?" Fab groaned.

"We'll be here the rest of the day," Creole snapped. "What's your big idea?"

I kicked the man in the butt. "Run," I whispered.

"You can't do that," Creole groaned. "He dies, and you're in deep water."

The man hobbled to his feet and ran to his car. The four of us watched as he tripped and caught himself, heaving himself inside and slamming the door. He fired up the engine and jerked toward the exit.

"Call it in to one of your friends." I matched Creole's irritated look.

He pulled his phone out his pocket, going back and leaning against the table.

"He's headed south," I yelled. "The eyesore he's driving will be hard to miss."

Whoever Creole called, it wasn't 911. After the first terse moments, he was laughing with the person on the other end.

"Why did it take you so long to shoot him?" Fab grouched.

We'd moved back to the SUV and leaned against the hood.

"Me? What about you? If you hadn't been making googly eyes at that criminal and put your foot in his face, we'd be out of here already," I grouched back.

"Do you two want to walk home?" Didier said sternly.

"News flash, people," I yelled at the top of my lungs. "It's *my* damn coach."

Just then, Creole walked up. "Don't get her worked up, or she'll want to drive and we'll be tomorrow getting home." He traded a grin with Didier. Creole's phone rang. "Load up," he said after he'd hung up.

We weren't far down the road when we caught sight of the flashing lights. The would-be thief had made apprehending him easy, as he'd run the front end of his car into a ravine and was crawling out on his hands and knees.

Chapter Thirty-Two

The day after our adventure, Creole called in contagious, we turned off our phones, and I treated him to tacos on the beach.

Spoiled by our day together, the next morning, I decided to suggest that we have breakfast out before going to our respective offices. I yanked on his foot, which was sticking out from under the blanket. "If you get your tuchus out of bed, I'll take you for coffee and something yummy."

Creole lifted the pillow off his face. "What are you buttering me up for?"

"You're so suspicious."

He continued to stare.

"It beats cereal."

That sold my offer, and we ended up at the Bakery Café, scoring our favorite people-watching table. We'd just finished eating when my phone rang. Creole held out his hand, snapping his fingers.

"It's a toss-up as to who's more annoying—you or Fab." I handed it over, knowing that when it rang this early, it was never good news. Let him handle it.

"She'd have jerked it out of your hand." Amused at whatever name popped up on the screen, he answered, "What do you want?" He smiled at me and pretended to turn away so I couldn't hear. "Since I'm an investor, shouldn't I be invited to this sit down?" he growled, enjoying himself. He listened for a moment, then covered the phone and told me, "VP is calling a meeting. Apparently, the motel has a sketchy past. He's not sure that it means anything, but he says you like to know everything." His face registered faux shock. "I know that comes as a surprise." He spoke to VP for another moment, then laughed before hanging up.

"I've been needing an assistant—you're hired." I leaned over and kissed his cheek. "I'll route all calls to you, and you weed out the felonious requests."

"The biggest offender is Fab, and me hanging up on her wouldn't be a deterrent; she'd just hunt you down."

I wrapped my arms around him. "Coming to the meeting?"

"I'm meeting the code guy and need you to drop me at the job site. I'm not worried about getting signed off, since we don't cut corners, but I like to be there so if there's a problem, I can get it handled pronto. Thanks to your connection—the man takes my calls, and I don't have to wait days for a return call."

"Another friend of my aunt's." When Elizabeth died, she left me an address book of connections that never said no. "We should do this more often." I sipped the last of my coffee. "Just you and me."

He leaned forward and kissed me. "We need to take a few days and run away, leaving a note so they don't send a posse."

"What did you find out about the highway robber?"

"He's got an arrest record a mile long, mostly petty stuff. This was the first time he used a gun with a history; it was stolen and used in a previous crime."

Creole finished his coffee, and we got up and crossed the sidewalk to the SUV. He held the door while I got behind the wheel, then circled around to the passenger side.

"Double check your seatbelt, since I'm driving. Can't be too careful."

His deep laugh filled the car. "I'll take my chances."

I dropped Creole off, then drove to JS Auto Body and pulled up to the fence, laying on the horn. It took several minutes before it opened. I pulled up to one of the bays. "I'd like the Cadillac service," I told Kevin. "If possible, I'd like to know what blew out the sidewall."

Kevin laughed at me. "We aim to please and will call you when it's ready."

I rounded the front of the Hummer and saw

Spoon standing in the doorway between his office and the garage. I waved and veered in his direction.

"What happened?" He tossed his head and hugged me, then ushered me into the office. I sat in my usual chair, and he sat behind his desk.

I'd already reported back about our meeting with Janey, having called him from the car. I updated him on the rest of the road trip and ended with Creole's news.

"What did you think of Janey?" Spoon asked.

"Hard to read, cold, wound tight. Tipped her off and gave her the replacement list. She got up and flounced down the dock without so much as a 'have a nice day.' I'd be interested to hear if she takes the advice and makes the change."

"Sorry she was rude."

"No big deal. It was one of our few jobs that didn't erupt in gunfire. That's a win." I laughed. "The guys picked a restaurant for breakfast afterwards, and the food was good. I'm happy that Creole was driving when the tire blew, although I have every confidence that Fab would've handled it just as well."

"Where is your sidekick?"

"I like that." I beamed at him. "Especially since that's usually my title. She's swinging from the chandelier with her husband."

Spoon wolfed out a laugh and made an X in front of his face. "TMI."

"Can I bum a ride to the office?"

"I've got a new toy, and you can be the first to ride." Spoon stood and led the way to the door. We made our way to the last bay, where he wheeled out a jet-black, two-passenger scooter.

"Where did you get that?" I asked in awe and walked around, inspecting it.

"A guy short on cash heard that I collected cars and motorcycles, and since the pawn shop only offered pennies, he hit me up. I gave him a fair price. Frankly, I would've bought it even if it wasn't in such pristine condition and fixed it up myself." Spoon held out his hand, and I stepped up and sat down.

One of the mechanics opened the gate, and we zoomed through and down the street. My hair blew all around, and I didn't care; the wind in my face felt great. The ride ended all too soon, when he pulled up in front of the security gate and hit the button. It opened without question. He drove in, u-turned, parked, and helped me off.

"So much fun." I reached out and hugged him. "Mother's going to love your new toy."

I waved as he drove out, then climbed the steps. Xander had the door open—he worked it like a pro. I knew Fab was there because I'd seen her car.

"Bon Morning." I waved like a pageant contestant.

Fab shook her head and smirked.

I rounded the corner and dropped my purse

on my desk, then went back and took a seat at Fab's desk. Xander had moved from his usual seat on the couch to the other empty chair.

"I call this meeting to order." He reached out and slapped the desk with a grin.

Fab glared.

Stop, I mouthed at Fab. "Ignore her," I said to Xander.

He blushed. "The motel property has an icky past. Almost everyone associated with it has ended up dead, and it hasn't been pretty."

"That matters how?" Fab asked.

I shook my head.

"It might have nothing to do with the price of peas. Is there a smoking six-shooter?" Xander made the appropriate noises. "No. I'm just sayin' there's a history."

"Just ignore her facial antics," I said. "I want to hear what you've got. Pretend she brought her party manners to the office today."

"You already know that one of the original owners died of a heart attack and made a widow of Isabella. The surviving owner, Abe Greer, swindled her, and you know the rest of that story. What never got mentioned was that after Isabella's death, her three children went to live with the grandparents of the surviving owner, who pretended they were blood relations. It took a couple of years for the deception to be uncovered, but nothing changed, as no one in Isabella's family had the money to fight for custody. Shortly after that came to light, the supposed grandparents' home burned down with them in it. The kids escaped and were finally reunited with Isabella's family."

"That's a heartbreaking story." I squirmed in my chair.

Fab leaned forward. "How did the fire start?"

"Arson," Xander said matter-of-factly. "No one was ever charged. At the time, it was reported in the news that the kids were questioned, but I haven't been able to find anything to substantiate that that ever happened. The neighbors on both sides of the grandparents' house thought it was weird that the kids' explanation for how they escaped the fire was that they were playing outside in the middle of the night."

"And that links to the current murders how?" Fab snapped.

"You said check the history. I did," Xander defended himself.

"I didn't know what it would yield, just..." I said. "At the time, you thought it was a good idea. Did you forget that part?" I turned to Xander. "Go on."

"Ten years later, the motel, which was still owned by the Greer family, got torched. His kids were running it at the time. While in the process of being rebuilt, it burned again, and that was the final blow that caused them to go into bankruptcy. Shortly after that, their father was found dead—murdered."

"Let me guess, that also went unsolved?" Fab asked.

"Were Isabella's kids questioned?" I asked. "I'm not sure that's a logical leap, but I'd be interested in where they were and what they had to say."

"I have an answer to that." Xander smirked. "By that time, they'd moved to the northern Arkansas border and disappeared into the bushes, and that was the last anyone heard of them. At the time, there weren't a lot of communication options up there."

"Went on a road trip through there one year, and in one small town, not everyone had plumbing." I made a face at the memory. "For some, an outhouse was the only option."

"You want to hear about the court fight that got dismissed?" Xander squinted at Fab.

"This is your meeting, *VP*."

"Before the fire and Abe Greer's murder, Isabella's kids sued him, saying their mother had been swindled. The case was on the verge of being thrown out when the kids' lawyer bailed, knowing his fees weren't going to get paid."

"Then Greer turns up dead?" I guessed. Xander nodded, and I raised my brow. "Wow. Is there anyone still alive?"

"Isabella's side is still sucking air, and the ones that aren't all died of explainable causes. The Greer family, not so much. Their family tree is dotted with murders, accidents, and other untimely deaths."

"No one thought to check out the history of this property ahead of time?" Fab zeroed in on me.

"You already know the answer." I turned my attention to Xander. "So, after it burned down again while being rebuilt, the Greers were bankrupt or dead, and this steal of a property was bought by someone else. I'm afraid to ask what happened to those owners. I hope murder isn't the reason they went out of business."

Xander continued. "They overestimated the cost of doing business and ran out of money before all the repairs could be made. They paid someone to sign off so they could open, in the hopes of recouping something and to keep the place filled they rented to a seedy clientele. Neighboring businesses were in an uproar because, as you know, renting to the dregs is an issue. Mainly, they're an unreliable lot, and every day, it's something new."

"If your stare is your way of saying I should know that, you're right, I do." I glared back at Fab without any heat. "I learned the hard way that you can't elevate sh**. It only brings you down to its level. I fought against that premise and lost."

Fab stood and crossed to the kitchen, coming back with a soda and two bottles of water and distributing them. "Are you about ready to get to the happy ending?"

"It's all in how you look at it. That's what I heard Kelpie say once."

I laughed at Fab's exasperation.

"The last owner went broke and drank himself to death. The property stood empty for years. The loan sold several times, but legal ownership was an issue, and the motel drew trouble like a neon light. There were several offers, but none came to fruition because they all had grandiose plans they couldn't back up with cash. Over the years, ghost stories and rumors of multiple murders having been committed on the property circulated and served to keep away the squeamish, even though they weren't true in the case of the last owner. The veracity of the ghostly stuff depends on who you talk to—not all the sightings came from drunks."

"Isabella can hang out as long as she wants; she gives the property a little mystique, and so far, she hasn't been a problem," I pointed out. "If that changes, then I'll have a talk with her—woman to woman."

"And you look so normal," Fab said.

"We both know there's no fun in normal."

"What I'd like to know—" Fab flicked her feet up on the desk.

"Oh no." I finger-wagged. "Boss lady doesn't like feet on the furniture."

"Where was I? Oh yes, the two recent dead chicks—do they have any ties to Isabella's or

Greer's side of the food chain?"

"That's going to take more research."

Chapter Thirty-Three

The information dump had me leaning back in my chair, eyes closed, hallucinating about margaritas lined up, frosty and ready for my consumption.

Fab's phone rang. She picked it up and, with a mumbled, "Hold on," headed out to the deck.

"That better be Didier," I yelled. "Listening in goes two ways."

Xander smirked—he'd been doing a lot of that lately. His phone dinged, code for someone at the gate. He hustled over to the window and whistled. "Nice ride," he said in awe.

I jumped up and joined him, oohing at the classic black-and-silver sports car that rolled through the gates on a flatbed. Perfect in every way, it shared the trailer with a Mercedes. I traded a *what's going on?* look with Xander.

"I gotta find out what's up." He ran downstairs while I watched the oversized vehicle maneuver to the far side of the lot.

It surprised me to see Toady jump from the truck cab and meet up with Xander. After a short conversation, Toady unloaded the sports car, hopped behind the wheel, and drove it into the garage. He came back and unloaded the Mercedes, which I recognized as one of his cars, then moved the hauler off to the side.

"What's going on?" Fab joined me at the window.

"Maybe you can tell me. Getting a new car?"

"Remember that dog-sitting job that wasn't a dog?" That job was supposed to seem funny in time, but it hadn't happened yet. "Toady worked the neighborhood, leaving his card everywhere with a friendly, 'I'll make it happen.' A week ago, a rich woman called, wanting to surprise her husband with a half-million-dollar present." She pointed down to the driveway. "Toady picked it up and needs to keep it out of sight until the big day, then deliver it to the manse in pristine condition. Meaning no dust."

Fab had set her phone on the desk, and I reached for it before she could figure out my intent to grab it and scroll to the last call. She was too quick, though, and knocked it out of my reach.

"You could just ask who called," she said snootily.

"Why? You wouldn't ask me. And you're teaching Creole your devilish tricks." I raised my eyebrow, prompting her to continue, which she ignored. She would make me ask.

Toady and Xander came tromping up the stairs, and Xander flung himself down on the couch.

"Cool car, huh?" Toady bee-lined to the refrigerator and took out cold drinks, handing one to Xander. "Stopped by see my girl up close and personal." He flashed a grin.

"Good timing," Fab said. "I've got a job for you."

I heard a phone ring outside, but it didn't register until I heard voices coming up the steps. Assuming it was Creole and Didier, I was surprised when the door opened and Mila ran in, Brad right behind her.

"Hiiii." Mila did a convoluted handwave, twirled around, and ended with her hands in the air.

I held out my arms, she ran to me, and I pulled her into a hug. "Not to be rude, but how did you get in?" I said to my brother, who grinned down at the two of us.

"The boss gave me the code."

It surprised me when he looked at Xander and not Fab.

Mila wiggled to get down and kissed Fab's offered cheek before she ran to Toady, kissing him. Then she skipped over to Xander, climbing up to sit next to him and peer at the screen of his phone, which was never far away.

"When did those two hook up and become besties?" I asked.

"When he and Liam took Mila to a carnival thing. Rides and all kinds of fun, I heard. At least, they didn't return her all sugared up. She did score a stuffed camel that had sat on a shelf somewhere for a looong time, based on the smell." Brad scrunched up his nose.

"Maybe you should take it to the camel groomers."

Brad half-laughed. "Can you watch Mila until Mother gets here in about half an hour?" He didn't wait for an answer. "You're the best." He kissed my cheek and did the same to Mila, grabbed a cold water from the refrigerator, and with a wave, headed to the door. Once there, he turned and said, "Call Mother for me about the change of plans." He closed the door.

Knowing him, he ran back to his car.

"What the heck just happened?" I stared at the door.

"Too bad Mila's not old enough to question." Fab laughed.

"I forgot to tell you..." Xander started. "Brad called an hour ago—some kind of last-minute meeting. I told him you were on your way. You wouldn't say no, would you?"

"Of course not. My favorite part is that he's having you inform Mother about the change of plans." I laughed.

"Brad meant you. Mrs. Spoon doesn't like me." Xander squirmed.

I shrugged. Poor kid, if he'd grown up with a sister, he'd know how devilish we could be.

After a moment of silent eye contact, Xander caved, standing and holding his hand out to

Mila. "I'm going to need your help. I'll deliver the news and hand you the phone, then you babble until she hangs up." The two of them went into my office space.

"Can we get down to business?" Fab asked in an exasperated tone.

"A lot goes on around here." Toady laughed.

"Call this meeting to order." She banged her hand on the desk. "Gunz called, and he's got a couple of family issues."

"That's a shock. Hurry it up," I yelled to Xander. "Something tells me we're going to need your skills."

Fab swiveled her chair towards Toady. "Gunz has another family member or something, it's hard to sort them all out since there's so many and every one of them in crisis mode. Anyway, this time, it's a husband and wife who run a business out of their house. They get a fair number of packages delivered, and three times now, they've been stolen out of the garage. An open design one under the house. I need you to check it out."

"You want my opinion, for which I'm paid so handsomely?" I asked.

Fab ignored me.

"You want me to question the neighborhood?" Toady asked.

"I've already recommended installing a security system and have it scheduled with my guy, but it will take a few days."

"There's a couple of options here," Toady reasoned. "It's either neighborhood thieves making the rounds, following delivery trucks in hopes of making a quick buck on fenced items or an inside job." Fab waved a piece of paper that Toady leaned forward and grabbed. "I'll get right on it."

Fab folded another sheet in the shape of an airplane and sailed it in Xander's direction.

Mila laughed and clapped. They'd come back and taken seats on the couch, where Mila sat on his shoulders, her chin on his head, staring down at his phone.

"I told Gunz that he'd be expected to meet your fee," Fab assured Toady.

"You've never screwed me." Toady stood. "Overpaid me a couple of times. I'll get back to you."

"Your other option..." I said to Toady. "Gunz's relatives are full of it and making up the story, which wouldn't be far-fetched in his family. Although stealing packages is big right now."

Toady waved and hit the door. "Third time," he said, shaking his head. "You'd think they'd start having them held for pickup, unless they're stupes."

The gate buzzer rang. Xander checked his phone, showing the screen to Mila.

"Gammi." She clapped.

Xander stood. "Mrs. Spoon has another

appointment, so I need to hustle downstairs." He walked Mila over to me, we nose-kissed, and he did the same for Fab, then returned Mila to his shoulders for the ride downstairs.

I crossed the room and returned with waters. "The second job?"

"One of Gunz's nieces, Pam Davis, met the man of her dreams and has run off to parts unknown. He wants her found."

"We're going to interfere with true love?" A bad feeling washed over me, and I hadn't heard the details yet.

"She's seventeen and met her prince online, according to her sister, then waited until she hit the road to tell anyone."

"How do we find her? Gunz give you an address?"

Judging by her glare, the answer was no. "That's where Xander comes in. He puts his snooping skills to work and tracks her down."

"We were just talking about you," I said as Xander walked back in. "Or she was."

"Whatever it is, I didn't do it." He laughed, clearly amusing himself. "Mrs. Spoon said family dinner soon and no excuses will be accepted."

"That number—can you ping it or whatever and get a location on the owner?" Fab asked. "If not, hack into her computer and find out anything you can on the guy she hooked up with." She ran down the case. "You need additional info, call Gunz."

Xander picked up his laptop and went to his desk.

"Let's hope Xander can come up with a lead so you have something to tell Gunz when he starts burning up your phone."

Chapter Thirty-Four

It took Xander two days to get a lead on Pam Davis, during which Gunz burned up Fab's phone. It turned out the girl had hooked up with Albert Johnson Jr. on social media. Details on him were sketchy.

Xander passed the information to Fab, and she showed up at my place and came close to dragging me out of the house. "I want this case over with."

It didn't surprise me that Pam had run off, young love and all, but why not contact her parents and let them know she was okay? She had to know they'd call the police, and if not them, then Gunz, who I was certain every member of the family had on speed dial.

"We can't force her to go home," Fab said as she blew south on the Overseas.

"First, we make sure she's okay. Then we come up with some options, one would be blackmailing Albert. He's twenty-one, according to his profile, and her being seventeen makes this a felony. I'm thinking he'd be willing to boot her out the door to keep from landing in jail."

"Chances are good that this is his parents'

home. The door opens… then what? And not the missing cat."

"I'd suggest handouts, except my box of pamphlets got trashed one of the times the SUV got cleaned out." I shot her the evil eye, letting her know that I knew she was the culprit. Her ignoring me only strengthened my conviction. "I'm tired of our overused ideas; I suggest something new-ish. We pass ourselves off as friends or family of Pam's and say we'd like to speak to her."

"This area is…" Fab hung her head over the steering wheel, having turned onto a side street. "It's remote, and the buildings are rundown."

"Appears it suffered significant damage from one of the recent storms and hasn't recovered."

New construction was popping up, interspersed between rundown buildings with pieces of siding and roof tiles lying in the dirt and a few with red "keep out" posters tacked to the doors. Others showed signs of tenancy, as evidenced by kids' toys, piles of trash, and the occasional car.

My phone rang. I retrieved it from the cup holder and glanced at the screen. "Hi, hon."

"Where are you?" Creole demanded.

"Fab and I are doing a welfare check for one of her clients."

"That's the same vague story that Fab gave Didier, except she sent him a text, which is now banned and you have to speak to one of us." His irritation was audibly ratcheting up.

"We're going to knock, inquire about my missing cat, and leave," I said, trying to placate him with a bit of humor.

"What could go wrong with that ruse?" His voice dripped with sarcasm.

"I'll call you as soon as we leave." I made a kissy noise, hung up, and shoved my phone in my pocket. "We're in trouble. That's been happening a lot these days."

"Thank you for not mentioning Gunz. I didn't tell Didier, as he wants me to dump him as a client. He's 'too high maintenance'—a direct quote."

"Didier's right. But I know you're loyal to Gunz, as you've been friends for an age. If this job looks like it's going to south in any way—which if we're being honest, it has every chance of doing—then we leave and call in reinforcements."

Fab rumbled down the gravel road. The farther she drove, the more evidence there was that rehabilitation of the neighborhood was in progress. The lots were larger, and the houses that were completed didn't sit on top of one another. She parked across the street from a faded blue shotgun-style house that had been red-tagged as unsafe.

"I suggest we get straight to the point." I blew out a sigh, checking out the dump of a house. "The sooner we get back on the road and call the guys, the better. We go with the 'her family's worried' story, which is true, suggest she call Gunz, and hand her a phone."

Fab looked at me for a long moment. "Sounds good to me. If she wants a ride back to town, all the better."

"You could park closer to the house. No need for me to get rocks in my flip-flops."

"I know you can afford a real pair of shoes."

I ignored her and got out, following her across the street and pausing to check out the rest of the block. It was quiet, not a person in sight. The house on one side was vacant, and the other showed signs of being lived in, but no cars were parked in the driveway.

We hiked across the gravel yard and slowed to check out the lone vehicle, a white panel van that once had advertising on the side, which had been removed, leaving holes. We stopped at the rotted-out wood-slatted porch, and Fab gave it a kick before climbing the steps to the door. She knocked loud enough to be heard over the sounds of a game show blaring from the television.

A middle-aged man threw open the door, half-dressed, his shaggy grey hair hanging in his face. "Yeah, what?" he grumbled in an irritated tone. At the same time, he eyed Fab up and down like a yummy morsel he'd like to nibble on.

Fab bristled. "I'd like to speak to your son."

"For the second time, what do you want?"

"Albert?" she asked in a conciliatory tone. "I'm here to check on Pam, whose family is worried about her since she left town so abruptly."

His eyes narrowed to a mean glint. "Never heard of her." He slammed the door with a resounding bang.

"He didn't acknowledge having a son or correct you when you called him Albert," I said. "Maybe this isn't a case of young love but of Pam hooking up with a perv three times her age."

"Get your Glock ready." Fab banged again, rivaling my cop knock—I was so proud—and continued until the door cracked open.

"You hard of hearing?"

"Pam is a teenager, and if you don't want the cops surrounding the place, I suggest you smarten up and let us take her home," Fab said.

They engaged in a glare-off. "Hold your shorts." He banged the door closed again.

The door opened moments later. Albert brandished a handgun and, without hesitation, pulled the trigger. If I hadn't moved to Fab's other side, I'd have been laid out on the rickety porch. I pulled my Glock and shot back, and he dropped his weapon, blood oozing from his shoulder. He kicked the door closed.

Screams came from inside the house.

Fab shot the lock off, and shoved the door open, striking Albert. Having produced another gun from somewhere, he fired.

Fab shot back, and he went down, not moving. When she kicked him, he moaned. "I think he's still alive." She kicked his gun out of reach, then bent down and removed his belt, securing his hands.

The entry was dark, but a little light filtered in through the drapes on the opposite side of the room. The odor of mold and mildew assailed my nostrils. I wanted to pull my shirt up over my face but needed to maintain control of my firearm. I pulled out my phone and called Gunz, who answered on the first ring. He had a connection with the local police that was unparalleled and assured me they were on the way.

"Stay here," Fab ordered me.

"Don't be ridiculous."

"Over here," came a weak voice.

Fab moved into the living room, weapon ready, and scanned the room, then moved past the stained couch and into the dining room. There were three young women lined up against the wall, hands tied to the rungs of overturned chairs. A brunette that matched the photo of Pam Davis was the person who'd spoken. The other two, who appeared to be much younger, were crying. All three were dirty, their hair matted, and pale, with big circles under their swollen eyes.

"Please, help us," Pam begged. "We need to get out of here before his friends come back."

"You're lookout," I informed Fab and proceeded to untie the girls. Not usually my area of expertise, but the knots were simplistic and easily came undone.

The girls stretched, shook out their hands, and huddled together.

"It's best if you stay right where you are," Fab told the girls. "This is a crime scene and needs to be preserved. That way, there will be no doubt about the evidence the cops need to put the pig away." She made a check of the remaining rooms.

"I don't want to go to jail." Pam started sobbing.

"That's not going to happen," I reassured her.

Pam calmed enough to say, "Albert was so sweet online. And so cute. But when I finally met him, he laughed when he told me he never loved me and that I was stupid to even think that." She sniffled.

Another girl spoke up: "He planned to ship us to a ranch in New Mexico, and then who knows from there."

Fab had her eye on Albert, who had come to and was trying to crawl away. His attempt failed miserably.

I moved to the front door, keeping one eye on the road. "Shall we flip to see which of us gets to shoot him again?"

"You know..." Fab half-laughed. "...it's too bad he's unarmed. If he can get out the door with his hands tied, let him crawl down the street, and the cops can run him over."

Speaking of… police cars blew up the street and squealed to a stop in front of the house.

I holstered my gun and exited the house with my hands in the air. Fab did the same.

Two more cars rolled up, along with an ambulance. Fab and I were separated and questioned while two of the cops went inside to investigate, guns drawn.

"Before I forget, the girls claim Albert's friends will be coming back." I admitted to shooting the man in self-defense and relayed my version of events. "I swear the bullet blew right through the side of my friend's hair." At the request of the cop interrogating me, I lifted my top, took out my gun, and set it on the ground.

The cop asked a few more questions, and I was forthcoming about how we got involved. He walked me over to the SUV, where I produced my ID and carry permit.

Another officer walked up. "You doing okay?" I nodded. "Gunz wanted me to make sure you two were unharmed."

"I know that you can't answer any questions, but Albert Johnson is a really bad guy, based on the condition of the girls, and they said that he was about to ship them out of town. They also told us that he wasn't in it alone."

"Unfortunately, trafficking is big business. I'm hoping that knowing how much trouble he's in will make him want to spill his guts for a lesser sentence."

"Doesn't it make you sick to make deals with the devil's disciple?"

"It does." The officer gave a sad smile. "Unless we get the head honchos, get to the bottom of what's going on here, and put them out of business." He went to meet the two additional ambulances that rolled up. Medics jumped out and, after a short conversation, grabbed their bags and went into the house.

I had mixed feelings about the fact that the man was still breathing, especially if he'd sexually assaulted the girls inside… or any others, for that matter. I leaned against the door of the SUV and hung out on the roadside.

Fab joined me. "We stumbled into something big," she confided. "The cop interrogating me told me that Albert's part of a sex trafficking ring they were in the middle of investigating. We got here just in time. I heard one of the girls tell the cop that the road trip was planned for tomorrow."

"One day. We'd have missed them and possibly never found them." I shuddered. "What happens to the girls?"

"They're going to the hospital to be checked out. Then they'll be released to their parents."

"They're all underage?" I shouldn't have been surprised, because they looked it.

"So, I assumed when I heard talk about calling

their parents."

"Old Albert's a real piece of filth," I ground out. "I never wish people dead, but in his case... except they need him for information."

"He'll survive being shot. But how long he stays alive remains to be seen. Sex criminals are at the bottom of the prison hierarchy. He'll also be on Gunz's s-list."

"Tell Gunz to hold off until they've wrung every last detail out of him." After that, who cared? Albert wouldn't be missed.

"We've got another problem."

I groaned, knowing that she meant our husbands. There was no way to pretty up an exchange of bullets.

"I've got a plan for a change. We hit the liquor store and see if they've gotten in any new Euro beers. That always makes them happy. Then we pick up takeout, head home, and get them liquored up before giving them a sanitized version of events."

Fab's sneaky smile should have had me second-guessing her plan, but what the heck? "I'm in."

Chapter Thirty-Five

To say the guys weren't happy to find out about the events of the day was putting it mildly, and they'd shut down the plan to beer them up before prettying up the news. They'd broken up the dinner party before it got started, and Didier dragged Fab home. The only thing that saved me from a long lecture about personal safety was that Creole's phone rang, and I fell asleep while he fielded another problem.

A new round of annoyance sparked when the phone rang just before dawn. Who called that early? Trouble.

Creole hung up after getting news from Cootie about a blaze at the motel and that the fire trucks had arrived and were in the process of stamping it out.

At such an early hour, it was hard to function without coffee, but I didn't dare complain after Creole said, "You can stay here, and I'll call you later. To Cootie's trained eye—" He snorted. "—that's his description, not mine—the damage is minimal."

"Fat chance." I pulled on a variation of the

same outfit as his—sweatpants and a t-shirt—and slid my feet into tennis shoes. When we got in the SUV, I said, "Anytime you want to stop being mad over yesterday's shootout is fine with me."

Tarpon wasn't a town that woke up at the crack, so the streets were empty. One other car poked down the road that Creole blew around.

"I'm frustrated that a sleepy beach town has a scumhole like Albert Johnson in its midst—running around, preying on young girls. I talked to an old detective friend last night, and he was happy to hear about the arrest." He unleashed a long sigh, brushing his dark hair back in frustration. "Happy ending for law enforcement, but not at the cost of you or Fab paying the ultimate price. Where does Fab find her clients? They're all lunatics."

Good question. "She's maintained connections from her old life as a member of Miami nightlife. That was back before I met her. As for Gunz, they've been friends a lot longer. *Fixing* his family problems is a new gig."

"He's a criminal."

"Reformed. He should get credit for turning his back on his past and becoming a legit businessman. That counts. One thing I know for certain—he wouldn't knowingly put Fab in danger, unlike some of her other clients, who couldn't give a flip what happens to her." I sighed at how far she'd been hung out to dry by a few of them. "Gunz was genuinely worried about his niece, figuring she'd run off with another teenager, not an old perv. If he'd had any inkling what was really up, he'd have done the job himself and killed the man."

"I want to meet Gunz."

"I'll send him over to the Boardwalk, and you two can mark your territory."

"I doubt we'll be peeing on one another." Creole's lips quirked up at one corner, just enough for me to see that he'd calmed down... somewhat. He pulled around the back of the motel, where both fire trucks were parked diagonally, and managed to squeeze out a parking space next to the dumpster.

We got out and split up. He went to talk to the firefighters, who were loading equipment back on their truck, and I went into the office. I headed straight to the coffee machine, chose a flavored brew, and stuck it in the machine. I only had to have a minute's worth of patience before the warm concoction appeared in the paper cup below. I picked it up and turned toward the front desk.

"Take a seat, have a sip or two." Cootie smiled big for someone who'd rolled out of bed and looked it, what little hair he had sticking on end. "If you were Rude, I'd need to give you time to consume the whole cup."

I turned and pointed to the cat stretched out from one end of the coffee table to the other. "I see Trouble's back. Not that I'm not sympathetic, but someone going to jail, meaning Rude, isn't a good solution."

"All taken care of." Cootie dusted his hands together. "Rude got a happy ending for both her and the cat. I can't tell you how, since it's her story. If I do, she'll kill me."

I'd bet on more weirdness. "Back to the fire. What happened? I'll take the short version."

"Arson. According to the security feed, a woman snuck up to Isabella's room, bottle in hand, a rag hanging out of the end, lit it, and pitched it through the window. Luckily, the room was empty at the time."

"Good thing." I drained my coffee. A better ending would've been for the ghost to scare the wits out of her before she tossed the bottle.

"It's lucky that I never enforce the pool hours." At my raised brow, Cootie added, "Unless someone's making an ass of themselves; then I'd be right out there. Anyway… there were two couples in the jacuzzi at the time. They heard the glass shattering, saw the flames lick the curtains, and started hollering. One came running to the office, and another got hot on the phone to 911."

"So, a woman sauntered up and started a fire?" I asked in disbelief. "What if someone had been in the room?"

Rude poked her head up from behind the front desk. I hadn't seen her sitting there. "It was a woman, all right." She went back to staring at her computer screen.

"The curtains were open, so she knew no one was in the room at the time. Not in bed, anyway. They could've been in the bathroom," Cootie added.

I walked around the counter and peered over Rude's shoulder as she reran the security footage. Sure enough, a person of slight build, dressed in sweats and a hoodie with strands of long hair sticking out the side, walked up with confidence, sent the bottle flying, and calmly walked away.

The woman's only mistake was she turned, and the camera picked up a shot of her face. I stared at the freeze-frame, searching my brain for any glimmer of recognition, any feeling that I'd seen her somewhere before. "Has there been anyone—man or woman—lurking around?"

They both shook their heads.

"Forward me a copy of the image." I tapped the screen. "I'll have Xander come over and go over all the security tapes. Maybe he'll find another sighting."

"There was that one young woman a week or so ago." Rude swiveled in her chair. "She specially asked to rent the haunted room, and when Cootie told her it was closed for remodeling—that's the excuse we're using right now when someone asks for that room—she threw a hissy fit."

"Until someone gets locked up, the room's not

available," Cootie said. "The murderer can dump the next body at another motel; there's plenty around."

"If the murderer is specifically attracted to this motel, then a body will turn up in another room. Wonder why this particular place?" I'd mulled over the whys and come up with nothing. Maybe it was someone with a grudge against one of us owners. To my knowledge, though, none of us had done anything to inspire that kind of enmity.

"I'm thinking we need a security guard." Cootie walked to the door and hung his head out, then came back inside and grabbed another coffee. "Someone to patrol the grounds at night until this person is caught."

"Got anyone in mind?" I asked. "Don't be offering to work round the clock. You're needed here in the office, not traipsing around in the middle of the night. I'll ask Creole; he'll probably know someone."

"Talking about me?" Creole came in the door and, like me, headed to the coffee pot. He made himself a cup, then came over and sat next to me.

"Since it's your idea, you pitch it," I said to Cootie. And he did.

Rude checked her watch, then jumped up, crossed the lobby, and began setting up for the continental breakfast. "Donut and danish delivery will be here in fifteen minutes."

"Night security is a good idea," Creole said. "The fire has officially been classified as arson.

Thanks to the fire department's fast response, the damage was contained to the one room."

"That's good to hear." I turned to Rude. "Cootie says you wrangled a resolution to freeloader cat."

"Furrball's mine now." Rude beamed.

"Short's not going to go for that." I groaned, picturing a knock-down fight. "He's desperate to hang onto the cat."

"Short agreed. I have it in writing from a lawyer, and it's all wrapped up legal-like."

Creole shook his head, not quite believing her. "Why don't you start at the beginning?"

"Turns out Furrball is a trust fund cat. Even has his own lawyer. When I found out it was Tank, I went to him and appealed to his inner animal lover, telling him the cat would be better off with me and I wouldn't take a dime. I knew my plan would only work if Short wasn't cut off. I detailed instances of mutual hate between the cat and the fat odious man and said that surely the dead owner would have wanted what was best for her beloved feline."

"Short agreed?" I asked.

"He didn't have much of a choice," Cootie grunted.

"Tank loathes Short and the monthly visits he's obligated to make. He drew up a new agreement and told him to sign it or else. Gives me ownership, and Short keeps the income from the estate as long as he never bothers me or sets foot on this property again." Rude beamed.

Creole laughed. "One less problem."

Chapter Thirty-Six

Deciding we were done, Creole grabbed my hand and headed out the door, slowing with an admonition to Cootie: "Call if anything out of the ordinary happens."

"That could mean anything," I grumbled as I slid into the passenger seat. Almost immediately, my phone started ringing. Doodad's face popped up on the screen, and I debated whether to answer, waiting until it was nearly ready to go to voicemail to pick up.

"Hi." He hemmed and hawed and stumbled until I was ready to scream, then finally blurted, "Someone tried to break into the bar, and I'm not sure what you want me to do."

"Call the cops." Duh!

Creole, who'd slid behind the wheel in time to hear what I said, leaned over and attempted to eavesdrop, accidentally bumping his head against mine. I giggled and blew him a kiss, then pulled away and ignored his gesture to put the call on speaker, which earned me a growl. I laughed again.

"Are you paying any attention?" Doodad demanded.

"I am now," I said sweetly. "The reason you called me and not the cops?"

"In a word—Kevin. I know there's more than one cop on the force, but somehow, he's always drawing the short straw—his own description—and he doesn't stop his bellyaching even when I remind him about the free soda," Doodad grumped. "We voted, and it was unanimous—no one wants to deal with him today."

"I'm not going to go into all the ways this call is irritating. You're in luck—I have another cop I can corral to investigate. I'll need to incentivize him, but I'm sure I can get him to agree without too much complaining. See you soon." I tossed the phone in the cupholder and grabbed the front of Creole's shirt, pulling him in for a kiss. "Hey, babes?"

"What?" Creole squinted at me.

I knew that he knew exactly what I wanted, but he was going to make ask. "You think I'd dance you?" At his raised eyebrow, I almost laughed. "There was an attempted break-in at Jake's. As you probably heard, no one wants to call the law. You'd think my employees had outstanding warrants, but I checked before hiring and they don't."

"I'm in."

"That was easy." I knew he'd say yes, just not so quickly.

"Keep in mind that the incentives better be good. Or next time, I'll bail with a lame excuse."

I turned away to hide my laughter, but lost the fight.

"Done now? I hope you have aspirin, because I need two," Creole grouched. "You get any details out of your *manager?*"

"It's going to be a surprise. Won't that be fun?" I handed him the aspirin and kept the bottle out.

It was a short drive from the motel to Jake's. Creole slowed to allow a forklift that cut in front of him to turn into the parking lot of the bar. Both of us stared, not sure what the operator was doing, when he headed straight for the front door, not veering off course and not hitting the brakes, and rammed it. Then, the big piece of machinery backed up, and with a squeal, the driver threw it into gear, taking another hit.

"What the hell?" Creole hit the brakes and stopped in the middle of the driveway before parking off to the side. He cut the engine and jumped out. I was right behind him and skidded to a stop when Creole jumped on the ledge next to the operator.

The man yelled at Creole and followed it up with a fist to the face. Creole ducked and, at the same time, managed to jerk the key from the ignition. The driver roared something unintelligible and pulled a gun, the shot going through the metal roof. Creole knocked it out of his hand, and it skittered to the ground, the driver attempting to dive after it. Creole gave him some help, planting his foot on the man's backside and sending him flying. He landed face first on the asphalt.

I ran over and kicked the gun from his grasp. He rose up with a roar and attempted to launch himself at me, but I pulled my Glock and pointed it at him, taking several steps back. He registered no fear of getting shot—his only mission was getting his gun back.

Creole leapt down from the forklift, jerked the man off the ground, and landed a solid punch. He collapsed to the ground and didn't move.

Two cop cars blew into the parking lot, tires squealing, and came to an abrupt stop. Kevin jumped out of the first car, a cop I'd never seen before out of the second. Must be a new guy. I'd welcome him to the neighborhood later. They ran over to Creole, and it took both cops to subdue the man, who'd come around and was attempting to shake them off and avoid getting cuffed.

"Dude's on drugs." Creole brushed his hair back from his face. "Ranted that you owe him money? Not you specifically, but Jake's."

"I've never seen that man before. And you know that all the bills are paid on time. Besides, Cook has a hard rule that he never does business with any supplier whose owner or driver has substance abuse problems."

Kevin and the second officer dragged the man across the parking lot and shoved him into the back of a cop car. He'd stopped struggling about halfway there but continued to spew an expletive-laced rant. The cops stood by the car, talking, for several minutes.

Kevin broke away, waving to the other cop as he drove out, and walked over to where Creole and I still stood in the parking lot. "What's your side of the story?" he asked Creole.

Creole ran down the facts.

"What do you know?" Kevin asked me.

"Same thing he does." I gave him my side of the story, which was pretty much the same.

"It's about your dead friend Werner…"

Not him again. "I never met him," I practically spit, calming when I noticed the amusement in Kevin's eyes.

"Got it." Kevin winked. "Roger—the fellow on his way to jail—loaned money to Werner that he borrowed from a loan shark. Or as he put it, 'a friend that wants his money now or else.'"

"Old Roger doesn't keep up on the news?" Creole asked. "If he did, he'd know that Werner blew himself up and he's not getting paid back."

"Since Werner was partners with Madison here, he figured to collect from you." Kevin eyed me.

"Werner circulated that story?" I flinched at how many more lowlifes might show up.

"Apparently, Roger called you several times, and when you continued to dodge his calls, he decided on a face-to-face, figuring that was the way to get your attention."

"Doodad probably took a message and threw it in the trash. He's good at fielding my calls."

Kevin shook his head.

"Does this have anything to do with last night's break-in?" Creole asked.

"Yep." Kevin grinned. "Roger spotted a couple of cars around back. Thinking it was a good time to collect, he blew his cork when no one would open the door and got aggravated when he couldn't force it open. He was vague on how he came to the conclusion that stealing a forklift would be a good idea or how he knew that there was one sitting on a jobsite down the street." Kevin surveyed the damage. "Claims he didn't mean to mangle the door."

Yeah, right. "What did he expect would happen when he hit the door head-on?" I sighed. "Too busy thinking about ways to spend the money he hadn't collected. You know if he hadn't been caught here, he'd have taken the forklift for a joyride before dumping it beside the road."

Kevin snorted. "Speaking of… as I pulled into the parking lot, a call came over the radio about the stolen forklift. I laughed, happy not to be the one to respond to that. Oh look." He pointed. "I'm thinking a 'thank you' is in order, now that I have to deal with getting it towed to impound."

"One more case solved." Creole half-laughed. "When Roger comes down from whatever he's on, let me know if he mentions any of Werner's other friends."

Kelpie, who'd been peeking around the corner, made her presence known, strutting out in a ruffled denim skirt that barely covered her butt cheeks, a gingham print crop top, and worn cowboy boots, yelling, "When are you going to get that thing moved? It's a business-killer."

Kevin stared, a stupid smile on his face. He was a man who loved an overabundant cleavage, and Kelpie's was on display.

Creole turned a raised eyebrow on me.

"I'm thinking it's National Cowgirl Day. You know it's important to celebrate these occasions," I managed to say with a straight face, ignoring his telegraphing that I'd lost my mind. Later, I'd show him proof and subtract an indulgence.

Kelpie skidded to a stop, hands on her hips, and worked Kevin's rapt attention. "Would you like a cold drink, officer?" she cooed.

I didn't hear his response because I gagged, which earned me glares.

"Is the door useable, or are we going to have to route people through the kitchen?" Kelpie asked.

"You could close down," Kevin said sarcastically.

"When pigs fly." Kelpie accentuated that with 'oink, oink.' "Tips will be hot once they hear how the guy was impaled and hung there, dripping guts."

I stepped next to Creole and banged my head on his shoulder. "If I hear one word of that story, I will hunt you down."

Creole shook his finger at Kelpie, who responded with a big smile and shook her chest.

I peeked around him in time to see that and leveled a glare at her. "Don't think I won't maim you if you do something untoward."

"Yeah, got it—you're not a sharer."

"Just another day in crazyland. I knew that when I got the call." Kevin strode over to his car.

Creole went to inspect the front door.

"What do you know about this current mess?" I demanded of Kelpie.

"Nothing. But the second I find out *anything,* I'll be hot on the phone."

Creole rejoined us. "You're going to need to reroute traffic until I can get someone over to fix the door and frame."

"Who do we know with low motivation—two someones—that we can get to sit out here and direct foot traffic to the kitchen entrance?" I asked Kelpie as we walked inside, leaving Creole to answer his phone, which had started ringing. "The job requirements are to look alert and answer coherently when someone wants to know what the heck is going on. If you've got a live one, don't forget to mention the good pay, free meal, and under no circumstances liquoring it up on the job."

"I got this handled," Kelpie assured me,

performing a dance in the kitchen to the delight of the line cook, who was ogling her.

Chapter Thirty-Seven

It was rare that Creole took the day off, and thus far, we'd spent it curled up on the couch, both of us working on our laptops, Jazz and Snow asleep on the other end. His phone rang, interrupting the peace, and I groaned when he got up and took the call out on the deck.

It was several minutes before he came back inside, bending over to kiss my cheek. "Call your friend and tell her to get down here. I've got some news she's going to want to hear."

I fisted his shirt and kissed him again. "Fab doesn't like to be ordered about."

"I know." He smirked and went into the kitchen.

I leaned over and scooped up my phone. "A hint would be helpful."

"Tell her not to dawdle."

I called, got no answer, and called again. That was the signal it was important, which she ignored. "Sorry babe, no answer." I flashed a pouty face. "No worries, I can be a rapt audience."

He reached over, picked his phone up off the counter, and made a call. "Impromptu meeting,

ASAP. Since your wife is too busy to answer her phone, you can leave her at home and give her the details later." After a pause, he laughed. "You're going to want to hear this." He hung up, then reached into the cabinet, pulled out an enamelware bucket, and filled it with ice. Stocking it with beer and water, he carried it out to the patio.

I followed him outside and claimed a chaise, curling my feet underneath me. "Do I get a preview?"

"Remember the sex trafficker? He escaped from custody."

I sucked in a breath, ran back in the house, and grabbed my laptop off the coffee table. Sitting back on the couch, I typed in his name. The article said he'd escaped while being transported to court. He shot one of the corrections officers, who thankfully was in stable condition at a local hospital. "So, that phone call…" I called out and went back outside. "Shouldn't someone in an official capacity have given us a heads up?"

"They would've gotten around to it. Eventually. Thank goodness I still have friends on the force."

"It's really creepy that Albert's on the loose." I shuddered.

Creole pulled me down on a chaise, wrapped his arms around me, and hugged me hard. "So, you won't be complaining when I handcuff you to my wrist?"

"For about five minutes. Then the novelty will wear off."

A sudden banging noise made me jump. In order to be that loud kicking the door down, Fab must have worn tennis shoes with the intention of being obnoxious. "Good thing we don't have a glass door."

Creole stood and glared into the house, but didn't make a move toward the offending noise.

"Someone should answer the door." I pointed and leaned back against the chaise, making it clear it wouldn't be me.

"The door's unlocked. Which she'll figure out when she inserts her lockpick."

"She's been admonished to curtail those activities under penalty of no sex."

Creole laughed.

Fab kicked again.

I swore it was louder. "Heads up: I'm about to be a killjoy." I yelled at the top of my lungs, "It's unlocked."

"You're mean," Creole said as the door burst open.

"We're here," Fab shouted as she stepped into the kitchen. "What, too stressful for you to open the door?" She eyed Creole, who stood inside the patio door.

Didier hooked his arm around her, hauling her against his chest, and they joined us on the deck. "Beer. My favorite." He traded smirks with

Creole; it was good for his health that Fab couldn't see that.

I waved Fab to a chaise next to me. She sat down, and I pushed my laptop in front of her and tapped the screen.

Creole filled Didier in.

The cats, who'd moved to the bed, caught sight of Didier, jumped down, and came running, weaving their bodies around his legs. He stepped over them, and they meowed, following him into the kitchen. He found canned food in the refrigerator, which he gave them, and came back outside.

The guys claimed chairs across from us.

"This Albert Johnson character is on the loose, and thus far, there've been no sightings," Creole said. "Investigators believe he had a ride waiting, which means he had someone helping him. He could be anywhere, but most likely, he's still local. You wouldn't think he'd come back to this area, but criminals aren't the smartest."

"I'm thinking you need to give Gunz a heads up," I told Fab.

Didier growled at the mention of the man's name, much like Creole.

"I suggest the three of you meet at the Boardwalk and introduce yourselves," I said sweetly. "Won't that be fun?"

From the looks that Creole and Didier shot me, the answer was no.

"I've met the man," Didier huffed.

"The wormy version," I reminded him. "He's shined up and is a hard-working entrepreneur now."

"You never know, you could all be best buds." Fab winked at Didier, who shook his head, not enjoying our humor at their expense.

"I called this meeting to advise you two to keep your eyes peeled," Creole said to Fab and me.

"You think Johnson will be looking for them?" Didier asked.

"Not specifically, but who knows what he'd do if he ran into either of them. I'm certain he hasn't forgotten what they look like—you don't tend to forget someone that shot you." He grinned at Fab and me. "My contact told me that the girls who were held in the house have all gone to live with out-of-state relatives, with the hope that they can resume normal lives with no one the wiser about what they've been through."

"Since Johnson is looking at possibly never getting out of prison, you'd think he'd want to keep a low profile, lessen his chances of getting picked up," I said. "Let's hope he's left town."

"There's always the chance that he's cocky enough to resume his old life and start enticing other girls," Fab said.

I hope not. I'd like to see his network put out of business and quickly.

"Speaking of low profiles..." Creole shared his serious look between Fab and me. "You two should also adopt one."

"Is that your way of saying you don't want us driving the streets, hoping for a sighting?" Fab smirked at Creole. "I'm certain that you have even more good advice for us."

Creole and Fab engaged in a staredown.

"Be aware of your surroundings," Creole ground out. "Double check before you get out of the car. Things you're probably already doing, but a reminder doesn't hurt."

"Is this portion of the meeting over?" All eyes turned to me. "Have you two been updated on the motel fire?"

"Rude called," Fab said. "She's not as scattered on the phone as I thought she'd be. She ran down the facts, then hung up, which I appreciated."

"I thought she was delightful," Didier said, ignoring Fab's snort. "She also called and updated me."

"Another one you've scared," I said to Fab. "If she quits, I vote that you work her shifts until we find a replacement."

Fab ignored me. "Xander forwarded me the isolated frames from the security feed. Our fire bomber is definitely a woman—bleach blond, slight frame, baggy clothes, and ugly, oversized trench coat. She scoped out the property ahead of time. At first, I thought maybe she was homeless, then decided it was probably a disguise."

"Great week—a sex trafficker and an arsonist

on the loose," I said.

Creole and Didier engaged in some kind of secret code, which Fab missed because she had her back turned. If she knew she'd missed something, she'd never do that again.

Chapter Thirty-Eight

Two days later, Fab and I were returning home from a meeting at the office after stopping for lunch at a little hovel that served sandwiches on homemade bread. It was a peaceful ride until Fab hit the gas and swerved around another car, nearly sideswiping it. The driver blared his horn. Fab waved, which I knew he couldn't see through the tinted windows.

"That's Johnson," she said excitedly.

"What are you talking about?" I flipped down the visor, expecting to see the man walking along the side of the road.

"He just blew past us in that small sedan." Fab gripped the wheel, staring intently at the highway. We jolted forward as she was forced to hit the brakes when the light turned red to avoid hitting the car in front of us. She banged the wheel when the sedan squealed through the red light, accompanied by the screeching brakes of cross-traffic, who'd just gotten the green.

"Are you sure?" I wished I knew how she could both drive and scope out the occupants of other cars.

"Johnson was on the passenger side and rolled down the window to flick his cigarette out. That's when I saw him." She tapped her finger impatiently on the steering wheel. The uncooperative traffic light was slow to turn green, and she had a car in front of her that she couldn't push out of the way.

At last, the light changed, and the chase was back on. She lurched around the car in front and barreled down the highway.

"How far ahead do you think they are?"

"Two blocks. They've caught just as many lights as we have, so they haven't been able to blow down the road and leave us sitting here."

"We should call the police." When Fab was slow to respond, I said, "I'm not happy to be dragged into another dangerous situation."

Fab finally said, "Just a little farther and we will. We need to tell them something more than that Johnson is in a red Ford and headed south. There's a miniscule chance that I'm wrong."

A pedestrian ran in front of the car beside us, and the driver hit his brakes, horn blaring. The jaywalker, who'd just escaped being smooshed on the asphalt, paused in the middle of the road, then sprinted to the curb, waving his middle finger. The driver honked again, and the finger-flashing duel was on.

Once again, we were brought to a complete stop, which nearly drove me out of my skin because I knew Fab wouldn't give up.

"Make the call," Fab said in a resigned tone. "We're going to lose him."

As I slid my phone out of my pocket, there was an intense explosion ahead, the car we were following going up in a fireball in the middle of the street. The shockwave was so loud that it literally shook the SUV. Fab hit the brakes and came to a screeching stop, cars behind us doing the same. The fiery cloud boiled upward and turned inward on itself until it evaporated in orange plumes of smoke. There was an eerie moment of what seemed like absolute silence before people jumped from their cars and either ran toward the explosion or away from it.

As usual, Fab's shock wore off faster, and she opened her door with the intention of getting a closer look, inspecting the chaos herself. I grabbed the back of her shirt. "You're staying here."

"I just—"

"No! For once, we're going to stay safe and let the cops handle it. You can get the grisly details later from Creole or one of your connections. Better yet, call Gunz. He'll have them, and if not, he'll get them pronto."

"If I'd had you call sooner—"

"There was no way to prevent whatever that was. If the cops had been in pursuit…" I shuddered. "At least, there are no dead officers."

"I wonder if the explosion was meant for just the driver or if someone knew the two of them would be together. There will be barely enough left to identify them."

"One of us needs to update the guys. I vote for you." I was surprised when she didn't insist that I do it. "Creole can inform his law enforcement friend. I'm assuming the hunt for this man is intense since he shot a cop, and now they can call off the search and close the case. Though, they'll probably wait until the coroner's report comes back."

Fab hung her head out the window, waving to another driver as she maneuvered out of the standstill traffic. She got turned around and headed home before law enforcement showed up and we ended up sitting on the highway all afternoon. Once she hit an open stretch, she called Didier. "It's on speaker," she informed him after finding out that he and Creole were together, then gave the two men a more thorough rundown of events than I would've been able to give."Good riddance," Creole said. "I'd guess that those higher on the ladder than Johnson were worried he'd name names and share incriminating information. I'll let my friend know." He asked a few more questions and ended with, "I appreciate your calling."

"I'm surprised you didn't ask him to keep you updated," I said after he hung up.

"Taking your suggestion and calling Gunz," Fab said. "He's got cop connections and will get all the good dirt."

"He sure does. When he's called 911 for us on cases of his, the cops who've shown up have all been upstanding members of the force and not shifty pretend cops."

We were almost back to the Welcome sign when the car in front of us slowed while someone hung out the passenger window and hurled a briefcase to the side of the road, then sped off.

I twisted in my seat. "What do you think?" I wasn't going to have to wait long for an answer, as Fab got over and hung a u-turn. "It's probably trash, and even if it's not, we don't need to stick our nose into everything."

Another u-turn later, she pulled up to the side of the road and slowed until she found the case, which had surprisingly held together.

"I'll check it out; you sit here." Fab patted my hand.

I shook it off. "You know the saying about curiosity killing the poor cat? It could as easily be a human."

"What else do we have to do?" Fab jumped out and rounded the front of the SUV.

I'd have to run that excuse by Creole and see where it got me. I rolled down the window and hung my head out. "In light of recent events, I suggest you be careful picking it up." I made a kaboom noise.

Fab walked around it, gave it a kick, then bent down to open it, tugging her sleeves over her hands to avoid leaving fingerprints. Locked.

Not for long.

She took out her lockpick, set the square case on end, and flipped the lid open in record time. After a quick look, she closed it back up, hiked into the weeds, and tucked it up on the low-hanging branch of a tree.

"What? You're leaving it behind? That's not like you," I exclaimed when she slid back behind the wheel.

"This is a case for the cops." Fab answered my shocked look with, "You heard right." She took off like a rocket and turned down a side street toward the office.

"That's shocking." My words dripped with sarcasm. "The suspense is killing me."

"It was crammed full with bundle after bundle of hundred-dollar bills."

I whistled. Sort of. It needed work. "Why throw it out the window? Some stupe's idea of a drop-off? If that's the case, then someone is going to be showing up to fetch it and not be happy."

Fab took an alley shortcut. It surprised me she didn't cut across the dirt lot; it would've been faster. One shouldn't waste that extra minute.

Chapter Thirty-Nine

We trooped up the stairs, where our doorman, Xander, had it open and flourished his arm as we walked in. I faux-yawned, and he took the hint, letting me have the couch and going into our office. He grabbed my bag and tossed it on the desk, and I stretched out and closed my eyes.

Fab sat at her desk and got hot on the phone. In this case, eavesdropping would only have worked if I were fluent in French. The few words I knew were limited, and that was a kind assessment. So much for that beginner's class I was briefly enrolled in. The tone of the conversation was spirited, which was a word she'd used once when insisting that she and her sexy husband didn't fight. She'd smirked, and I knew she was full of herself.

I didn't realize I'd fallen asleep until I heard the undisguised sound of footsteps and voices coming up the stairs. "I assume you know who's about to burst through the door," I said to Fab, "and it's not an intruder."

The door flew open before she could answer. Creole and Didier, both in work jeans and t-shirts, entered, laden down with shopping bags from one of our favorite restaurants, and set them on the kitchen table.

I licked my lips and sat up. Creole crossed to me and leaned down for a kiss, pulling me to my feet.

Didier unloaded several boxes that contained a variety of seafood favorites while Fab got out plates and silverware. I didn't bother with taking a drink order, instead choosing an assortment, shoving it in a bucket, and setting it in the middle of the table.

Creole went into my office and came out with Xander in tow. I was happy that Fab hadn't forgotten about him.

"I've got a business proposition for you," Didier said to Xander.

I sighed and grabbed a skewer of shrimp. "This better not be about permanent employment elsewhere."

"When we have commercial space open, I'm thinking it would save a lot of time to have potential clients checked out before we sit down to discuss contract details. We just ran off a man who had a criminal record as a con artist. If one of the other tenants hadn't recognized him, who knows how badly we would've been ripped off. One of his so-called deals ended up in court, and it took two years to undo his machinations."

"Sounds good to me." Xander nodded excitedly.

While we ate, talk drifted to how the project

was going. Every bit of food disappeared in record time.

I heard a phone ringing in the distance. Recognizing the ringtone, I looked around, realized it was coming from my office, and got up and crossed the room. As I reached for it, the logo on an envelope lying on Xander's side of the desk caught my eye, and I momentarily forgot about why I'd gone in there. Okay, none of my business, but when did that stop me? I picked it up, checked out the return label and saw that it was addressed to Xander, and flipped it over. Unopened. That was about to change. I went back to the table, holding it behind my back.

Instead of sitting, I stood at the end of the table next to Xander and waved the envelope in the air. "Can you believe it? It hasn't been opened."

All eyes turned to me.

"Yeah… well…" Xander stammered. "It might be bad news."

I slipped into my seat and handed it to him. "Bad news is you'll be dead tomorrow or the world is ending. Short of that, we can make things happen. Besides, they should be freaking honored to have you."

"You're like a—"

"If you say mother, I'm going to drag your ass out of that chair and dump you on the floor."

Fab made a clucking noise.

I turned to her in a huff. "You'd think you

never used any questionable language, and we both know that you do."

Fab actually blushed. Score one for me.

I flicked my finger at the envelope, which Xander had dropped as if it were contagious.

"Madison," Creole whispered in my ear.

Xander ripped open the envelope and pulled out one sheet of letterhead, reading it aloud. "'I am delighted to inform you that the Committee on Admissions has admitted you…'"

Everyone clapped, and Fab and I whooped.

"I knew it." I plucked it from his fingers. "'Please accept my personal congratulations for your outstanding achievements,'" I read. "I knew they weren't stupid."

Xander's eyes filled with tears. "Crum had these big ideas of me finishing my degree in California, then one day decided that maybe I should be closer so he could meddle in my life if necessary, and he's made it happen."

"Just when you think the man doesn't have a redeeming quality. Crum scored on this one." I clapped, and everyone joined me.

Xander blushed.

"The old weirdo comes through," Fab said.

"Happy for you," Creole said.

"Agreed." Didier fist-bumped Xander.

The guys stood and cleared the table while I refilled the bucket. We stayed seated around the table.

"There is a little minor something that came

up earlier," Fab attempted to slide in, possibly thinking that shady news would go over easier on a full stomach. Since all eyes shot to her and stayed glued to her, if that was her plan, it didn't work.

Xander tried to hide his grin and failed. He loved the drama, but he preferred it second-hand, after having a ringside seat with a gun stuck in his face. I sat there in total support, a smirk plastered on my face as Fab relayed the details of the discarded briefcase in a matter-of-fact fashion.

"I just had to go back..." was Fab's response to both men growling. "Check it out."

Creole and Didier rolled their eyes.

Xander's phone rang once. He picked it up and looked at the screen, then cleared his throat. "Sorry to interrupt."

"Go ahead," Fab said, happy not to be the center of attention, even if only for a moment.

"There's one... no... make that two guys climbing over the fence."

Creole jumped to his feet and ran over to the window. "Well, hell," he grumbled. "They're armed."

Fab shot back to her desk, unlocked the bottom drawer, and handed guns to Creole and Didier.

"I've got the door." Creole raced across the room, slowing to exchange a couple of words with Didier.

I jumped to my feet and pointed at Xander. "I apologize for once again—"

"Don't worry about me," Xander cut me off. "I'm taking cover." He disappeared into our office.

Fab motioned me to join her behind her desk. If the two got past Creole and Didier, we'd have a clear shot.

The door opened, and two scruffy thirty-somethings in worn, baggy jeans stepped inside, guns drawn. "Left the door unlocked," one of them laughed.

In seconds, Creole and Didier had the two cornered and relieved of their weapons. Then, Creole poked the muzzle of his gun in the middle of their backs, encouraging them to move forward. One leapt around and took a swing at him. He deflected the punch and sent the man tumbling to the ground. He didn't attempt to get up and instead glared, rubbing his face.

Creole hauled him to his feet and frisked him before shoving him into a chair. The other man backed up against the wall, and Didier frisked him, then ordered, "Sit."

Both men glared, but their expressions were laced with fear.

"We're going to have a little chat," Creole told them. "We can do this the easy way or the hard way. It's up to you."

"What's it going to be?" Didier had his gun trained on the pair. "Ready to talk?"

Fab reholstered her gun and sat behind her desk, and I took my seat in the corner.

Creole pointed his Glock at first one, then the other. "Why don't you introduce yourselves?" When one mumbled something incoherent, Creole cuffed the side of his head. "I'm not going to ask you again. Not nicely, anyway."

"John," the one who took a swing muttered.

"Steve," said the other, making it sound like a question. Guess he wasn't sure.

Creole moved over to Fab's desk and leaned against the corner. Didier leaned against the kitchen table. Both had their weapons aimed at the men.

"Why are you trespassing?" Fab flashed them her "scary girl" smile. "Don't waste our time with something made-up; stick to the truth or risk a bullet for wasting our time."

"You got something that belongs to us, and we want it back," John spit out, holding the side of his face.

"Don't pretend you don't know what we're talking about," Steve sneered. "We saw you."

"Describe what you're looking for, and maybe I can help you," Creole offered.

"The briefcase," Steve said in a tone that said Creole was stupid. "Hand it over and we'll go. It doesn't belong to us; it belongs to our boss."

"Shut up," John barked.

Steve ignored him. "It's way better to deal with us than have Boss Man on your ass."

"Boss got a name?" Creole asked.

"No, he doesn't," John said adamantly.

"Sorry to say you wasted your time coming here," Fab said with no sincerity. "The briefcase never left the drop point."

"You're a liar," John said. "You know how we know? We were sitting across the street watching you."

"You didn't pay close enough attention," I said. "I'm telling you that she didn't take the briefcase."

"We've got a half-hour to make the delivery." Steve tapped his forearm, apparently forgetting he wasn't wearing a watch. That something bad would happen if they failed hung in the air.

"Let me see if I got this," Creole said. "Two of your associates toss a briefcase by the side of the road, and it's your job to pick it up? And deliver it where?"

"Warehouse in Homestead," Steve said.

"Dude, keep your mouth shut," John barked.

"Does it look like we're going anywhere without offering up some information?" Steve barked back.

"What's in the case?" Didier asked.

"We got strict instructions to deliver, not snoop," Steve said. "If we want to live past tonight, we need that briefcase. Our boss doesn't like problems and has a short temper." He grimaced.

"Make sure these two don't go anywhere,"

Creole said to Didier, then went out onto the deck. I watched as he made a call and wished I could read lips. At some point, Xander had come out of the office and taken a seat in the corner.

"How about you let us go?" John suggested. "We promise not to come back."

Yeah sure. That kind of money says you'll talk, spill where to find us, and then die. Someone scarier will show up, and we may not have the advantage next time.

Fab stood. "Hon, if either of them moves, shoot him." She winked at Didier, who grinned, and walked across the room, going out on the deck with Creole.

"I say we shoot them now," I said. "Haul their bodies to the crematorium and light them up. End of story."

Both John and Steve yelped.

"I say we take a vote," Didier said, not hiding his amusement.

"Damn voting. I'm always outnumbered." I pouted, then trotted out a "crazy girl" face of my own that I'd been practicing. Judging by their reactions, I'd gotten it down.

"Maybe not this time." Didier laughed.

The two men started talking over one another.

"Quiet," I yelled. "Senseless chatter gives me a headache."

Creole had shoved his phone in his pocket while he and Fab talked.

Oh, to be a fly!

They came back inside.

"You get your case back, and we never see you again?" Creole demanded.

The men nodded and fell over themselves saying yes, relief on their faces.

"When you were told the case never left the drop spot, it was the truth," Creole informed them. "It's still out there, but in a different location."

Fab grabbed her purse and holstered her gun. "Follow me back to the site," she told the two men. "We'll show you where it is." She motioned to me to follow.

"Hurry it up," Creole said gruffly.

To my surprise, Fab didn't take offense, which meant they must have a plan, leaving Didier and me as the odd men out.

"We'll be waiting here and go to dinner after you get back," Creole said in an off-hand manner.

Sure they will.

"Can we get our guns back?" John asked.

"No," Creole barked. "Get out of here before I change my mind about letting you two walk. And to be clear, don't show up here again. In fact, stay out of the Cove altogether."

The men ran down the stairs and out to the gate, which was closed. Apparently not inclined to climb over this time, they stood staring. Then finally looked around, *What the heck?* on their faces.

I gave Creole a quick kiss, picked up my purse, and followed Fab, sliding into the passenger side.

"They're so stupid." Fab sniffed as she got behind the wheel, pulling out of the garage. She eyed the men as they ran down the street to a truck parked on the side of the road and jumped in, gunning the engine and easing away from the curb to fall in behind Fab.

"What's the plan?" I took note of the evasive look on her face and added, "Don't skimp on the details—you'll hate the payback."

Fab fumbled for her phone, but before she could make a call, my phone rang, Didier's face popping up on the screen. Taking a not-so-wild guess, I asked, "You behind us?"

"Remind Fab to stick to the speed limit. We need to buy a little time for everyone to get in place."

"That will be a first." I hung up and repeated what Didier said. "Creole got the cops involved?"

"Of course," Fab said, clearly disappointed.

"This is better for us and our longevity. There's zero chance that Dick and Jane weren't going to rat us out and give our address to someone way scarier. You have a tendency to forget that Creole is always, mostly anyway, forthcoming on the details. So, you have details to look forward to. Happier now?" I made a face.

Fab grunted, which I took to mean that she

was in agreement with me. Then laughed to myself.

She was quiet on the boring, uneventful ride back to the field, her eyes glued to the rearview mirror. Once there, she u-turned and parked in almost the same spot as before. Steve, who was driving, parking right on our bumper. John got out, and he and Fab trooped through the weeds to the hiding place, which she pointed out to the man.

John grabbed the briefcase, exchanged words with Fab, and beat it back to the truck. Midway there, two cop cars converged on our location and drove into the middle of the lot.

Steve hit the gas and tore down the highway.

It surprised me that neither of the cop cars gave chase. Must be another one close by.

John danced in a circle, clutching the case to his chest. With no obvious escape route, he made a run for it across the field in plain sight of everyone. One of the cars sped after him. Two cops jumped out and wrestled him to the ground, leading him back to the car.

Fab put her hands in the air and was led to the other car and placed in the back. My junker truck pulled up on the other side of the street, and I recognized the two men inside. Not sure what to do, I stayed inside the Hummer and decided to let events play out. If I was going to be arrested, I'd know shortly.

The cop car with John inside pulled back onto

the highway and sped away.

The cop in the second car opened the back door, and Fab got out. Didier, who'd run across the street, scooped her up in his arms for a hug, then put his arm around her, and they walked back across the street and left in the truck.

Creole, who'd gotten out of the truck right behind him, talked to the cop for a long time, then walked over, got in the SUV, and gave me a big kiss before driving away. "It's not likely that we'll hear from those two again."

Chapter Forty

It had been a quiet few days. Fab had overseen the installation of a home security system for one of her clients. Creole had been kept up to date by his undercover friend on the information they'd been able to squeeze out of John and Steve. They got the location of the warehouse out of the pair, along with a heads up that it housed a variety of illegal enterprises, including drugs, and shut it down. My guess was the two got some kind of sweet deal. The investigators hadn't identified the top man yet, as everyone arrested in the sting had clammed up, but they did get a few clues they were following up on.

The guys called a meeting to go over motel issues, announcing that it would be at the property, out by the pool, and I suggested that in the future, we could just as easily meet on the beach, since it was convenient and wouldn't require shoes.

I finished dressing, strapping my Glock to the small of my back, and pulled my top down, then twirled for Creole, who shot me a thumbs up. My phone rang. I picked it up, and Rude's face flashed on the screen.

"She's here," Rude's hoarse whisper came through the phone.

"Who?" I shrugged at Creole, who blew out an exasperated breath that I translated as *What now?*

"The woman on the security feed." She continued to whisper.

"Under no circumstances do you confront her yourself," I said firmly. "I'm en route and bringing muscle that will know what to do." I winked at Creole.

"Will do."

Rude's easy acquiescence didn't indicate whether she planned to listen to me or not. If she was like everyone else I employed, she'd be on the snoop the second she hung up the phone. While telling Creole about the conversation, I took off my sandals and shoved them in my bag, sliding my feet into tennis shoes.

Creole hooked my purse over my shoulder. "Let's hope mystery woman doesn't have another victim in tow."

"To be fair, we only have evidence linking the woman to the fire, not the murders."

"You sound like an old boss of mine," Creole teased. "Is this where you tell me not to come back without hard evidence?"

I patted my Glock. "I'm your backup, which means you get to boss me around."

He grabbed me and pulled me into his arms for a kiss. "Same rules apply. You do nothing to get hurt, not even a scratch."

I saluted.

He pulled me out the door and opened the passenger door of the SUV. I slid inside, took out my phone, and made a call. "Didier and Fab are meeting us at the property," I told him when I hung up. It rang immediately, and Xander's face popped up on the screen. "What's up?" I asked.

"I've got information for you on the arsonist."

"Meet us at Beachside."

Traffic cooperated, and we made it to the motel in record time.

We entered the property from the back and split up. I cut across the lobby to the coffee maker, brewed cups for Creole and myself, and took them out to the pool. Excellent vantage point for spotting the arsonist, as long as she didn't suspect something was up. While I pulled chairs into a semi-circle, I made a surreptitious survey of the property and didn't see anything out of the ordinary. No one loitering. There were only two guests, both carrying plates loaded high with breakfast and headed back to their rooms.

Out of the corner of my eye, I caught sight of Creole skulking around the property, checking every blind corner. Cootie trooped in from the rear, and the two men met up and exchanged words. Fab and Didier, arriving on Cootie's heels, joined the conversation. I'd have to get an update later.

Fab looked bored, and if I were to venture a

guess, it was because she wasn't the one calling the shots. With a look around the property, she left the men and went into the office. Before disappearing inside, she acknowledged me with a tip of her head. It wasn't long before she joined me poolside, coffee in hand.

"While scanning the security feed, Rude caught sight of the woman who threw the fire bomb lurking around the front of the property," Fab reported. "The guys are splitting up to do a search. The second or third one, at this point, and still nothing."

It surprised me that I didn't have to drag the details out of her. "If the arsonist notices that she's attracted attention, she'll be long gone. Hopefully. That is, until her fire-starter itch brings her back."

"I asked Xander to research how many arson fires there've been in the area. He got back to me to say that it wasn't even a handful, and that goes back years."

"Did you see Rude while you were getting coffee and snooping around?" I asked, realizing I hadn't seen the woman since we arrived. "I told her to lie low until we got here."

"Rude called in one of Cook's relatives, the one who fills in when we have meetings, and he's working the desk, so I wasn't able to so much as get behind the counter. He had those massive arms of his crossed in a militant stance. Didn't want to start the morning off by shooting him. Well, I did, but I restrained myself."

Cootie jogged up, out of breath. I didn't know he had it in him. "Can't find Rude." He threw himself in a chair and huffed out a few breathes. "She's going to be pissy if she misses the meeting. Likes to be in the know, even if it's about the neighbor's hangnail. She better be the first to get the information or she bends my ear about the injustice of it all."

I immediately thought of Mac and Kelpie. "I believe her two sisters from other mothers live close by."

"And you employ them all." Creole had come up behind me. He leaned down and kissed my cheek, then sat next to me. "We just searched the property, and no sign of the arsonist or Rude."

Didier dropped into a chair next to Fab.

"I hope she's not off on her own looking for the arsonist." I shot Cootie a questioning stare.

"I haven't seen the cat either," Cootie said. "Wouldn't surprise me if she's somewhere chasing him."

"We're going to go ahead for now. I want to thank you all for coming," I said, meeting the smirks of those seated around me. Probably at my audacity for taking control of the meeting. If anyone wanted to jump in, they could.

Fab coughed, *hurry it up* implied.

Before I could proceed, Xander appeared out of nowhere, handed me a folder, and took a seat. Fab jumped up and hung her head over my shoulder. Creole leaned in. I winked at Didier, who was odd man out, and moved to the table, setting the paperwork in the center so we could all read at the same time.

Xander had gone over the security tape frame by frame and found several shots of the same woman lurking around the property. She appeared to know all the places to tuck out of sight and evade attention and had been caught going in and out of the ghost room, even after we'd made the decision to stop renting it out.

I flicked through the report and gasped when I read the highlighted section where Xander had identified our arsonist—Phoebe Gardener, a distant relative of Isabella, our resident ghost. That didn't explain the woman's fascination with the place, as ownership had changed hands long before she was born.

Xander had included a copy of Phoebe's arrest record, all old charges. There were a couple for trespassing and one for breaking and entering, all at the residence of a man. The charges had been dropped because the complainant had been a no-show in court and moved out of the area. Xander had noted that those types of charges were often seen on the records of stalkers.

"My neck hair is standing on end," I said after reading the report. "Maybe everything's just fine, but I'm worried about Rude. We need to fan out and find her. If this turns out to be some amusing game of hers, she's fired."

"She's flaky," Cootie attested, "but not like that." He went back to their residence to check there.

Creole said, "Spread out, everyone. If by chance you catch sight of Phoebe, back off and call for backup."

The guys went one way, Fab and I the other.

Fab and I exchanged a look and, in silent agreement, headed for the ghost room. It surprised me that none of the men had thought to start there.

As we approached the room, I knew something was off. It was a nuisance at times to be detail-oriented and always remember what was supposed to be where. In this case... the room was undergoing post-fire renovations, and the windows had been left open to air out the paint fumes and discourage the mildew stink that would build up in a nanosecond in this humid weather. They were now closed. The blackout curtain was supposed to be left closed whenever there weren't any workers inside, but only the sheer curtain was partially drawn across the window. If there was anyone inside, they could easily watch the comings and goings along the walkway.

I pointed to the windows. "They're closed," I whispered. Mostly, anyway—they'd been left slightly cracked open on one side.

Fab jerked my arm, and we sidestepped back towards the pool area, made a wide arc, and approached the room from the other side.

While I hung back on the far side of the door, Fab crept to the window and peered inside. She motioned me over and drew her weapon.

Phoebe Gardner, easily recognizable from the mugshot Xander had supplied, paced around the room, growling to herself as she stepped over Rude's inert body, which she'd secured with duct tape. "Why couldn't you just mind your own business? Following me." She snorted. "You're stupid. The first time I laid eyes on you, I pegged you for trouble. You couldn't let it lie, you nosey bitch. You had to get involved. And for what?" She kicked Rude in the hip, eliciting a muffled groan. "Ready to get your face on video?" She waved to a tripod with her cell phone attached to it on a nearby ladder. "I'll get your last moments recorded, just like the rest." She crossed to a lump in the corner and lifted the corner of the tarp covering it. "Yep, still dead." She chuckled.

"Nobody deserves to make a dime off this property, and when I'm done, it will stay a vacant lot for years to come—no one will touch it," Phoebe continued to rant. "It's been a family mission—one my mother started when she set the first fire. She almost got caught. The detective on the case wouldn't give it up. He drowned when his boat capsized. So sad." She brushed away a non-existent tear. "She always said killing was the easiest crime to get away with, and she proved that true."

Rude appeared to be somewhat alert, making blowing noises out the sides of the tape covering her mouth.

"Wakey-wakey. Time to make you a star." She ripped the tape off Rude's mouth, and she yelped. Phoebe bent down, firearm sticking out of the back her pants, and put her arms under Rude, dragging her to a sitting position, which Rude fought. Phoebe pushed and pulled until she'd maneuvered Rude into the only chair, and even then, she slumped over. "No fast death for you. I'm going to cut you." She took a knife from her pocket, and from the other, she drew a small bottle and held it up. "Got this from Eddie the dime dealer. Guaranteed me that any noises you make will be faint. Can't have you alerting anyone. It's the weekend; no one's going to be coming down to this end unit. Drink up. Time to knock you on your ass so you can't cause any trouble. Don't worry, you'll still be aware of what I'm doing to you and feel the pain. A slice here, one there..." She cut the air with the knife.

Phoebe circled the chair, ranting about the history of the property, Isabella's murder, and how her children never got over the fact that the co-owner hadn't been charged. The last straw was his kids taking over the management. Phoebe had promised her mother before she died that she'd get the property back in the family name, no matter what it took. That hadn't happened, but it would satisfy her if no one else profited off it.

"Last words?" Phoebe cackled, the exact sound you'd expect from an unhinged person on the lam from a mental hospital.

I drew my Glock and scanned the property, seeing the backs of the guys as they headed out to the rear entrance. Luckily, no guests were hanging around.

Fab reached over and turned the knob—locked. She held up three fingers, then true to her nature, shot the lock off on one and barged through the door.

Phoebe had her back to the door and was caught off guard, turning with her knife above her head. Fab didn't take the risk of firing, since she was too close to Rude. Her hand shot out, grabbing the woman's knife hand and pulling her close as she brought her other arm up, landing a fierce blow to the woman's face with her elbow. Phoebe attempted to reciprocate, her arm shooting out, but Fab deflected it and leveled another punch. The woman staggered, and Fab landed a final blow to her face before she fell to the floor.

Phoebe didn't stay down for long. She clawed at the floorboards where the carpet had been removed and rolled onto her side, scrabbling for the gun in her waistband. Without a moment's hesitation, Fab shot her. She screeched and grabbed her backside while Fab kicked Phoebe's weapon out of her reach. I tossed Fab a piece of rope that was lying on the floor, and she tied up the shrieking woman while I untied Rude.

"Oh man, thought I was goner," Rude moaned, shaking out her hands. "Bitch is off her rocker, and it runs in the family."

Creole and Didier burst through the door, weapons drawn. After scoping out the situation, Creole holstered his gun and dragged the still-ranting Phoebe into the chair Rude had vacated while Didier called 911.

Cootie rushed in and scooped Rude into his arms, rocking and whispering to her, and walked her outside.

"Good job, bestie." I beamed at Fab.

* * *

When the cops arrived, Kevin led the pack, an arched eyebrow leveled in my direction.

I held up my hands in self-defense. "It could've been worse. Two bodies instead of one. We've done your work for you, handing over a killer."

Kevin snorted at that.

"Careful of your man goods," I told Kevin with a smirk. "Phoebe tried to stick her foot in Creole's groin. She's having a bad day."

The first ambulance rolled up, and Kevin pointed them to where they could find Phoebe. The next arriving paramedics were directed to the lobby, where Cootie had carried Rude to the office, mumbling the whole way about the "really crazy chick." Both women were strapped to gurneys, rolled out, and loaded in the back of ambulances headed to the hospital.

The guests—a hearty bunch in the mood for some first-hand action—had poured out of their rooms and filled the chairs and chaises. The coffee pots and a tray of danishes were moved to a nearby table, and they downed their coffee, watching the ensuing drama with rapt attention.

Why did I expect them to pack their bags and hit the streets? I should've known better.

When Kevin finally got around to questioning Fab and I, he found us in the lobby. Fab was able to better describe events, since she was the first to enter the room. I'd stood back and out of the way, ready to shoot if Phoebe somehow got the upper hand. I was able to report the woman's rantings and that she'd said it had been a family affair.

"The upside is that you two always give me a concise report." Kevin flashed a cheeky grin. "Must be all the experience you have with murders, shootings, and the like."

"Officer, you think you're so..." I stopped before telling him what a pain in the backside he could be.

"Careful, or I may have to arrest you for littering."

"Just when I think we're making progress." I

shook my head. "Cold drinks in the refrigerator." I pointed across the room.

Kevin stood. "It would help if you could learn to appreciate my sense of humor."

I winked at him.

"Coroner's van just pulled up," Creole said as he and Didier entered the lobby and sat down across from us. "We're getting quite the rep."

"Can any of you ID the dead woman?" Kevin asked.

"No clue who she is," I told Kevin. "Don't even know why Phoebe killed her."

"That was a gruesome sight." Fab grimaced. Of course, she looked before leaving the room.

Kevin walked off without so much as a "see you," but not before he helped himself to a couple of sodas.

"Bye," I said in a slightly snarky tone and waved to his back.

"You could be nicer." Creole gave me a stern look.

I bit back a grin. "I sort of am. You know, half-assedly." I pointed at Didier, who was laughing. "That's why you're my favorite."

Chapter Forty-One

Two weeks was a record. In that time, there'd been no dead bodies, fires, or drunken antics reported at any of the properties I owned. It was the perfect time for a getaway, even if only overnight.

Phoebe had been carted off to the hospital, and instead of being booked into the jail upon her release, she was admitted to the looney bin. She'd flipped out in the hospital and slipped into another world, where she didn't communicate with anyone but herself. She'd made it easy for the cops, having kept a scrapbook and videos of her felonious activities.

Creole leaned over, chin on my shoulder, and said in my ear, "Tell me again why we're going out to Caspian Island?"

It was a beautiful day, the sun beating down on the glimmering water as we skimmed across the Gulf on Caspian's boat, a short ride to his namesake private island, which he'd purchased to be close to his only daughter.

"Because Caspian is planning a big surprise for Fab." I gave him a coy look. "He wants my input."

Creole scowled at me, not amused. "And we need to spend the night for that, why?"

"You had plenty of time to call Caspian back and inform him 'no way' on that point."

"Old Caspian is a master at playing people."

I giggled at his description.

"It didn't escape my notice, the casual way Caspian threw out the invitation, took our non-committal response for acceptance, and hung up. And you mean, wife, that *you* refused to call back with 'wait a damn second.'" Creole glared, but his lips quirked.

I leaned forward and kissed him. "I've paid for that egregious mistake… a couple of times."

"It should be made clear upon our arrival that when Fab finds out about her 'surprise,' we want immunity from death. Caspian would be better off letting Fab help plan her own surprise—she'd like that better."

The boat coasted up to the dock, and one of the dock hands ran over and tied it off. A golf cart sat ready, driver included, to take us to the house. Our suitcase loaded, it was a short trip to the mansion through the lush landscape, trees and tropical blooms dotting the pathway to the opposite side of the island that was a good example of what double-digit millions could buy a person. It had everything—swimming pool, tennis courts, lawn games, water toys, and that was just the outside. It would be hard to believe that one could think of something it didn't have.

We rode past the pool, where loud noises could be heard. Liam waved before cannonballing into the water, drenching Brad. Mila squealed at the top of her lungs.

"At any time in the invitation process did Caspian mention 'group affair'?" Creole's eyebrows bushed together.

"I don't know anything."

Creole laughed. "The old man's up to something."

"I dare you to call him that to his face."

Creole laughed again. The driver had overheard and laughed as he pulled up to the curved stairway that led to the front door. Sunshine glimmered off the endless row of windows. Another tropically clad gentleman awaited our arrival. He introduced himself as Charles, and we followed him up the stairs, into the house, and to the bedroom suite at the end of one of the hallways that had been assigned to us.

"If you need anything, just press the intercom button." He pointed. "When you're ready, everyone is gathering at the pool, or you can wait until dinner. Drinks at five."

"Do you know who was invited?" I asked Charles.

Creole poked me in the back.

Maybe rude, but we both wanted to know.

"I've been sworn to secrecy regarding the details." Charles zipped his lips with a smile. Not waiting for a response, he closed the door behind him.

"You want to change into bathing suits and go down to the pool? It'll be easy to squeeze information out of Liam."

"I'm not in the mood for a swim." He crossed the room and locked the door, then scooped me off my feet and tossed me on the bed. "I've got something else in mind. Whatever surprise Caspian has in store can wait until later."

* * *

I knew, when packing, that Caspian didn't do casual for dinner and packed accordingly. I'd found a tropical print dress in shades of blue in a local store, paired it with low nude heels, and accessorized with lapis jewelry. Creole wore the new silk shorts and shirt I'd bought him on the same shopping trip. It didn't escape our notice that no one had knocked and told us to hustle it up. I double-checked for a 'Do Not Disturb' sign on our way downstairs for drinks and didn't find one.

We found our way down the stairs and into the cavernous living room—large windows on one side, sliding pocket doors on the other, all open to the equally large patio and the water below. In addition, there was a tiki bar, a fully stocked outdoor kitchen with first-class appliances, an island top with barstools that could seat eight, and plenty of comfortable outdoor seating.

"Hmm… okay," I said as I took a head count of the family and friends that were seated on the chairs and couches that faced the railing overlooking the water. All were accounted for. "I'd say the surprise is on us."

"Or that Caspian's a lying toad," Creole said with humor.

I laughed and made a sound I thought mimicked something in the frog family. Creole rolled his eyes. We crossed the threshold to a chorus of hellos.

Caspian waved and shouted, "Welcome."

Another man appeared to take our drink order. I ordered a margarita, "Pitcher, please."

Creole snorted and walked over to the bar to peruse the beer choices, choosing a label I didn't recognize.

I cruised over to Mother, trotting out my beauty queen wave, and kissed her cheek.

"You here for Fab's surprise?" Mother giggled.

"That's right." I turned to Fab and yelled, "Surprise," throwing my hands in the air. Good thing Creole was carrying the tray of drinks. He set it down next to Fab's pitcher of martinis and full glass of olives and snagged us chairs next to Fab and Didier.

She flashed me the "crazy girl" smile. Maybe she didn't know what was up, but I doubted it.

Caspian, not the least bit embarrassed by his

antics, sported a huge grin.

I playfully smacked my brother in the back of the head.

"Ouch," Brad grumbled.

"Oowie." Mila mimicked from where she was sitting on his lap. She pursed her lips, then laughed.

I leaned down, and we rubbed noses.

I reached out and messed up Spoon's hair as I passed on the way to my chair and, before sitting, whispered in Fab's ear, "How did daddy dearest get you out here?"

"Something important to discuss," she said casually. "I'm a little surprised to see everyone." Except she didn't sound it.

Caspian stood. "I want to thank you all for coming. I hope you find it as amusing as I do that I got all of you out here on a made-up pretext. The same one for each of you, essentially, with a variation or two."

The women giggled, the men half-laughed, and all our faces registered surprise. Mila clapped her hands. Caspian reached out his arms, and she went eagerly. He lifted her to his shoulders, and she laughed in delight.

"This is the kind of family gathering that Madeline would plan." Caspian smiled at Mother, who blushed. "Frankly, it's not fair that she has all the fun. I thought, you know, Caspian, you could pull a trick or two out of your bag too. It was fun," he said unrepentantly.

"That's so weaselly." I reached over and took a healthy sip of my drink, draining half the glass.

"Young lady..." Caspian shook his finger at me.

"You *do* know that these family get-togethers have a tendency to go off the rails," Brad said, a warning tone in his voice. "You should've kept the bar closed and just served water."

"Food and drink? No other ulterior motive?" Spoon grinned at his friend.

"I've got an agenda," Caspian said.

"I bet," Creole grumbled. He and Didier laughed.

I held out my glass for a refill.

Creole filled my glass. "Try not to get sauced too fast. You might miss something good."

"Gotcha." I clinked rims with Fab, who'd also requested a refill.

"I think it's cool." Liam stuck his fist in the air and exchanged a knuckle bump with Caspian.

"Where's Emerson?" I asked.

"Her grandmother went to heaven, and she flew to New York for the services," Brad said, eyeing Mila, who was distracted by pulling Caspian's hair.

"Why didn't you go with her?" I asked.

"Really, Madison," Mother said, insinuating *none of your business*.

"You want to know too... unless you've already wrestled it out of him," I shot back.

"You remember her mother, the obnoxious

lawyer? She doesn't like me. I'm not up to her standards for boyfriend material. And out of respect, since it was her mother, I decided it was best to stay home, knowing that she'd wouldn't appreciate me putting in an appearance."

"If it makes you feel any better, old Ruthie never warmed up to me and girly here either." I poked Fab's arm.

"In case it ever comes up, I sent a big a-s-s arrangement of flowers and put all our names on the card." Brad held out his arms to illustrate the size of the bouquet.

"That was thoughtful." Mother reached over and patted his hand.

"So, Trickster," Didier called to Caspian, "what's on your agenda?"

"Let's have a toast." Caspian lifted Mila down and handed her to Liam, another favorite play partner. He picked up his glass and held it up. "To family," he toasted. "Since we're all here, I thought it the perfect time to discuss a business opportunity that's come to my attention."

"More Boardwalk business?" Didier asked. "Or are you talking about something new?"

"I've got an option on the wooded acreage to the south of the Boardwalk—the area with the crumbling two-story house—and thought it would be a prime location for an *upscale* hotel."

I groaned loudly enough that all eyes shot to me, then downed the rest of my drink.

"We seriously considered partnering with a

chain on a boutique hotel, but that didn't work out," Didier said. "None were interested in outside partners. Or anything on a smaller scale. And as the four of us know—" He circled his finger around. "—owning the Beachside has been…"

"Chaotic," Creole supplied. "Hectic. Downright weird."

"Love the idea, though." Fab smiled at Caspian. "But in light of recent events, another project so soon would be too much."

"It would be nice if you were exaggerating about Beachside and its weirdness," Spoon said. "But on the upside, you guys have made the motel a go-to place, and it's the talk of the town."

"For all the wrong reasons," Mother grumbled.

Caspian clapped his hands. "Hear me out." He snapped his fingers, and a man appeared with a stack of reports and handed them out. "My CPA has put together the figures to show that this would be good investment. Since it was previously ordained that everyone has to contribute equally financially, my thought is that you could sell the motel, which frees you up to invest in an upscale resort that will bring a better return." He flashed a big smile. "Here's the best part—I've got an interested buyer for your motel, willing to pay top dollar and with no plans for a high-rise, which I knew would be important to you."

"Hell no." I put my glass down with more force than I intended. "What about the employees? Are their jobs secure? And for how long?"

"We didn't discuss staffing." Caspian's brown eyes bored into mine. "The new owners will need employees to keep the place running smoothly, and I see no reason that they'd bring in all new people. Except for the couple that run the office. They're a hard sell."

"Do these 'buyers'—" I made quotes. "—have any idea how damn difficult it is to find someone to run a twenty-four-hour business in crazyland and speak the language? Certainly no one of your ilk would apply for the job." It took everything I had to maintain eye contact with the formidable man.

"Ilk?" Caspian's eyebrows shot up.

"You know, billionaire dude with money to burn or invest," Fab said with a huge smile.

Everyone laughed, lightening the tense moment.

"You've always been so loyal," Mother said to me, adding, "Which is good," when I turned a huffy look on her. "At least, think about the idea before discounting it."

"I suggest that we read the report, look at the numbers, and reconvene to discuss the project," Spoon said. "A drive-by of the intended property might be helpful."

"Just so we're clear," Creole said. "As in our

past deals, anything new has to be mutually agreeable to everyone." He held up his bottle in a toast.

"We can take a vote now, if you promise that we don't leave any employees hanging without a job." I stared at Caspian. I didn't mind selling, as what started out as a fun project had turned into an ordeal that had rapidly drained the excitement out of me. I knew if we kept it, I'd spend my time anticipating more problems—deadly ones. "I know," I said with a teasing smile. "We could relocate them to your island to work at Caspian house."

Caspian laughed. "I like it. The island's named after me, why not the house?" His dark eyes sparkled in amusement. "Are you sure?"

I nodded.

"The ayes," Caspian called out.

All of us raised our hands.

"Done deal." Caspian smacked his hand on the table.

"I've got some news," Mother announced.

"You're pregnant," Fab said.

Spoon laughed.

"That's an old joke," Brad grumbled.

"I'm going to lighten up and try not to worry so much. You're going to see a funner Madeline. Purchased a new handgun, Spoon and I have hit the range, and I'm ready to be backup. One less worry if I'm in the middle of the action."

"To quote Madison, 'Hell no.'" Brad turned a

glare on Spoon.

"Mother went out on a job with us and was great backup," I said. "Turns out she has rapport with our funeral friends."

"Oh, Madison." Mother groaned.

Everyone laughed.

"You'll see; this will work out great," Mother reassured us.

"Any more breaking news, announcements?" I asked, which was met with laughter.

Fab rolled her eyes.

~*~

PARADISE SERIES NOVELS

Crazy in Paradise
Deception in Paradise
Trouble in Paradise
Murder in Paradise
Greed in Paradise
Revenge in Paradise
Kidnapped in Paradise
Swindled in Paradise
Executed in Paradise
Hurricane in Paradise
Lottery in Paradise
Ambushed in Paradise
Christmas in Paradise
Blownup in Paradise
Psycho in Paradise
Overdose in Paradise
Initiation in Paradise
Jealous in Paradise
Wronged in Paradise
Vanished in Paradise
Fraud in Paradise
Naive in Paradise

Deborah's books are available on Amazon
amazon.com/Deborah-Brown/e/B0059MAIKQ

About the Author

Deborah Brown is an Amazon bestselling author of the Paradise series. She lives on the Gulf of Mexico, with her ungrateful animals, where Mother Nature takes out her bad attitude in the form of hurricanes.

Sign up for my newsletter and get the latest on new book releases. Contests and special promotion information. And special offers that are only available to subscribers.
www.deborahbrownbooks.com

Follow on FaceBook:
facebook.com/DeborahBrownAuthor

You can contact her at Wildcurls@hotmail.com

Deborah's books are available on Amazon
amazon.com/Deborah-Brown/e/B0059MAIKQ

Made in the USA
Las Vegas, NV
16 August 2024

93931511R10210